THE
SHADOW
GUARD

THE
SHADOW
GUARD

DIANE WHITESIDE

BRAVA

KENSINGTON PUBLISHING CORP.
www.kensingtonbooks.com

BRAVA BOOKS are published by

Kensington Publishing Corp.
119 West 40th Street
New York, NY 10018

All Kensington titles, imprints, and distributed lines are available at special quantity discounts for bulk purchases for sales promotion, premiums, fund-raising, educational or institutional use. Special book excerpts or customized printings can also be created to fit specific needs. For details, write or phone the office of the Kensington Special Sales Manager: Kensington Publishing Corp., 119 West 40th Street, New York, NY 10018. Attn. Special Sales Department. Phone: 1-800-221-2647.

Brava and the B logo Reg. U.S. Pat. & TM Off.

ISBN-13: 978-0-7582-2519-1
ISBN-10: 0-7582-2519-9

First Kensington Trade Paperback Printing: April 2011
10 9 8 7 6 5 4 3 2 1

Printed in the United States of America

To Ann Jacobs and Jean Marie Ward, who guarded my back.
Thank you for great critiques when I
most desperately needed them.

CHAPTER ONE

Snow coiled like serpents through the trees' barren branches and flung a silent net over the Potomac River below, as if warning the water to be wary of onlookers. Icy frills marked where a wave dashed over a boulder or tumbled too long in a pool, isolated from its fellows in this rocky wilderness.

Twin beams of golden light lanced across the sky, followed by an SUV's sullen rumble. A few dead leaves from last fall shuddered for an instant on the trees, then began the long, slow fall through the gorge.

Astrid Carlsen froze into position, her skin colder under her jacket than the mid-March temperature called for. If that vehicle turned into the overlook above—or worse, its driver climbed out to see the famous view—she couldn't hide.

She hadn't spun a spell strong enough to stay invisible from farashas, the ordinary mortals who walked the earth. If any passersby looked down, they'd surely spot the silvery glow wrapped around her and her partner.

Guard law would demand she cast their memories, and possibly their minds, into the shadows as penalty for seeing too much.

The headlights scythed through the tree branches and swept past. The river torrents quickly drowned out any sounds of the SUV's departure.

Astrid allowed herself a small, silent sigh of relief. It sent no warmth through her veins before she started scanning again.

A snowflake tumbled from a tree onto her cheek and clung for a moment, chilly as the late winter blizzard or her stomach's unhappy contents.

Only high summer would see humans visit this landing often, with its deadly currents tumbling so close to the shore. Late winter should bring nobody here except the wild animals.

"Where did that scream come from?" she muttered and tilted her head back, hoping against hope she'd see an honest buzzard shredding its prey.

Her partner Nathan Bradshaw braced himself against her until his heavy coat rasped the nape of her neck. They stood back to back, of course, in the only safe formation for two sahirs working magick alone.

"Nothing up there big enough to shriek like a banshee," Nathan growled, his native Boston accent thick and harsh. "It'd take a strong life force to wail that loud and long."

Astrid flinched, ice ripping into her veins from fading magick. She'd find out who was wounded, no matter what the cost to herself.

She set her jaw and began to reframe her spell.

"Can a magickal death really be heard from far off?" Nathan asked. "They say the sound cuts you to the bone, even from miles away."

Astrid's hands shook and nearly lost their grip on Nathan. Only his wrists' quick twist saved their vital contact.

"Yes," she agreed in hoarse tones that bore little resemblance to her usual polite instructor's voice. "Mages can hear someone killed by magick for a long distance, certainly as far as the main highway."

"Where we were."

"Yes." It had ripped all joy from their souls until ice carved apart their bones. Agony and anger shrieked through the skies until no man could hear the banshee wail and not act.

Or even worse. Seventy years ago, a similar scream had torn twenty-five years of hard-won happiness from her heart.

This time, her partner shot the car across three lanes of traffic to reach the nearest icy exit before she even asked him to.

She caught her breath and forced herself back to the present. She'd had decades to cry a river of tears until she built a new life.

"Can you see anything yet?" he asked. Seventy years since she'd been his first trainer but Boston still thickened his vowels.

She spread her legs a little wider and reached deeper into the earth for strength. But pulling it back felt like sucking a milkshake through a broken straw. Sustenance was out there somewhere; she simply had no way to reach it, not without a kubri.

She shook her head in frustration. She'd spent an entire week interpreting for the FBI before and never failed a basic scrying spell afterward.

Dammit, they should still be able to solve this puzzle. Something else was wrong than simple exhaustion.

They'd both already taken off their gloves to let the magick flow more easily. Now they'd just have to go further.

"Give me your hands."

"What?" Nathan was so surprised that he turned to look her in the eyes.

She hissed in alarm and jabbed his ribs with her magick, a trainer's sharp warning to a reckless student. If they'd been strangers partnered in a spell, she'd have scorched his face for risking both their lives with a direct glance when they weren't safely anchored by a kubri.

Nathan jerked away in surprise but quickly flattened his back against hers with only a guttural curse. He hadn't made the mistake of trying to watch another sahir from within a spell since his first semester at the academy.

Still, she was wryly glad he'd satisfy his lust with somebody else that night, not her. Nathan loathed yielding to anyone's magick, even if he owed a student's duty to serve his instructor.

"We'll pool our power and extend the spell that way." She cast another wary eye around the small grotto, listening for more than the ice-shrouded river. Instinct still insisted this was the only place to look.

"Right," Nathan agreed. "But make it fast, okay?"

She snickered at that statement of the obvious and stretched out her arms. An instant later, his fingers twined with hers and they stretched their arms out.

The magick, which had circled and howled inside her, snapped and snarled its disgust around her head, then suddenly swung into smooth, clean lines of force. They charged through her bones like horse-drawn chariots, prancing and snorting their eagerness to do her will.

Nathan huffed once, then settled more solidly against her back. Red flames danced along the magick coming from him but they couldn't stop to let him take the lead, not now.

She stretched her fingers slightly and pushed the magick out. It swirled forth in a shimmering haze that snatched her breath away.

She choked—and the silvery mist sagged back toward her before it had entered the river of time to find out who had summoned them.

Crap, that was weird. Even so, she managed to catch the slippery mass of not-quite-real stuff.

"We can come back tomorrow, after we recharge," Nathan suggested, pragmatic as ever.

The woman's scream echoed in her memory again, long and heartrending as Astrid's husband's death cry. She'd tried to gate to him, only to slam into an icy black wall. She'd collapsed, the loss echoing through her body and soul for years.

Now another family would be wracked by the same despairing grief, dammit.

Even so, Gerard had at least made his attackers pay a high price for his death. This lady deserved the same justice.

"Like hell." She'd find out what had happened if she had to spend every drop of blood in her body.

She wheeled slowly and Nathan moved with her, as steadily as if they wielded this much power every day.

The spell's silver strengthened into a ball of light, as bright as a candlelit hall. The magick had finally dived through time's murky waters and found a responsive eddy.

The river and its boulders suddenly danced into a new pattern. A large pool lay at the water's edge, shaped like a teardrop, deep at one end but pouring into the main channel like a grand prix racetrack at the other. Moonlight spilled into its darkest recesses—and every wave turned crimson.

Astrid forgot to breathe. Her legs screamed their exhaustion again and she ignored them yet again.

"What is it?" Nathan tapped his boot against hers.

"Two people, a man and a woman. She's much smaller and he's got her in a choke hold with a knife against her throat."

"The bastard."

What else could she see? She forced the magick forward but the Potomac drank the spell down, melting its edges as if a new waterfall had just joined it.

"I can see her face but not his. He's wearing a ski mask, dammit." Astrid nodded, useless tears touching her eyes.

"Can you describe him?"

"Bigger than she is. Tall, perhaps your height, and heavier. He's wearing true cold-weather gear, not lightweight, fashionable stuff." She hesitated and tried to push the magick through time and the snowy vortex in the air. "His ski mask has a black-and-white pattern."

"Not solid black?"

"No, its design blends into the snow so I can't see him very well."

"Damn," Nathan said with more emphasis that he usually allowed himself to express. Astrid couldn't have agreed more.

"She's arguing, but I can't hear the words over the water's roar."

"Does he know about us and magick? Enough to use water as a barricade?"

"Or simply trying to block farasha forensics?" Astrid shook off useless questions impatiently. She had a job to do somehow—trigger justice for that beautiful young woman. "He's laughing at her words. And then. And then . . ."

She closed her eyes too late. The memory seared its way like a welder's torch deep in her heart.

She'd need a very long session with the healers tonight, when they finally returned home to Georgetown.

She forced herself to speak, to give the memory voice. That beautiful woman's ghost deserved a little peace.

"He cut her throat and tossed her body into the deep water. The blood went everywhere." She stopped, her empty stomach now a rocket headed up her throat.

Nathan's hands clasped her hips in silent sympathy. Strength poured back into her. She allowed herself to accept it for an instant, knowing he risked his life to offer the closer grasp during this spell.

Then she leaned her head against Nathan's back and firmly relinked their fingers.

"When I lock onto that moment and scan," Nathan said briskly a moment later, "I can spot the corner of a single car's hood in the parking lot up above."

"Can you describe it?" A trickle of hope brightened her heart.

"Dark colored, since it was just before today's snow started, and square." Nathan hesitated. "It's hard to see much more. Maybe because I have a bad angle on it from here or maybe—"

"What?" She focused her power and poured it into her partner. The murderer's ghost shrank into a puff of smoke and vanished into the late afternoon mist. She'd seen enough of his body to describe it, and she'd recognize his black aura anywhere.

Just give her the chance to hunt him.

"The car might be warded—there's a faint shimmer around

it." Nathan shifted on the balls of his feet, in a knife fighter's deadly search for an advantageous position.

Astrid dragged in another breath and wished she could find a straightforward clue in the air.

"Shit." Magickal protections were almost more frightening than a psychic scream loud enough to alert two Shadow Guard members. Only registered sahirs were permitted to set wards this close to Washington, D.C., with its treasures. The penalty for disobeying that law was death, a price that hadn't been exacted since the Civil War.

"Exactly. Can't prove it, though. There were absolutely no witnesses."

"Maybe no farashas but—"

"Not even a spider was nearby when this happened."

Hell and damnation, that took serious power—which the killer himself didn't reek of. He was hidden death, like arsenic added to narcotics. Did he have enough magick to set such wards?

If that tall hellhound had killed so easily once, he'd probably do so again. But where and why would he do so? How much of a threat was he?

"She died screaming about duty." Astrid allowed herself to relive the memory's last few moments.

"Let the local police handle it." Nathan stretched to unkink his larger body. "They'll have a corpse to study, once she washes ashore."

Ghostly waves, livid in the moonlight as if the river itself bled, washed over the lady's body and swept her downstream across Astrid's memory. Far, far too similar to her last glimpse of Gerard.

Astrid gagged and hunted for a more useful image. "He marched her into the water upstream from here. The rocks are snow-covered by now."

"Making it impossible for anybody to find evidence." Nathan rolled his shoulders to stretch them. "There's no reason for us to make the cops search here."

She frowned at his logic, even though it followed paths she'd taught him.

Still thinking, she closed down the spell, her duty as elder.

"We need to get back to Georgetown and report to the Shadow Council on what we learned from the FBI." The Boston banker turned weapons master stepped away from her, his voice animated as a child anticipating Christmas Eve delights. "If we could combine some of the FBI's stuff with the military's . . ."

Astrid gave the river a long, considering stare. Even without the scrying spell's aid, her magesight showed long tendrils of blood weaving through the water. How many more miles of rapids would batter that poor woman's body before her brave spirit could find rest? And justice?

"I'll make some phone calls tonight," Nathan went on, "after I have something to eat and recharge. We could wind up with some great stuff for our troops." His voice faded, accented by the sound of snow and ice crunching under his boots.

Astrid frowned. The blizzard was forecasted to bring heavy snow, followed by another, wetter storm in a few days.

The woman had fought valiantly against her killer, even when she knew it was hopeless. Her body could be damaged during the days it journeyed downstream, so badly her family might not recognize it.

The possibility was intolerable. The lady deserved a proper funeral.

Astrid gathered what remained of her strength, raised her hand, and cast a fine sheen of magick across the river. The delicate dust collected itself into tiny sprites that dove under the water, like dolphins riding the current.

Astrid sagged and the cold, dank air sank into her bones as if her sturdy coat was paper. Then she turned to follow Nate out of the gorge.

She'd cast just enough of a spell to protect the gallant lady, yet not enough to cause trouble for herself with Shadow Guard regulations.

If she was lucky.

Two days later

"What did you find, Miller?" Jake Hammond jogged the last few steps down the steep hill, vaulted over the sandbag barricade, and landed silently on cobblestones. Nothing more than puddles here, now that the floodwaters had finally gone down.

Plus, of course, whatever corpse had raised alarms amid the ancient taverns and shops on a starless night.

This alley had been old before the Revolution was fought. Hell, George Washington probably slipped along it to plot treason against the British and Bobby Lee undoubtedly used it to play hooky from school. Belhaven had built it narrow as a thieves' path to the docks, and nobody had widened it in the centuries since gold stopped coming in from selling slaves.

The light from Miller's flashlight was a bright bubble that disappeared quickly against the dark, wet bricks all around, like a miner's headlight in a tunnel. Behind Jake, a bar's single backlight fizzled and turned his shadow into a giant, onrushing silver-edged mist.

Water rippled beyond Miller, black and quiet, as predictable and patient as the winter runoff that had birthed it. Dawn would find it vanished into the Potomac River again, underneath the marina's boats. Now it formed a moat against the old munitions factory's thick stone walls. Nobody could pass without paying heed to what it had brought forth.

Something shimmered under its surface, like a network of stars.

Jake shrugged off the ridiculous idea. No way could a cop's flashlight produce something like that. He stooped down beside the canny beat cop, careful not to disturb anything, and flashed his own light on the scene. "Oh, hell."

A woman's corpse lay curled into an oddly regal posture, like an Egyptian mummy protected from time by the embalmer's art. Well-made, fashionable clothing shrouded her long limbs, and muddy water slowly crept away between the cobblestones like mourners. A diamond glinted on her left hand, large enough to snare any thief's eye.

Her head canted back helplessly at an impossible angle, held only by her spine. Gray blurred her once chocolate skin, as if hell had sucked out her color with her life. Her eyes were dark pits of blackness, lost between heaven and hell. Her right hand reached out, palm open, fingers extended, begging for help.

Somehow, if Jake tilted his head back just a little and the city lights blurred a bit on the wet streets until they offered a halo rather than sharp spotlights, she looked just like his mother the last time he'd seen her. Lying on the gurney at the morgue with her hand lying loose to one side and the gunshot wound that killed her hidden by her thick, dark hair . . .

He'd puked for along time after he'd identified her and Dad.

Jake beat on his thigh with his fist, his stomach knotting faster than rush-hour traffic. The older he got, the less welcome murder became. But this one—this hurt more than anything he'd faced before.

I'll find your killer, pretty lady, he promised her silently. *We'll bring him to justice, no matter how long it takes.*

Feet pounded down the alley toward them and sirens keened atop the hill, behind the fancier nightclubs and bars. The headquarters dudes had finally pulled their gear together to come help the victim who'd landed halfway between the two oldest government buildings in town.

Jake's eyes met Miller's in perfect understanding. Jake had only arrived so soon because he'd been at Duffy's Tavern a block away, eyeing his prospects for getting laid after a week of nothing but overtime. He hadn't lost anything by bolting out of there to come down here. Hell, even his best pickup line wasn't getting him far tonight.

"Glad you got here first, Sarge," Miller said, a little hoarsely. "She deserves the best homicide cop."

"Most senior." Jake shrugged off the compliment to his record.

Something hissed softly, just below a whisper.

Jake frowned but began to circle the victim, looking for clues. He squatted to look more closely at her boots.

A spark flashed beside his hand. His skin sizzled and fire danced through his bones. For an instant, her clothing faded into a shadowy outline until he could see the womanly curves underneath.

No damage there whatsoever, other than the gaping hole in her neck and a little bruising to her wrists.

Jake jumped back, startled. His heart thudded in his chest, far faster than during any shootout.

He couldn't have seen that. He'd only glimpsed something like it once before, eighteen years ago.

What the hell caused that spark?

He automatically checked for a live wire lying hot and deadly across the damp cobblestones. Nothing there but the same uneven gray stones he'd learned to run across as a child.

Static electricity, maybe?

He suddenly wanted to stutter more than any rookie cop. How could he ask Miller if he'd noticed anything?

"What have we got, Hammond?" Chief Andrews loomed suddenly behind Miller, his thick form compressed into a tuxedo. He was probably grateful to escape another political fund-raiser before it transitioned from dining to dancing.

Jake responded with familiar, comforting cop speak, his haven since he was twenty.

"Unknown female murder victim, sir, of a knifing."

CHAPTER TWO

Jake took another long pull from his double mocha latte before he picked up the bulging folder. No matter what anybody said about the modern office, cops still depended on coffee and paperwork. Belhaven's volunteer grant writer had earned her spot by providing restaurant-quality cappuccino makers for every department. Her latest achievement was decorating the squad room in the latest office furniture to match their new computers.

It didn't matter. Big cases produced mountains of paper, unlike the sleek tables they hid. Jake preferred his coffee on the heavily caffeinated side to match, especially after only six hours of sleep in two days.

The squad room's TV newscaster's voice blurred into an all-too-familiar sound bite. "And now we're returning to last night's interview with Belhaven Police Chief Andrews about the drowning in Old Town . . ."

Two men groaned. A third cop aimed the remote like a pistol and sent the news station tumbling into blessed silence.

Jake nodded his thanks, grateful he hadn't needed to spend time chatting to journalists.

Two stations in town had interviewed the chief about the murder victim and the local cable channel was running their longer piece every few hours. They'd promised their listeners updates, too.

Jake wished he had some to offer.

At least the youngest homicide dick on the squad had de-layed his skiing vacation in order to help out on the phones, which were ringing off the hook. It wasn't often a corpse showed up in the largest nightclub district on the East Coast between New York and Atlanta.

Citizens were eager to make suggestions and everything had to be checked out. At least the media still thought it was a drowning case; God knows how intense the hysteria would be if the public knew how viciously his mystery lady had been knifed.

So far, nothing had smelled worthy of taking his tackle out for deeper investigation, as his father would have said. All he had was his corpse; an Egyptian mummy would have been chattier.

Hell, he couldn't even make a guess at her name yet.

"Hey there, Hammond." Danica Jones's honey-flavored Al-abama accent turned the greeting into an invitation.

Jake smiled lazily at her and pretended to give the offer due consideration. Twenty years of marriage and five children later, Sergeant Jones was a lucky man to find Danica in his bed every night. She had more curves than a Ferrari, a better ear for gossip than an FBI wiretap, and a bigger heart than a char-ity telethon.

Somehow their union had even survived her part-time job as a civilian employee, which meant she knew every detail of her husband's workday—good, bad, or indifferent. It made SWAT operations touchy for everyone—the two of them and the rest of the department. Everybody hated seeing her worry during those high-risk moments.

Seeing them together usually sent Jake straight to his fa-vorite meat bar to pick up a partner for some heavy screwing, unhampered by thought. Far better to do that than remember how his folks had gazed at each other the same way.

"Hi, Danica." He sat down at his desk and set the new folder on top of the older, larger pile of leads to be followed up. He could take a few minutes to chat with her before he read them. "You're looking good today. Have you been training for the Tidewater 5K?"

"Oh, real hard." She laughed at him and made a swatting motion. "Can't you see how I've firmed up?"

She rotated and he obediently ogled her, while the detectives across the aisle clapped and cheered.

"You'll make all those other runners sweat when you hit the starting line."

"Runners?" She hooted, her double chins jiggling slightly. "Walkers, honey, walkers. I intend to stroll through the park for the 5K. My wardrobe won't stand up to breaking a sweat."

"Good God, no, you shouldn't have to do that." He rose to his feet and hugged her enthusiastically. "You'll be the most elegant athlete there. In fact, I think I need to pledge more for the battered women's shelter the funds will go to."

"You will?" She squeezed him hard.

"Definitely. They've been in business for a long time."

"Decades." She sniffled. "They're the best around, maybe the best in the state—and we're *this* close to paying off the mortgage. Elswyth will be so thrilled."

"Awesome. The good guys deserve to rescue at least one home from the bank, especially when so many are going down the foreclosure toilet." Jake patted her on the shoulder. "Do you have a blank pledge form?"

"Really? In that case, I'll help, too." Other detectives stirred and moved forward, pens at the ready. Almost all of them had sent a woman and her children to Enfield House at least once. It wasn't the closest shelter to Belhaven, but it was sure as hell the safest.

Danica beamed, bright as headlights burning through fog.

Jake handed her his pledge form. She glanced at the numbers and blinked.

"You deserve it," he said quietly. "Both for the shelter and yourself."

"Thank you." Her smile trembled, then grew. "I'll make record time, I promise."

"Looking forward to seeing it."

"And, Jake—"

"Yeah?"

"Two guys from the FBI are talking to the chief. I think it's about you." She dropped her voice to a near whisper, too quiet to be heard by the other detectives.

"Why?" He stared at her, disbelief icing his veins. Feds were never good news. Either they complicated the case—or the case itself was pure hell. "They'd never get involved with a simple murder, not unless we asked them in."

"Just what I overheard." She shrugged slightly. "Thought you should know."

"Hey, they probably just want help guarding a courtroom." The Federal government had given Belhaven a brand-new, high-security courthouse in exchange for use during badass criminal trials. Belhaven cops liked it as an easy way to earn overtime, as long as it didn't interfere too much with their normal duties. He squelched her far more unsettling suggestion. "Chief always pulls my unit in last for guard duty, especially with a high-profile murder like this one going on."

The other detectives crowded closer to hand over their pledges, and she broke off the conversation with Jake to talk to them.

He glanced back at his messages and shook his head, then sat back down in his excuse for an office and logged onto his computer. One sergeant had always been more than enough to run Belhaven's small homicide squad, given the few murders that occurred in this city. Jake had been on the squad for years before he received the promotion. He knew the job and he knew Belhaven.

Murder cases frequently felt like a messy ball of string. But he'd always known where to find a loose end to pull for clues.

Forty-eight hours into the case—the grace period when he

could usually at least guess where to look—every lead had led nowhere. And the public was giving him mountains more stuff to track down every minute.

He cursed under his breath and drained his latte. Dammit, maybe if he looked online he could find a lead. The coroner's preliminary report might have something useful in it.

His cell phone buzzed against his hip, and he ignored it.

He frowned. How many people had the number to his personal cell? His brother Logan and . . .

The distinctive triple pattern sounded again.

He grabbed his phone and flipped it open.

Message from Andromache.

A slow smile spread across his face despite everything else demanding his attention. They'd played *Argos* together on the same server since the game had started six years ago. Now they were members of the same guild. He was a mage who specialized in blasting bad guys with spectacularly efficient spells, which removed them faster than any court system. She was a very sneaky barbarian warrior, notable for her boobs, black braids, and flying axes according to her online avatar.

He couldn't count the number of quests they'd gone on. He wouldn't have as many points if they didn't game together so often.

Hey there, he texted back to her.

Hi. Gaming tonight?
Sorry. Big case here eating up my time.

He kicked back in his chair, certain she wouldn't want to chat about his job any more than he would hers. She'd probably figured out he was a cop, based on his responses to some very illegal suggestions on *Argos* boards. But she'd never said so specifically and she sure as hell had never been interested in any crimes.

The Belhaven knifing victim?

A cold wave rippled across Jake's skin, faster than a trout rising for air. The number of people who knew exactly how the mystery lady had died were fewer than he had fingers on his phone's keys.

Why? he asked and wondered how fast he could subpoena Andromache's cell phone records, if she didn't tell him.

There was a long pause.

An e-mail announced that the coroner's preliminary report was available for review. Nothing helpful there; that doughty old broad had already phoned him with the results.

Jake started to compose a stronger demand for Andromache.

Do you have ANY leads to the killer?

His thumbs hung over the keypad and he gaped at the small screen like a stranded trout. Why the emphasis? Did she know how unusually hard this case was?

A million questions clamored in his head, but he couldn't send any of them on an open line. He settled for the simplest.

Why do you ask?

Seconds ticked past before an answer came, every letter emblazoned on a yellow flag like a giant warning sign.

I can help.
What do you mean???

Her answer shot back faster than the freight trains barreling into town.

Where can we talk? PRIVATELY.

Jake stood up so abruptly that his keyboard bounced onto the carpeted floor. Heads turned to stare and he glowered their owners back to their own business.

He could take her into an interrogation room, but that would be recorded. Years of friendship demanded better treatment, at least until he knew whether she was willing to tell the truth.

He chose every Belhaven cop's favorite hangout.

Duffy's Tavern in an hour?
Sure. See ya then.

She disappeared without asking how to find Duffy's. Only the trail of golden balloons and text across his phone's screen confirmed she just might have something helpful to say.

He blew out a breath and shoved his phone back into its holster.

The pile of message slips seemed to sneer at him, all spurious innocence in its demand for his attention.

Dammit, his brain would rather race through a thousand labyrinths in a quest to discover Andromache's secrets. Starting with what the hell she looked like.

His computer chimed. A small, orange square began to flash on his monitor's corner.

Jake gave it the same narrow-eyed look he'd grant an open door in a drug dealer's hideout. Then he clicked on it.

Hammond, I need you in my office now. The FBI is here. Over.

All of Jake's previous arrogance about the Feds faded into cold mush at the bottom of his stomach, together with every other stupid boast he'd ever made. What the hell could they do for his case except slow it down?

He gritted his teeth and typed. Roger that.

Maybe he'd catch a break, the second one of the day, and they'd only want to talk guard duty. Yeah, right.

* * *

"Hammond, these are Special Agents Fisher and Murphy of the FBI." Andrews' body looked more relaxed than Jake expected, and yet his eyes were more perplexed. Around him, photographs of him with foreign and national dignitaries radiated confidence. Highly polished examples of every rifle the department had owned for the past two centuries conveyed lethal competence.

Jake shook hands with the two pin-striped strangers and tried to hide his wariness. Their well-tailored suits couldn't disguise the weapons belts at their hips nor their direct assessment of him.

"Gentlemen, this is Sergeant Jake Hammond. He's the head of our homicide unit and is personally leading the investigation into Saturday night's murder case. He was the first detective on the scene."

"Very glad to meet you, Hammond," said Murphy, the taller of the two and a woman. "We'll be working closely with you on Division Director Williams's murder."

"Division Director? Williams?" Shock thudded through Jake's system and deepened his voice. "May I ask who you're talking about?"

"Melinda Williams is a GSA division director who was reported missing in North Carolina five days ago," Murphy answered quietly, her cool, black eyes measuring Jake like a surveyor's sextant.

"Five days? If she drove directly back here, then three days in the water—" The calendar arranged itself in front of his eyes, dates sturdy as soldiers standing to be counted.

"And two days in the coroner's office. Yes, the time line fits neatly." Murphy sipped her coffee as precisely as she'd folded the scarf at her neck. "Miss Williams took a rental car to Elizabeth City, since flights aren't readily available there, unlike Raleigh."

"But she was reported missing in North Carolina, not here." Jake doggedly pursued the victim's footprints.

"Because she didn't tell her office or her family that she was returning. When she didn't phone in, the search started at her North Carolina long-term rental apartment."

Chief Andrews watched them silently, his fingers steepled like a rack of guns ready to go to war.

"Why do you think it's her?" Jake pushed harder, determined to find all the secrets in the FBI's arsenal.

"Miss Williams is very distinctive physically." Fisher spoke up for the first time, his deep voice shadowing the room. "Height, weight"—his eyes met Jake's, and they shared a moment's masculine response to those statistics—"and a small zodiac tattoo on the small of her back all matched your victim. Her fingerprints came back positive just before Murphy and I arrived here."

"Good to know," Jake murmured. They'd probably rushed the tests through. "She worked for GSA, you said. The General Services Administration, right?"

He kept his tongue and, he hoped, his tone away from dismissing them as the bureaucrats's bureaucrats.

"Correct. She was in the Public Building Service, where Uncle Sam is the government's landlord." Fisher and Murphy's utter relaxation confirmed that they, too, considered Williams and her group to be just ordinary public servants, not critical to the country's protection.

"Report said that she was knifed, which is why we came over," Murphy added.

"Since she's a federal employee and disappeared while she was working, her death might be related to her job, making it an FBI issue." Fisher peered into his mug's depths, then unhappily swirled the dregs. "I never expected to find a vanilla latte with soy at a police station. Can we have another round of coffee, please, before we talk about today's real problem— the upcoming arraignment of those terrorists?"

"Sure thing." Jake pushed back his chair. He too could use a good drink.

Triumph flickered through the chief's eyes for an instant. He swore gourmet coffee won more interrogations and political negotiations than any other bribe.

"Once we nail that down, we can chat about how to conduct a joint investigation into Miss Williams's death. It shouldn't take more than a few minutes to make sure we cover all the basics."

Jake nodded politely and headed for the best stash of coffee fixings in the building. He'd need all the help he could get to wash down the FBI's ideas of partnership.

Then get out in time to meet Andromache.

CHAPTER THREE

The old pub was warm and cozy after the dank drizzle outside. Astrid pulled the door shut and allowed its golden light to enfold her like a blanket.

Duffy's Tavern boasted of never having closed its doors, even for the British and Yankee invasions. Baseball and football posters brightened the main room's white plaster walls. In a bow to politicians' delicate sensibilities, an ornate iron grille allowed the bar area to be closed when not in use. Paneled booths with well-padded leather seats and glossy walnut tables welcomed long conversations there and scarred tables sang of long use throughout the entire tavern.

It served doctors and tourists with an efficiency that showed no favoritism. But rumor said the iron grille was sometimes unlocked late at night for cops, after hell came out to play in Belhaven's streets.

It was almost empty now, on this early spring afternoon. A trio of bedraggled tourists stumbled past Astrid, a baby sleeping high atop one shoulder and stroller stuffed with shopping trophies.

Astrid automatically moved out of the way so she could scan for Jake. She'd glimpsed him on TV during press conferences, but not enough for a reliable description. Especially when every instinct told her she was a fool to say she could help.

If the Council found out she was here, they'd kill her—and him—for letting him know there were sahirs. She'd nearly turned around and refused to see him.

But she still heard that woman's screams echoing through her sleep. She had to help that woman's ghost.

She'd just have to bespell Jake so he wouldn't get any suspicions about sahirs, no matter what he thought of her story. After surviving two world wars and a dozen overseas conflagrations, now she was reduced to a rookie's campaign plan. She was late, too, having missed her connection on the Metro, D.C.'s subway, without leaving time for alternative transport.

Pitiful, purely pitiful.

She shook her head at her own idiocy and headed for the bar, her boot heels drumming softly on the old planks.

The bartender watched her, his hands full of clean towels.

The man standing at the end of the counter also turned his head to look, his leather jacket camouflaging shoulders broad enough to block the wall behind. Only a tumble of jet black hair across his brow softened features too harsh to be named handsome. He belonged in this ancient room, the same as the sweating rugby players on the wall or Washington's gaunt, defiant trooper above the fireplace.

He pushed away the glass in his right hand and slowly straightened up to a very imposing height.

A jolt of lust kicked Astrid's belly into her backbone. She sucked in a fast breath and ordered her libido not to be stupid. She'd had one obsession in her life already. That much joy and grief should be enough living for any woman.

She had a bevy of sex partners to choose from back in Georgetown, none of whom tested her self-control. She'd always had more than enough, ever since she'd left Nebraska. She didn't need somebody like him who'd probably never let her escape with half-truths.

"Theseus?" She barely remembered to use her friend's *Argos* name.

"Andromache. Good to finally meet you." They shook hands like idiots who'd never spoken before.

"Same here." Teenagers had more intelligent dialogue than that. "I'd hoped to see you at the last *Argos*Con, when you wore full Colchis mage costume."

Her careless mention of the notorious female-magnet costume made his deep-set eyes heat. His gaze stayed above her shoulders yet Astrid felt her insides melt, like a chocolate candy dissolving under the sun's rays.

She glanced away from his eyes and discovered his sensual mouth held under firm discipline.

Lord, what couldn't he do with those lips—and why was she reacting like this? She was more than a century old; she'd long since earned the discipline to control herself around any *farasha*.

She bolted into the mundane world.

"My real name is Astrid Carlsen. I'm an interpreter for the FBI."

"Sergeant Jake Hammond of the Belhaven Police Department."

"Thought so. I glimpsed you on yesterday's press conference."

He shrugged and ran his fingers over his glass. His level eyes now studied her with a professional hunter's dispassionate curiosity.

For a moment, she could have mourned the lost flash of intimacy. Then she met his gaze just as openly, daring to show a little of her nervousness. Wasn't that what any old friend would do who'd come to talk about a murder?

Inside her coat, her fingernails dug into her thigh.

"Would you like something to drink?" Jake asked, his big body far too alert. "Or we can go back to my office at the station."

Despite all her best intentions, she couldn't control her eyelids' flinch—and she knew those cop's eyes saw every millimeter of it. No social niceties after six years' friendship, just straight down to business, damn him.

His bluntness felt like a desert sandstorm, all-encompassing and all devouring, even though she'd have done the same in his shoes.

Stay composed, Astrid, just as if you were facing the Council.

"I'll take a cup of tea, thank you." She'd learned a good deal about civilization's trappings from the British during two world wars. Polite conversation would be easier if she held some of their reliable brew between her palms. If nothing else, it might be a distraction from him. "We can talk in here where it's quiet."

The bartender, one eyebrow askew, waved Jake toward a booth and started to fix their drinks.

Jake slid onto the bench opposite her.

Astrid gritted her teeth and told her idiotic pulse to slow down. Her skin would not turn clammy now, as if she were a delicate maiden about to faint. She'd never done that, not even when she'd arrived at Radcliffe from Nebraska and seen just how tight city girls had to lace their corsets. She needed all her wits about her for this conversation.

Two cups slid onto the table in front of them and sent their tempting aromas spiraling into the air.

"Thank you." She gave the bartender a grateful glance and pulled her tea closer. He disappeared into the back room.

Late afternoon quiet fell over the tavern, deadly as a courtroom's hush.

What could she say to grab control of this meeting? Pretty phrases fled.

Calluses roughened Jake's big hands, and a thin red scar circled his right wrist like war paint. Dozens of ancient nicks marked his skin, in an armorer's telltale pattern.

He gave her silence, dangerous as the deep pits that villagers use to trap tigers.

"It was the afternoon of the last big snowstorm, when the Beltway shut down. I was driving back to DC after helping with some exams at Quantico," she said abruptly. Best to stay as close to the truth as possible and tests described exactly what she'd been working on with the FBI.

Jake's dark eyes rested on her, impenetrable.

"I headed upriver along the Potomac and wound up . . ."

Dammit, her heart was beating faster than a jazz drummer's showcase. She stopped, wet her lips, and tried again. "I went to . . ."

"I don't need to say anything about where you were unless it's germane to the case," Jake said very gently. His voice could have lulled a screaming baby back to sleep in five seconds, tops.

Courtesy was almost harder to face than his earlier brusqueness had been.

"You haven't heard where I was yet." Astrid shot him a disbelieving glance.

He put his big hand over hers and warmth flooded into her, sweet as the first surge of magick into a newborn spell.

She gaped at him, her skin heating faster than beeswax beside a flame. Lust, her reaction had to be nothing more than lust.

He released her and withdrew to his side of the table. His expression was thoughtful and wary, his jaw clenched tight as that of a prison guard standing watch over dangerous inmates. He had to think she could be the murderer, finally come to confess.

She could have laughed, or maybe screamed in frustration. If he only knew how dangerous the real killer was.

"I was at—the nudist club." How else could she describe where she and Nathan had parked?

Shock whipped across Jake's face, followed by rapid calculation. "Good God, is that why you didn't come forward before?"

She shrugged, knowing her expression was very embarrassed, and let Jake draw his own conclusions. Actually, she and Nathan had needed a quiet place to park, so they could investigate the scream. The nudist club's members were old friends who would never talk about sahir business.

"Did anybody see you there?" Jake's voice turned deeper and more calculating.

"No, I just wanted to spend time with the river." Again, exactly true, whether or not he believed it.

"Go on." Jake leaned forward. His eyes were actually a dark brown, full of the same solid strength that steadied an oak grove.

She sucked in a breath. The murder scene dwelt in her mind's eye, vivid and unforgettable as the entrance to hell.

"After I parked, I went for a walk along the Potomac to get some fresh air." Astrid closed her eyes for a moment and plucked memory's strands for details. She had to re-create the murder for the one authority who could bring justice. "I saw a man standing on a large rock in the river, holding a young woman with his knife to her throat. They were arguing and she was fighting him."

"Are you sure?" Jake's voice was sharper than a judge's gavel demanding justice in a crowded courtroom.

"As sure as you are that Robert E. Lee is buried in Lexington," she retorted, then said more gently. "She couldn't break free, no matter how she tried."

"Oh crap." He rubbed the stubble on his jaw. His thick lashes veiled his eyes. "Could he see you?"

"He had his back to me and she was so much smaller that his shoulders blocked her view of me." *That is, if I'd been in the same time frame, instead of scrying.*

"I wanted to scream but couldn't," she added with unplanned honesty. "Women aren't supposed to die, not like that."

Jake squeezed her fingers briefly in a man's hard, restrained gesture of understanding. An instant later, he was all cop once again.

"How did he have her tied?"

"He didn't." Remembered pain and helplessness surged through her once again to choke her throat. "He simply held her wrists over her head in one hand."

Jake's eyes pinned her like a prize fishing specimen, on the rack to be judged for quality.

She glared straight back at him and let him see all of her rage and disgust. The poor lady had never had a chance; she hadn't even truly known how to fight.

Jake sighed and threw his head back, looking a century older. "What then?"

"He cut her throat and threw her body into the main current," Astrid said simply. "But before that—oh, dear God, how she screamed."

"Scream?"

"The way my husband did when he was killed. A banshee wail demanding justice from everyone within earshot, that went on for seconds—minutes?—until death silenced her. In this world, at least."

She stopped, her throat locked tighter than a five-sahir warding spell. Maybe retelling the murder would become easier the more often she said the words. Or perhaps she'd gain peace when the killer was caught—which was Jake's responsibility.

Jake smacked the table and cursed. "Can you identify him?" he asked sharply, his words a brutal growl.

"Maybe."

"Maybe?" Jake pulled his voice back from a roar that would have tumbled the rafters. "What the hell do you mean?"

"I never saw all of him. He was wearing winter clothes, about what you'd wear to a ski resort."

"Face? Expression? Coloring?" Every question shot out faster than the last until they barreled together like bullets from an assault rifle.

"He wore a black and silver ski mask the entire time."

"Like a football or Viking helmet? Those are rare but we could probably track it down." He frowned, his eyebrows stitching together.

"Maybe," she said dubiously. She'd tried to picture the killer before, but he always blurred like river mist. She couldn't bring up an image of him at all inside the aerie she shared with other sahirs—and that was possibly more unsettling than the murder itself.

"You'll show me the spot," Jake stated. "Now."

It was more a prediction than an order.

"And the nudists?" Astrid queried, well aware she was fighting a delaying campaign.

"They'll survive—unless one of them's the killer. Which was damn unlikely in that blizzard." His grin flashed in an intoxicating invitation to share the laughter.

Astrid joined in and her heart sank. Charm was not what she needed or wanted from Jake Hammond during a murder investigation.

Jake stood in the clearing and studied the thundering Potomac River less than five yards away. Barren trees and dry leaves marked the land around them like ancient sentries. Boulders crept through the underbrush and into the water, forcing anyone or anything who passed to follow their rules. Thirty-foot-high cliffs, covered with still more trees and brush, blocked most of the remaining daylight.

Astrid would have had more than enough cover to watch a murder unnoticed from here, at least during the winter when nothing grew. But could she move silently enough?

Could she have pulled off the murder?

"Where did you grow up?" Jake asked abruptly.

"Nebraska." Her tone screamed that she found the question idiotic—but was too disciplined to challenge him on it.

Crap, everything about her had challenged his discipline from the moment he saw her. Maybe because he hadn't gotten laid in so long. Yeah, right.

He shifted to a better view of the river shoal where the murder had occurred.

Dammit, where Astrid said it had happened.

On the other hand, she knew too damn much about the killing. There weren't many places along the Potomac River's steep sides where somebody could slip a body into the water. Even fewer possibilities when one considered how fast the river had been running and how long the corpse had spent in the water.

Yet, Astrid had led him straight to one of those very few choices.

Was she legitimate or the killer? An FBI employee should be on the up-and-up, but you could never be sure.

She followed him, her booted feet barely whispering through the thick leaves.

Mind and instinct fell into alignment with the answer. He snapped off half a dozen photos in quick succession. "You go hunting much growing up?"

She snorted softly.

"Yeah, I was a tomboy and horse crazy to boot." He could barely hear her above the river's tumult. "My father said having me bring home dinner that way was fair, since I never did much housework."

Shadows carved her expression deep and dark in the twilight.

Jake frowned. Where did kids hunt for supper these days? If she were twenty, he'd give up his next pay raise.

Yet his brother Logan, the Special Forces sniper, wore the same harsh expression when he didn't want to talk about shooting. Maybe she too was strong enough to kill.

"Got everything you need from the shoal?" she asked.

"Yeah. I'll have to come back tomorrow with a forensics team, of course."

"Of course. There was so much blood." She shook herself and turned away from the water, looking paler than before.

His gut bitched at him that she wasn't responsible for the killing. No murderer willingly went gray around the eyes.

"I'll need to take a statement from you." Dammit, where was some real evidence?

"I know." Her tone made a day in the dentist's chair sound appealing.

"It won't be that bad." Dammit, he could do charm better than this. Witnesses remembered more when they were comfortable and Astrid was an old friend. A very, very good friend.

He'd get the truth out of her, no matter what it did to their relationship.

"I think he parked his car in the old turnout at the top." She took off along a narrow trail up the cliff.

"The hiking dropoff?" He admired her rear view far too much, especially when he thought how well it might promise for the bedroom.

Get your mind out of the gutter, Hammond. You're on a case, and she's your only witness—if she is a witness.

"There's a loop trail leading to the parking lot, which offers several routes down to the river," Astrid commented. "The killer could have forced the victim down one and onto that rock. Then he could have returned along a different, faster route."

She stopped at the top, her voice a little ragged, and scrubbed away a single tear.

His heart did a most unprofessional flip-flop.

"There aren't many parking spaces." She looked around, as if the getaway car could appear at any moment.

Jake had long since stopped believing in fairy tales. He'd settle for more achievable aims, like a hug or a date with Astrid, his flesh-and-blood gaming partner.

"There was a foot of snow the night after the murder occurred." Good, he hadn't openly cast doubts on her account. "Plus, we've had three inches of rain since then. We're not finding anything here except mud—and lots of it."

He eyed the tiny lot and tried to remember where Jones had snuck in his wife's little CRV, the Saturday they'd gone hiking together.

"Over here," he decided and headed for the spot. Out of sight from the road, it also offered a glance at the valley floor.

Astrid obediently trailed him. The heavy mud was slick and smooth, innocent of tracks. It fought them worse than a battery of defense attorneys, clinging to their boots and pulling them down with every step.

"How many points do we get for crossing this?" Astrid muttered. "It reminds me of Colchis, where we both died twice."

Jake was startled into a bark of laughter. Once more, her wit had lightened a quest.

"We may not find anything," he cautioned when he could speak again.

"Yeah, yeah, yeah," she muttered. "You and your famous caution."

"Yup, just like that." They halted at the last parking spot, in the corner—the utterly, completely, totally empty gap in the parking lot. There wasn't even a shred of tire track to hint that somebody had ever placed a vehicle in this location.

Icy disappointment swept Jake's heart into the soul-sucking mud. He'd been so sure there'd be evidence here, the one place the killer could have left something heavy while he did his filthy crime. Astrid would never lead him to proof of her own guilt.

She slammed her fist into her palm, then spun away, frustration etched bright as flame in her every line.

Jake started to speak but stopped. She'd see through a platitude in a moment.

He turned around slowly, to scan every detail and buy himself time before he drove a stiff, unhappy beauty back to Washington, D.C.

Something shiny winked at him, bright as the underworld's sky in *Argos*.

He ran for it, heedless of the mud's treachery.

A black and silver piece of cloth lay under a barren shrub, away from fallen leaves and out of the dirt.

Could it be a ski mask? Astrid said the killer wore one.

She was innocent!

Long habit, not intelligence, brought his camera out of his pocket to shoot a half dozen photos.

"The mask." Astrid arrived at his shoulder. She whispered something under her breath that sounded like a prayer.

Jake forced himself to take down notes about the fragment of cloth. He made sure every important detail was documented, such as the complete lack of footprints nearby, whether man or beast. The mask must have been flung under the bush before the snowstorm, to have left the ground so undisturbed.

Astrid stayed close the entire time without speaking to him, although she watched that telltale scrap like a prophetess seeking signs of foul weather.

Finally Jake was free to act.

He snatched up a broken tree ·branch and fished for the priceless artifact. It shrank away from the spiked tip, seemingly content to stay in its lair.

Astrid cursed under her breath in a foreign language, a long guttural string of syllables vicious enough to make a gang leader turn cautious.

The scrap of wool snagged on the branch and came sullenly free. Jake lifted it into the last rays of daylight like a captured pennant. It hung stiff and still for a moment before a vagrant wisp of air stirred it into motion.

A Nazi helmet unfurled before their eyes, the faceplate turned into a skeleton's death mask, hungry as a crematorium's gaping ovens. For a brief instant, arrogance and confidence filled the little clearing like smoke from a thousand burned villages.

Astrid gasped and her hand shot out toward the mask.

Before Jake could stop her from touching it, the breeze disappeared and the ski mask collapsed upon itself. An instant later, it was once again only a sodden bit of black wool with a few metallic markings.

Jake sucked in his breath and his startled wits, then fumbled for an evidence bag in his back pocket.

Now he definitely had a witness to his mystery lady's murder.

With luck, he'd still have his best gaming friend when this was over, no matter how uncomfortably thorough she found his interrogation techniques.

CHAPTER FOUR

A strid stiffened her knees. Even that movement took effort, given the elevator's man-made metal and steel. If only she could reach a kubri or another sahir to draw power from.

"Hang on, we're almost at my desk." Jake glanced over at her. "You can have some coffee as soon as we get there. There may still be some doughnuts, too."

"Ah, doughnuts." She gave him a shaky smile and shifted the evidence case to her other hand. "Aren't they a cop's solution to everything?"

"Yes, especially when we're tired." His eyes saw far too much.

Warding him and herself against the ski mask during the drive back to town had taken everything she had. She couldn't remove its malevolent guardianship spells without direct access, an impossibility given how it was locked up.

Holy crap, she hadn't seen one of them in over sixty years, not since she'd helped clean out the Nazis' reeking bunkers. Where this one had come from, she didn't know—and she was looking forward to finding out. Even inside the case, its vicious power sneered at her warding spells like a Charybdis troll facing a single warrior, instead of a fully armed guild.

Mercifully, the station's protections had helped once they turned in to the garage. As a federal courthouse, sahirs had built wards into its foundations to guard against evildoers and their weapons.

A chime sounded, and the doors glided open to reveal a room full of more cops.

Lovely. She'd hoped Jake would head straight for the evidence room, where she could snatch a second alone with the mask.

"What have you got?"

"Is that the evidence you found?"

"Do you think it came from the victim or the killer?"

People crowded around the Plexiglas case to gawk at the mask, their hot hands and breath pushing it back and forth.

Jake swooped on the case and held it up high.

"Now, now, folks, you know it's going straight into the evidence locker."

Thank God for some small favors. There were extra wards in there so the mask shouldn't cause too much trouble.

She hoped.

Ten p.m. and the station was muted, noise and movement hanging somewhere between the day shift's roar and night's unpredictable bursts of violence.

Except for the hallway outside Jake's office. Like fish lured by a lantern, every bachelor in the building crowded around his door, trying to make time with Astrid.

Sometime during that interminable evening, she'd taken out the clip that held her blond hair. The rippling mass of golden curls tumbled to her waist, tempting the few guys still around to find any excuse to gawk.

In their shoes, he'd do the same. That didn't mean he didn't want to knock their wide eyes back into the Stone Age.

Damn, she was beautiful.

Shit, why had the elevator broken down again? Just to raise his blood pressure?

Jake quickened his step and told himself his guildie needed rescuing. Astrid had spent hours repeating her story to the county police while they cordoned off the crime scene, then again back here at the station. She'd never fretted nor com-

plained once, even when her lips thinned at some of his cohorts' less veiled suggestions about her motives.

But those duties were over now and he didn't need a live
witness anymore. Shit, she could leave now.

He shot a narrow-eyed glare over the lazy fools hanging
around her. They stirred and quickly drifted away on a cloud
of lame excuses.

He looked at her more warily. Had she wanted suitors? Or
had he correctly read those long glances she kept brushing
over him, intimate as a polishing cloth sweeping over a rifle?

"Hey there."

"Hey, yourself." Pleasure and relief danced in her amazing
eyes. She flicked an *Argos* salute at him, the casual movement
suggestive of an ancient Greek helmet.

He returned it, satisfaction easing into his bones.

Christ, he'd had a long day and tomorrow would be worse.
But it had turned out to be a damn fine one, especially because
he'd met her.

"Would you like to sit down?"

"There you go." Jake dropped into his chair and slid the
statement over to Astrid. "One official witness statement,
ready to be signed."

"Great." She held out her hand for the pen and he handed
her one without a word. She glanced at the statement barely
long enough for decency and signed it, driving the writing im-
plement across the paper like a sword.

Her hair slid forward to conceal part of her face, like a helmet's cheek piece. Beneath it, her features were beautiful and
determined, a battle maiden battered by another campaign.
Her eyes were a startling green from this close, almost the
same shade as leaves dancing in a spring forest.

"Did you get the mask locked away?"

"Yeah, it's in the Evidence Room, underneath the new courthouse. We're all part of the same complex." He kicked himself
back into a trivial conversation and tried not to think about

how her gaze lingered on his cheek, and how warm her lips would be.

"Good. I'm glad to know a little of that killer is safe behind bars." She slid the page back to him and he dropped it into his out-box. Daria would file it in the morning. "Do you think the forensic techs will find anything on it?"

He shrugged, unable to think of a lie that might satisfy his old friend's nimble brain. She had long, slender fingers which could wreck havoc on a man's anatomy or his libido. If she walked them up his arm or unbuttoned his shirt . . .

"That bad?" She settled back into her chair, distancing herself from him, dammit.

"You saw where the brute killed her." He capped his pen and jammed it into his pen cup with unnecessary force. "Do you honestly think anybody who'd carry out a murder on the one spot where there'd be no forensics would leave a shred of DNA behind?"

"No. He needed the ski mask for concealment and warmth. But he'd wear a theatrical bald cap underneath to trap every hair, the bastard." She clenched her hands and looked ready to wield her deadly axes.

"Hey, I'll know the minute the techs find anything." He squeezed her hand in reassurance and heat shimmered into life over his skin, like the first touch of summer sunshine. He gritted his teeth against the urge to grab her and forced himself into cop speak. "Whether it's a hair, where the mask was made, anything. The lab's here, too."

"Where the new federal courtrooms are?" Her gaze sharpened.

"Same building. The feds built us a hell of a fine courthouse and police station. We just loan them a courtroom from time to time."

Hell, the resulting vault in the evidence room made the courtrooms' precautions look blasé.

"And they let you earn overtime."

"Exactly." He pretended to smirk, more than willing to look foolish if it kept her with him.

"Well, as long as you're comfortable with the arrangement." She smiled, genuine relaxation softening her posture.

"You look a little tired." He could forget about being a cop for a while and just think about her. "Have you eaten anything?"

"Lunch before twelve and after that—"

He frowned at her, appalled she was so careless with her health.

"I had a half a turkey sandwich from the cafeteria right after we got back here. It's okay; I wasn't hungry and I understand why you needed so much time to fancy up my statement and put away the mask."

He searched her eyes and saw only gallantry there. Guilt pricked him. Surely he could have gotten her out of the station sooner, somehow.

"Jake." She leaned forward and her rich voice drew an intimate braid between them. "Please don't worry about me. Finding the mask changed everything. I didn't know that the murder was truly real until I saw something tangible." Her mouth quirked wryly. "Crazy, isn't it?"

"Not really. You've been under a lot of pressure for the past few days. Especially since you didn't know how to come forward."

She snorted and shoved her hair out of her face, clearly remembering some of his questions earlier. "Jake, you must be as exhausted as I am. You've been pushing yourself for two days on this investigation."

Color brushed his cheek and he could have growled. Homicide sergeants were not embarrassed. Worse, they didn't want to rub their faces against a young woman's palm like a puppy.

"Come on, let's get out of here," Jake said roughly. "Before we both congratulate each other too much."

Her eyes searched his for a moment before she smiled, laughter running bright and free through her eyes.

He didn't say anything else until he picked her up in his car outside the station, on the sidewalk between the police garage and the restored nineteenth-century law offices across the street. The air was cleaner here, full of river mist and the deep solidity of ancient brick buildings and sidewalks.

She blinked at his battered old Mercedes S430 but sat down and strapped herself in without comment.

"Did you take Metro or drive?" Did he have to sound as if he wanted her to leave right away?

"Metro, but they closed early tonight for track maintenance. I can take a cab back to my dorm in Georgetown." She swept her hair out of her short coat matter of factly, without any evidence of coquetry.

His chest tightened. For once, he almost wished he had a bimbo in his car; he could lip lock one of those and fuck her into tomorrow without worry.

Astrid required more consideration. Fellow guildie for six years—hell, she was damn near his best friend.

His mouth acted before his brain caught up. "Would you like to come over to my place?"

Her head snapped around to stare at him. Her eyes were enormous, dark, unreadable pools against the station's brilliantly lit façade beyond his car's windows.

His pulse sped up, faster than just before kicking in a door to seize a bad guy. *Go for it, man; she hasn't slapped you.* "It's too late for a restaurant except Duffy's, which will be full of cops."

She pulled a face and he shrugged in agreement, careful to rein himself in.

"I can make an omelet for each of us. After that, I'd be glad to drive you home."

"Thank you." Her expression made hope sizzle through his bones. "You're very kind and I'd enjoy eating a real dinner with you."

She leaned over to kiss him on the cheek. Instinct whipped his head around and he caught her mouth with his.

He kissed her for a long time, the hot sweet taste of two

people learning each other like two teenagers in high school when a kiss means everything and a car is the only place to be together.

She moaned, yanked her seat belt free, and kneeled up to press closer. He slid his hand around the back of her head, her silken hair caressing his fingers like fire running into his heart.

More, he wanted more.

He took her mouth like the first taste of water on a hot summer day, and she opened to him, denying him nothing.

Honk! A horn blew behind them, close enough to shiver the Mercedes' massive frame.

Jake jerked away from Astrid. She landed across his lap and the center console, caught between his chest and the steering wheel, her white skin gleaming under the streetlights.

"Shit." He glanced into the rearview mirror. A marked patrol car needed to leave the station.

He waved politely and hoped the gesture looked more controlled than he felt. His cock was hard enough inside his pants to shift the Mercedes' transmission.

Astrid slid back across the seat and into her own. She sat up, her sweater back in place and her hair a tumbled invitation to hedonism.

Jake somehow managed to get the car started on the first try but he didn't trust his voice for another block. "Do you still want to come back to my house?"

"Oh, hell yes." Her voice threaded anticipation through the darkness like a fiery lure and she twined her fingers into his. "How soon can we be there?"

"Five minutes, tops."

"Let's go, handsome." She brushed a kiss against his knuckle and anticipation jolted down his spine into his cock.

He gritted his teeth to hold back a groan and hit the accelerator harder. He knew every cop in Belhaven. Better yet, he knew every back alley and how each traffic light was timed. His car could fly when he wanted it to.

Like right now.

CHAPTER FIVE

Astrid allowed Jake to lead her into the old brick house in the staid, prosperous neighborhood. Their fingers were still tightly threaded together as if they were teenagers sneaking in from the barn. The big man beside her stole her breath away until she could look nowhere else.

At the station his calm and self-confidence had radiated through the other cops and, perversely, deepened her attention. She'd been hypnotized by his voice, ruefully understood when men ran to fulfill his slightest request, and frantic when she couldn't see him.

Heat and anticipation ran through her, faster than fire dancing atop a candelabra. She wanted more than stolen kisses in a car or the slow glide of entwined fingers. She needed whoever lay under all that clothing.

Surely that was only because she'd spent so much of the afternoon and evening protecting Jake from the ski mask's ensorcelled malignancy, right?

The door fell back before them and soft lights bathed the kitchen walls under the cabinets the instant they entered, thanks to motion sensor lights.

The plank floor was original but carefully refinished. Turkish rugs were scattered across it, more for function than to suit a decorator's eye. All the fixtures were new but chosen to match the house's age. A battered, antique table and two chairs held pride of place in one corner but the wine cellar looked recent.

It was the simplest, most effortlessly masculine kitchen that she had ever seen. Astonished by the room's comfort, Astrid half-stumbled on the uneven floor.

Jake caught her and swung her against the solid brick wall.

Strength poured back into her from deep within the earth, through the bricks' ancient clay. Her legs steadied and held her. Light and life tumbled over and over each other through her veins, faster and faster every time their eyes met.

He cupped her cheek in his hand and threaded his fingers through her hair. His gaze was unfathomably deep and dark, like a forest pool she could swim in for days. He delicately caressed her scalp and she shivered, tiny spears of pleasure racing through her skin. Her eyes drifted shut in sheer delight.

His mouth came down on hers and his hot breath stole her few remaining wits away. He kissed her as if they had all the time in the world, as if nothing mattered more than this moment, as if this kiss alone would satisfy him.

She answered him as openly, more than willing to enjoy the moment's diversions.

His hands swept down her back and pulled her closer. He stroked the long sweep of muscle until his fingers dared to slip inside her trousers' waistband.

She hummed her pleasure into his mouth, lust sparking like fireflies in her blood. She was surrounded by masculinity, enveloped by it—his wool jacket, cashmere sweater, trousers, the bricks behind her—sinking into her every time she writhed against his hard chest, stroked her leg over his, or kneaded his shoulders.

His cock was heavy and hard between them, hot and thick in its cage behind his fly, imprisoned like her by his will.

She slid her leg up his hip, lust drumming through her veins faster than any rock music.

"Astrid, dammit." His breath stopped in his lungs and he

caught her thigh. He dragged his lips away from hers with a muttered curse.

She went still, startled by his reaction.

Then he kissed her throat, tossed her up into his arms, and left the room at a dead run.

She gulped and clutched his shoulders, a shamefully eager burst of hunger tightening her breasts. Surely this simple display of barbarian tactics should not impress an experienced sahir like her.

Her long-practiced discipline, which had turned cohorts of previous sexual partners into eager fodder for her magick, was now far less important than the salty-sweet aroma of his musk. Or the smooth thrust of his legs under her ass as he carried her forward through the simple living room. Or his heated breath ruffling her hair every time his feet trod on the narrow stairs, steep as any guardhouse tower.

She was captured and on the way to his lair, yet more vibrantly alive than she'd been an hour ago.

What kind of body did he have anyway? His torso looked as if he subsisted on a cop's classic diet of doughnuts, coffee, and cheeseburgers. But when she was tucked this close, his chest offered the same massive reassurance that a weightlifting machine would.

She nuzzled his shoulder, soaking up the contrasting textures of rough wool jacket, soft sweater, and crisp collar, all draped over the taut lines of his collarbone.

"Yummm," she purred and pressed a kiss in between his shirt and sweater.

He jolted, then chuckled a little hoarsely. "Hedonist."

"Oh, you have no idea," she said honestly. He'd certainly never dealt with a century-old sahir before, let alone one eager to recharge her magick. She curled her hand around his nape, the same way she would with a kubri, and let her sheer, reckless enjoyment of this moment flow into him along with a bit of her magick.

"Pretty lady." His eyes darkened before his mouth came

down on hers again, hot and possessive. She answered him eagerly, more than pleased that he welcomed a two-way flow of magick, unlike most farashas.

She came up for air when he sat down on an enormous bed. A very modern TV sat atop a smoothly carved cherrywood chest that any antique dealer would have coveted. The streetlights' reflections danced like tiny candles among nicks and scars in the dark red furniture.

Photos covered the walls, of a laughing family with two sons and also exotic locations with no people visible. All were carefully framed, as individual as the photos themselves.

The room was efficient, well worn, and made Astrid's heart skip a beat.

"Astrid, sweetie." Jake lifted her chin with a finger and kissed her eyes. She closed them far too willingly, happy not to look at his tempting lair.

He kissed her eyebrows and the bridge of her nose, her temples and her cheekbones, her forehead and her upper lip.

Her breath stuttered and stopped. She turned to come up onto her knees and rubbed herself over him, only to meet with jacket and sweater and shirt.

"Jake!" She pulled back, disgruntled, then reached for his waistband. Dammit, she knew exactly how to deal with this problem.

"Astrid!" he mimicked and caught her by the wrists.

"You're wearing too many clothes." She glared at him. She was probably stronger than he was, especially with her magick. Did she want to betray that? Probably not. She frowned even harder.

"We are *both* wearing too many clothes," he pointed out, still holding her in that inexorable grip.

She glanced down at herself and beheld a matching array of jacket, sweater, and trousers. At least her jacket was a casual sports jacket, rather than a suit jacket. Then again, she was wearing high boots, unlike him.

"True," she agreed. "Do you want to undress together or one at a time?"

"What do you think?" He shifted slightly under her and his cock nudged, hotter and far larger than the flames dancing within the furniture.

She flushed—and a far stronger surge of lust knotted her belly.

"Together," she said hoarsely.

"Smart girl." He dropped a single kiss on her tousled curls, then released her wrists.

She leaned up and kissed him on the cheek, then slid off his lap. She'd have to take off her boots quickly, never easy with a pair that reached her knees. And then there were her skinny jeans, which peeled off slowly—if one was lucky.

She sat down on the chest under the windows and let Jake have the bed. She'd never get any traction on the boots if she was perched high atop that mattress.

The first boot came off without too much sweating and tugging.

A piece of dark woolen cloth flew across the room, hit the TV, and draped the chest of drawers.

Astrid froze, her heart pounding, then slowly went back to tugging off her second boot. If she thought about what Jake looked like, or the night's possible activities, then she might not get her boot off at all.

She gripped the heel a little harder, pulled more strongly, and—eureka! Her foot moved inside the boot. Another wriggle, another tug, and another piece of cloth flew past her head.

She closed her eyes and lowered her head, her heart thudding in her chest like a steam engine driving for the station.

Then she muttered a simple housekeeping charm under her breath, a trick utterly forbidden in any encounter with a farasha.

The boot promptly loosened and came off.

She looked up at Jake in triumph, more than ready to reclaim the advantage over her pounding pulse.

Barefoot and shirtsleeves loosened, Jake stood next to his bed. His crisp, cotton shirt and trousers outlined a body sculpted in muscles.

"Jake, perhaps you should..." Her throat closed down when her mind refused to supply words, only deeds. Astrid's fingers itched to undo that precise row of buttons marching down his shirt, that shiny buckle closing off his trousers, that crisp collar blocking his throat...

"Yes?" He slid his hand into his back pocket and accentuated an incredibly delectable ass.

Astrid's mouth watered. The boot dropped out of her hand, onto the floor.

A worn black leather wallet appeared in his palm. He flipped it open, checked the golden star inside, and snapped it shut.

Whap!

The rich scent of salt and sweat and Jake rolled over Astrid. Her knees almost buckled and she bit back a moan.

"Astrid?" Jake's voice deepened to a slow, enticing purr. "Are you a badge bunny, sweetheart?"

"A what?" She blinked at him, baffled, and tried desperately not to rub her legs together. How could she be creaming when all they'd done was kiss? This was the first time they'd met in person, dammit, even if they had known each other for six years.

"Somebody whose fetish is police badges." His Virginia drawl hadn't sounded that attractive back at the courthouse. "And cops."

"Certainly not!" A woman didn't live more than 130 years without understanding her own kinks.

"Sure? This here's my department-issue Sig Sauer." His hand came slowly out from behind his back carrying a large automatic, like a dildo on a salver.

Her core clenched again, and heat rocketed through her veins. Dear heavens, she was wet.

She gave a long, heartfelt moan.

"Getting eager, honey?" Jake teased.

Thank God he, too, sounded hoarse.

Astrid nodded, unwilling to trust her voice.

"And the magazines for my Sig."

She shot a frantic look at the small, ferocious boxes. Would he delay matters by loading and unloading his gun, marking his mastery of the situation—and her—by the soft thud of those deadly bullets sliding home?

"These are my department-issue handcuffs." Perfectly polished steel gleamed across his callused palms like the path to untold delights.

Far, far too many delicious scenarios immediately ran through her mind, all of them involving those handcuffs, her naked body, and his wicked grin. Her hips rocked toward him, borne by an irresistible current.

She was scorching hot, and her nipples were chafing her camisole. Impatient and desperate, she peeled her long alpaca sweater over her head. She wanted the man who effortlessly controlled those deadly items. Now. Before she crawled to him, as she'd never done to any man.

He caught his breath, and his brown eyes widened.

A purely feminine note of triumph, mixed with anticipation, ran through her. Two could play this game—but she still didn't know what he looked like under all that clothing.

She rose and thrust her fingers inside her waistband. She could unbutton it slowly, of course—right? Maybe not, especially when he was watching her like a hungry tiger eager to pounce.

Astrid's fingers grew clumsier and clumsier, her breath tighter and tighter.

He yanked his sweater off. His shirt was stretched tight over a broad chest that her family blacksmith would have envied.

She whimpered and forced her jeans down over her hips. If she didn't hurry, she'd hurl herself at him fully clothed and denim was a more effective barrier than any condom.

"Holy fuck, Astrid!"

Her head came up and she stared at him. She stayed bent over, her thumbs hooked into her jeans where they'd stalled just above her knees. "What do you mean, Jake?"

"A ruffled black thong?"

"Why not?" She shimmied her jeans down a little farther and wiggled her ass at him. "Have any objections?"

"No, of course not." He gulped audibly. Buttons popped and he tore his shirt off. "But how do you expect a man to overlook *ruffles*?"

She blinked.

"Why should I want you to?" she answered reasonably and kicked off her jeans. An instant later, his trousers covered hers.

"Minx!" He smacked a handful of items down on the nightstand. "Will you ignore this?"

He slid his hands underneath her camisole and kissed her again, harder and hotter than before. She answered him eagerly, pushing against him in a frantic quest to join herself to him in any way she could. He chuckled hoarsely into her mouth and caressed her freely, his rough hands fondling her, shaping her body to his, exploring her possessively.

She moaned into his mouth and rubbed herself over him. His breath heated hers, and his nipples caressed her chest. Even the rough hair on his legs incited her, sending hot jolts up her thighs and into her core to send her soaring.

He half lifted, half tossed her onto his bed and came down onto her. He was so big that he effortlessly covered her, yet every sensation focused more mind-shattering delight.

He knelt between her legs and rained kisses over her eyes, her throat, her breasts. She twisted restlessly, desperate to reach the heights that he alone held the key to. But he held her hips until she stilled.

Then his tongue swept lower, down her belly, along her thighs, across her mons . . .

"Jake, please," Astrid begged, too hungry for him to care about anything except satisfying them both.

He tasted her, delving between her folds as if she was the finest treat in the world. She thrashed under him, frantic for more, desperate to be closer to him. Her pulse thundered through her and she wrapped her legs around him.

He gave a choked laugh and pulled free.

Before she could blink, he returned. There was a *snick!* of torn foil and a condom packet fell onto the nightstand, beside his Sig Sauer.

She whimpered, too far gone in pure lust to cast her usual contraception spell.

A moment later, he was finally—finally!—in her arms, and his big cock nudged her entrance. She shifted, and he slid inside, to be promptly welcomed by her greedy muscles. He stretched her from the inside out in all the most deliciously wicked ways.

She threw back her head and loosed a heartfelt moan. *Heaven.*

"Come on now, babe," Jake said, "gotta give a fellow just a little time to prove he's not a pig." He started to thrust slowly, varying his angle and intently watching her face.

Oh, dear God, was he hunting for her G-spot, too?

A sudden shock wave ran through her, brighter than shooting stars. "Ah, Jake!"

"Better." His voice sounded tighter. But she wasn't listening, not really, not when he started moving again and again, faster and faster. Always against that one perfect spot, always triggering that shock wave, always breaking and re-forming her ideas of what pleasure truly was until—

Her bones shattered and she tumbled upwards like a child rocketing over a Ferris wheel. She shouted for joy and their voices mingled, his hot liquor pulsing again and again within her, deep inside his condom.

She clung to him afterward, content to lay her head against his chest and listen to their pulses slow down together from a mad gallop to the merely frantic.

He began to caress her hair, drawing each lock through his fingers slow and easy like a banker counting coins in his strong room.

If she didn't say anything, surely it was only because she needed to catch her breath. Not because he'd made her rethink what she needed to be happy.

Right?

CHAPTER SIX

Even the sun was smarter than to haul itself out of bed to greet Jake the next morning. Not that it mattered; he'd rubbed the cobwebs out of his eyes many times to make a predawn rendezvous with his fellow cops.

But his cock had never grumbled so much before about leaving a lover.

And how often had a woman simply brushed off his apology for waking her and rolled out of bed herself? Never. They'd always grumbled or complained or, worse, pleaded for another meeting, until he couldn't wait to shut the door on their sorry asses.

Astrid's ass—well, that was another matter, as it accompanied a beautiful face and a mouth that didn't say too much. Like right now.

Or that gorgeous body he hadn't had time to fully explore last night. Shit, you'd think he was a teenage boy the way he'd crashed and burned after one orgasm.

Don't think about that, Jake. Just finish getting dressed; you don't have much time left before the CSI van picks you up.

She swept her brush through her hair again, then shook her head to test the tangles. The golden locks swung free in a rustling mass of silk—and Jake's cock immediately surged hard against his guaranteed-to-meet-any-test tactical trousers.

He muttered a bitter curse, dictated by Murphy's Law. But

logic insisted he'd see her again. After all, he had her address and phone number on her witness statement. She'd return to testify when he caught the killer, right?

"Jake?" She glanced at him, all green-eyed innocence.

"Nothing." He latched his belt buckle with an unnecessary snap and ordered his unruly body to restrain itself.

Even if the prosecutor didn't call her in, he would still know where to find his guild mate for another round of *Argos*. Now he could suggest that they game in person, which would make questing together more intense.

His stuttering heartbeat refused to listen. His skin heated everywhere she came close, dammit. He threw a veil of words over his dawdling, rather than say he lingered over memories he hoped to repeat.

"Just double-checking my gear for today to make sure I have everything."

"Oh." She looked him over again, her eyes lingering approvingly on every inch of his rough garb.

He almost preened but controlled himself in time.

The horrified nudist colony had freely agreed to a search of its grounds, as long as its name wasn't mentioned. Jake was now dressed to explore dense woods and swamps in high boots and heavy trousers, plus a long-sleeved turtleneck and many-pocketed vest. He'd add a jacket just before he arrived at the scene with his team.

"You look as if you have everything you need," she remarked. She dropped her hairbrush into her bag and drifted forward to stand behind him.

His stupid pulse sped up again, intrigued by her proximity. What else could he want for today's search, that might interest her? Even if he didn't have an item on, he had its spare in his kit.

"I was wondering if—" He glimpsed the old jewel chest in his socks drawer. "I could wear my ear cuff."

"Ear cuff?" Curiosity sparked in her eyes. "You, a cop, wear that kind of jewelry?"

"Hey," he protested, "it's not a heavy piece of metal, like a tin can bent around my earlobe."

She raised a single eyebrow, elegant as a judge lifting her gavel to eliminate a nonsensical argument.

"Plus, I always concentrate better when I'm wearing it. You know, like acupuncture." God knows that was true. His intuition always flashed brightest with this jewelry. There was only one problem.

"But I don't know if my hair is long enough to hide it." He shook his head to emphasize its length. "I have to get it cut frequently. If not, I look like a shaggy dog."

"How very important the cuff must be." Laughter danced in her eyes. She drifted her fingers up his chest, then held out her hand. "Let me hold it against your ear and see if it disappears."

Jake obediently handed her the cuff. With luck, this would lead to a good-bye kiss that was both sweet and intimate.

Astrid stared down at the delicate gold jewelry. It curved across her hand like a vine, its stems and leaves seeming to catch the light like a living thing. Astonishment mingled with awe, then rippled through her expression and melted into hunger.

Her tongue darted out, swept over her lips, and disappeared like a crimson enticement to lust. The air suddenly turned thick and scented with rare spices.

He fought to drag in another breath.

"Oh, I believe you'll be very, very successful with this ear cuff," she whispered, her voice a throaty invitation to sin. She laid her palm against his thigh, up high, just below his cock. It promptly surged even harder against his so-called indestructible trousers. "Would you like to know how much?"

He managed to nod.

"Put it on and let me show you."

He slipped it onto his left ear, closest to his heart. For the first time since he'd been given it eighteen years ago, it locked neatly into place just under his ear's upper curve. The stems disappeared behind his ear, leaving only the delicate leaves as evidence he wore jewelry. Their long, sloping lines pointed upward until it almost appeared he had an elf's pointed ears—except for his shaggy black hair, which would be better suited to a barbarian.

His pulse settled and hummed. It was always happier when there was pressure on this ear. But, hell, an acupuncturist could probably make it do that.

Jake frowned at himself in the mirror. He'd be joining men from the FBI, his own department, and the home county today at the nudist colony. He couldn't afford to wear funky jewelry, even if doing so barely skated under department guidelines.

He took a step forward to yank it off and dump it back into his drawer.

But a pair of female hands on his hips stopped him in his tracks.

He staggered, caught totally off guard.

"Sexy," purred Astrid. "Very, very sexy, Sergeant." Her voice could have persuaded a sitting judge to close shop and join her in an orgy.

Jake's breath caught in his throat. Heat and strength blurred together somewhere below his knees like hot springs gathering for an eruption.

"Do you mind if I pay you some attention, Sergeant?" She gently fanned her fingers across his fly.

He shook his head rapidly, his chest tighter than the cloth stretched across his hips. He didn't trust himself to speak, lest he squeak like a schoolgirl or grab like a boor.

"Thank you; you're very kind," she murmured.

He was kind? No, he was greedy.

She murmured something under her breath, then carefully unbuckled his belt. It came undone far more quietly than he'd fastened it a moment earlier. Astrid sank to her knees in front of him.

Jake threw back his head. He should tell her to stand up. He should order her not to do anything. He should remind her—

and himself!—of everything he needed to do that morning and the strict schedule he had to adhere to.

She gently tugged the zipper past the crest of his aching cock.

He hissed in pain or anticipation. He didn't know which; he didn't much care.

"For the love of God, Astrid." His fingers cupped her head. He glanced at the nightstand and winced. *Don't think about when the team will arrive; just look at Astrid.*

Surely he could make up the time, if he did the driving and took his favorite shortcuts.

She lightly kissed the heel of his hand, sweet as the brush of an angel's wings. She slowly peeled the zipper down the length of his cock until it bobbed free, dark crimson and more swollen than he could recall.

Astrid hummed approvingly and heat roared into his groin to sustain his erection, down his spine and into his cock, vibrant and all-consuming.

"Irresistible," she whispered. Her slender fingers delved into his trousers and cupped his balls, playing with them like greater toys than found on any pool table.

He moaned, thrown far beyond words, and widened his stance to give his lover anything she wanted.

She stroked his cock and swirled her tongue over the tip. Precum dripped wildly, chasing her blandishments. She cooed against him and sucked him, blatantly enjoying every inch, every drop.

He panted and fought to stand erect when every cell, every iota, begged to explode inside her mouth and dive down her throat.

She pumped him, swirling her hand over and around his shaft in a spiraling, twisting motion that savored every inch. His hips surged toward her, his seed gathering stronger and stronger in his balls. Only Astrid and the magic she evoked mattered in this instant.

"That's it, Jake, honey," she murmured. Her heavy eyelids

barely cloaked her lambent green gaze. "Give it to me now, honey, just let it rip."

Her tongue swept over her swollen red lips, as if anticipating a rare treat. Then she lunged forward and took his cock all the way in, all the way down her throat.

He howled, immediately blinded by lust. He thrust once into her hot, velvet cavern.

She moaned around him, palpating his shaft where sight didn't matter, only intimacy and passion.

He thrust again and she bucked against him, the desperate cue of a woman hunting her own fulfillment. His orgasm surged out of his spine and into his balls, more powerful than a SWAT battering ram.

Her fingertip pressed into his asshole and released every inhibition.

He thrust once more down her throat, deeper than he'd ever thought possible. She caught him to her and he spilled himself down her throat, over and over again, in a series of cascades, mindlessly ecstatic. She shuddered around him and her hands bit into his hips, the pain spurring him higher still.

Waves of fiery hot orgasm washed through his bones and muscles, turning him inside out, like a starfish pummeled against a beach.

It seemed a long time before he heard a victorious marathon runner gasping for air. His brains needed a few moments more before he realized he was the athlete being held upright by the lady—and the bedroom clock hadn't changed its opinion of the time.

The doorbell rang downstairs on a long, sharp note. The CSI van, his ride to the crime scene search, had arrived.

"Listen up, guys." Jake could have grinned at the fine crew surrounding him but he needed to keep things serious.

Some were from Belhaven and the FBI, plus the well-funded suburban counties who hated any mention of knife killers. The local sheriff's office had done its best to make a good showing, even though they were probably still recovering from the snowstorm. Big snow, then a fast melt, meant lots of accidents from snow, ice, and floods to keep a department hopping.

"We've got two sites to concentrate on. First, we have to check out the hiking drop-off, where the only physical evidence has been found so far."

Nobody looked bored, even at this very obvious opening statement. Given the gorge's steepness, there were only two places to put a car—the hiking drop-off or the nudist colony, which required an electronic card key for admittance. Any and every search would include the public access.

"Next, we'll check out that granite ledge in the river, plus the path leading down to it."

Heads swiveled to look where he pointed.

"The witness?" squeaked a young man. "You mean she was telling the truth?"

Jake spun on the sheriff's deputy. He deliberately had not mentioned the source of his information.

Well, that ruined any chance of keeping his material witness a secret from the whole damn world. Or at least the cops in it.

"How the hell did you know, Schachter?" asked the local sheriff in a voice which would have made even a sleeping bloodhound spring to attention.

"I came out here with her and wrote down her report, sir." The kid glanced around for sympathy but found only hard, expressionless faces.

"I didn't see that in any of my summaries," his boss remarked.

"It sounded crazy when you look at the place. I mean, who'd wade out into a river to kill somebody when you can do it in comfort on the shore?"

"What happened to the report, Schachter?" the sheriff asked, still in that deadly cold voice.

Jake was glad he had only met the sheriff in a helpful mood.

"It's in my desk, sir. I haven't entered it into the computer yet because of the backlog and all." Schachter looked at his boss's face and went even paler. "Sir."

"Since you were here immediately after the attack, why don't you show us where you looked?" suggested the sheriff. "After that, we can talk about your next fitness report."

The kid blanched. To give him credit, he moved out into the front and started working.

CHAPTER SEVEN

Astrid placed both hands on her condo's glass wall and wished she could ask for an overseas post. Somewhere she wouldn't worry about Jake Hammond and his doings while she performed her duty.

This aerie, like all modern dormitories for Shadow Guard members, was a glass skyscraper. It curved into its waterfront location like a towering wave, set on one edge. Thanks to the magick embedded in it, any inhabitant could open a gate to anywhere in the world from here.

But a transfer was impossible, since she was on mandatory home rotation. Call it R&R, or recharging—or even letting the Council make sure she was still steady enough to stay in the Shadow Guard—nobody would let her fly out of here.

No, she had to stay and pay the piper.

"What did you tell the Council?" Elswyth asked. Her normally rich drawl had almost vanished, testimony to unusual agitation.

Astrid swung away from the floor-to-ceiling glass wall and offered a smile to her friend. It didn't soothe the older sahir, judging by the sharper frown lines between her brows.

"The truth, of course," Astrid said.

"But not all of it," Nathan cut in, his Boston Brahmin accent a harsh contrast to the women's voices. He was leaning on the sofa in a studied attempt at casualness, probably to remind himself how junior he was in this gathering. His Armani suit perfectly matched the room's sleekly modern perfection; a fool would have taken him for nothing more than a gigolo.

Six years ago, Astrid had taken some of her profits from his stock market advice and spent almost half a million dollars to decorate this condo in highly polished wood and marble. She probably needed to redecorate, just to give herself something new to do in the evenings.

"No, not everything. But you can never lie to the Council." Astrid sighed and gave up looking for an escape. She headed for the kitchen to make herself a cup of coffee and damned modern architects for creating open floor plans that didn't let hostesses hide.

"You admitted to farasha police that you'd seen a murder? And then told the Council what you'd done?" Elswyth spun her chair to stare at Astrid across the breakfast bar. The vivid afternoon sunlight turned her complexion sallow, rather than pure cream, below her raven black hair.

"We all know it's okay for sahirs to help farashas when there's been a crime," Astrid put on her most reasonable tone.

"Minor problems like pickpocketing, or perhaps attempted rape." Nathan snorted harshly. "Certainly not anything involving magick."

"Well, of course I didn't mention the scrying spell!" Astrid slapped the brewer's faceplate. It immediately began to grind and brew her beloved, very strong, organic Sumatran coffee beans.

"But you did go to farasha police, even though Shadow Guard agents are supposed to keep a low profile." Nathan crossed his arms and leaned against the door jamb, effectively boxing her in. "What excuse could you possibly have for that?"

"What?" Elswyth's shriek shattered a crystal champagne flute. "Sorry." She flicked her fingers and the shards gathered into a cloud, then dove into the trash can.

"Girlfriend," she said more temperately, "you can't just

spring a surprise on your friends like that with no warning. You know the Council does not like to have sahirs anywhere near farasha police."

Coffee splashed into Astrid's cup from the disgustingly high-tech machine. A percolator, like the one she'd first learned how to make coffee in, would have given her more time to compose herself. Or perhaps make up a suitable story.

"The cops didn't ask me why I was there," she mumbled. She wouldn't readily admit how much the woman's scream had sounded like Gerard's. Reliving either death cry meant reawakening nightmares that had shattered her soul for years.

"But cops are trained observers and might spot something wrong, something we couldn't arrange a spell fast enough to block." Nathan set his coffee cup down on the counter, clearly preparing himself for a long interrogation.

"The detective believes I work for the FBI."

"So what? Lots of baby J. Edgar Hoovers in this town." Elswyth sniffed haughtily. "That's not enough reason for a cop to be polite."

Astrid splashed unnecessary milk into her best coffee. "*This* farasha cop is my old friend."

"We're not supposed to be—" Elswyth began, her voice deadly soft.

"You should have known before—" Nathan interjected, sharper than an executioner's blade.

"*Argos* is my only recreation!" Astrid roared. The condo walls vibrated and the stone fireplace hummed, amplifying the truth in her statement. Every wineglass and pitcher echoed their song and she ruthlessly fed magick into the spell, using oh so very little of what she'd gained from Jake that morning.

Nathan stiffened, then bowed low in acknowledgment.

Elswyth flung up her hands in acquiescence. She wouldn't lose her temper again here today.

Astrid nodded slightly and gently released the spell. The magick slipped away, back into the room's foundations, ready to feed her needs again at a moment's notice.

"*Argos* is my only recreation," Astrid said again, much more gently. "Hundreds of thousands of people enjoy it and it's impossible to check out all of them. I didn't consider notifying the farasha police about the killing until I realized my longtime friend led the investigation."

Elswyth grunted, clearly still unhappy. Astrid couldn't read her thoughts behind those brilliant black eyes.

"First law is that the needs of the many—" Elswyth intoned an uncomfortable moment later, like a high priestess starting the confessional.

"Outweigh the needs of the few." Astrid rubbed her thumb over her cup's rim. She'd dueled the Council long and hard for permission to proceed. If only she trusted their acceptance as much as her favorite spell book.

"But if I could pass on a hint to somebody I trusted, surely that doesn't infringe on my service to the many?"

"You'd let *him* hunt for the murderer, and thus look out for the needs of the few?" Nathan cocked his head. "Interesting."

"Too risky!" Elswyth countered. "You're Shadow Guard, the finest of all sahirs. He's not one of the farasha cops, like those FBI we work with, who're bespelled not to see what we really are. Even those who employ you believe you're truly one of them."

"No, but the detective and I *are* friends. He won't make trouble for me." *I hope.* "Besides, I pointed out to him how close the site is to that nudist colony. He thinks that's why I'm trying to keep my testimony low-key, so it won't embarrass the Bureau."

"What!" Nathan choked.

"Did he ask who you were with?" Elswyth asked. She studied Nathan, a wicked gleam in her eyes.

"No, I told him I went there after some tests at Quantico."

"Not a bad description of your FBI work, given all the special translating jobs you do," Elswyth mused.

"If he asks about companions, I'll say that the club's policy forbids me to say." Astrid shoved the conversation into smoother channels.

"Quite true." Elswyth was still thinking hard.

Astrid flicked her fingers and milk obediently began to heat for Elswyth's beloved cappuccino. Sweetening her mood never hurt and might help.

"Unless either of you would like to join me at the farasha station?" Astrid asked her oldest friends among the sahirs.

"Like hell!" Nathan jerked upright. "A murdered farasha is not worth risking everything for." He gripped Astrid by the arm and half shook her. "You're a fucking idiot to even think of it. Where the hell is Astrid, the ice bitch, who taught me how to stay alive in occupied Europe and serve my country so damn well?"

His harsh voice flayed Astrid's spirit raw and she flinched.

"Nathan," Elswyth purred, deep and rich like a voodoo princess offering up the poisoned goblet, "have you asked yourself yet why the *Council* permitted Astrid to live after confessing to this reckless deed?"

Two heads spun to stare at her.

"What do you mean?" Nathan asked slowly and freed Astrid.

She didn't bother to voice the words; she'd worn grooves deep into her brain by asking herself the same question.

"We all know the usual punishment for such behavior is death," Elswyth reminded him.

Astrid poured her coffee's dregs down her throat without flinching. Their bitter taste was no fouler than that potential destiny.

"But she's still alive." Nathan studied Astrid as if seeking signs to disprove that theory.

"Maybe they want Astrid to go out on a limb."

"Not because I'm the most deadly sahir in the country," Astrid protested.

"They don't know that."

"What do you mean?" Astrid frowned at Elswyth. A frisson of magick shimmered into life under her skin as if summoned by its mention.

"Most sahirs only live to be fifty, perhaps eighty years of age, before they shatter and die while working magick."

"Yes, trying something beyond their powers. Everyone's told me about that, and Christ knows I've seen it." Nathan flapped his hand at the old bogeyman from academy days. "Go on."

"But striving to climb higher is the only way to learn what peaks a sahir can reach."

"The amount of power he can channel?" Astrid turned the idea over in her head, more intrigued than she wanted to admit. Back in Nebraska, those who wished to survive learned caution, particularly women. She'd learned that lesson before she'd gained words to express it.

"What if the Council is willing to let you be reckless, just to see how powerful you are?" Elswyth's eyes were dark and unfathomable, as if they held more knowledge than even she could voice.

"It's just a murder investigation: I'm not working magick for this," Astrid countered. Elswyth's explanation was colored with far too many dark motives for her taste, even if it did sound like the Council.

"If you're reckless enough to risk your life, why wouldn't you go further and work magick by yourself?"

Astrid's stomach knotted but her skin hummed in anticipation. Her brain stalled, racing over and over the same phrases, both attracted and terrified by their potential.

"You did at Oslo," Nathan said slowly. "You didn't have any backup there."

Astrid set her cup down on the counter with suddenly nerveless fingers.

"I was in my ancestral country, in the ancient fortress which guarded its capital," she countered carefully.

How many times would she relive in her dreams the moment when the great battle fleet loomed out of the morning mists? Early on a Sunday morning, while so many fluttered over whether the risk was real, she'd looked down the fjord's mountain-girded throat and imminent death.

"You had no artifacts with you for aid, nor time to work spells to draw upon the ley lines." Damn it, Elswyth had been asking her about this for years. That didn't make her gaze any easier to meet now.

"You didn't even have a kubri who could channel magick into you." Nathan's eyes narrowed, as if envisioning himself on that battlefield. "If you'd had a powerful kubri there—"

Somebody who could have fed her power from the earth itself to fill her magick, hotter and brighter than any sex with a stranger. What couldn't she do with a brilliant kubri at her side?

What more could she have done if Jake had been there?

"Were there any Norwegian sahirs on duty that morning?" Elswyth wondered.

"Nobody, not in the beginning." Astrid clenched her fists, icy cold rage coming to life once again through her veins. "It was Sunday morning in Norway, a neutral country. Why should they be armed and ready for an attack? They'd given no provocation and received no diplomatic notice."

"Instead the entire Nazi invasion force sailed down the fjord to attack the capital." Nathan's face was all harsh lines and stubborn angles now, stern as during the Spanish Civil War's last, bitter hours. "How many sahirs did Hitler send with his finest ships? A dozen? Two dozen? More?"

"I didn't know and I didn't care." Astrid shrugged and set aside old what-ifs. "I still don't."

"Instead of taking up guard duty at the American Embassy, as was your duty as a Shadow Guard member—"

"And the conservative tactic," interjected Nathan.

Faugh! Cower in the American Embassy with Gerard's death blow still clawing at my gut? Never.

"The Nazis would never have attacked the American Embassy." Astrid poured herself a slug of Courvoisier from her cooking wine stash, the closest place to find good booze. "They'd already proved that while raping far too many capitals."

She tossed back the cognac like water, as if it could wipe away the bitter memories. Rage still surged through her veins every time she remembered that dawn.

"You stayed and fought with a group of naval reservists." Elswyth's measured tones allowed no evasion.

"A split-second decision." Astrid shrugged off any heroics.

"Their single, antique torpedo took out Hitler's finest battleship." Unaccustomed awe rang through Nathan's voice. "How? It would have been a damn difficult shot, even if Hitler's sahirs hadn't surrounded the fleet with every protection, every disguise they could manage."

Nathan caught Astrid and swung her to face him.

"What did you do? That was a masterwork, worthy of a trio of sahirs backed by their kubris! Or even a country's sahir council."

"I was furious." Astrid caught his hand and looked at Elswyth, old angers thrumming hard and fast through her. "Norway was my family home; I was angrier than I'd ever been before to see it betrayed like so many other countries. The Nazis killed Gerard the day before."

"And so you acted," Elswyth said softly.

"When you see evil coming, you take any weapon you can find," Astrid forced the words out between her teeth. "I bespelled it and hurled it at the best target I could find . . . I didn't care if my death was needed, so long as it struck home."

"How very reckless of you," Elswyth commented, so softly the hairs on Astrid's nape stood up. "No wonder you spent a month in a coma afterward. It's amazing Nathan was able to get you out of Norway alive."

"Don't remind me," he muttered. He dumped whisky into his coffee and knocked it back.

The memories made Astrid shudder, too, before she escaped back to today's worries.

Could Elswyth be right about the Council's motives? Astrid had spent years fighting for her own survival and for others.

But she'd never hurled herself against magick's boundaries, except for that one brief moment.

"You'd have done the same in my shoes." Astrid poured herself a double slug of brandy and drank it down, wishing sahirs could get drunk. Maybe she should have another cup of espresso.

"You're saying we're the three oldest sahirs who aren't rated for power." Nathan's agile banker's mind was back to gnawing at the Council's motives again.

Astrid frowned at him. "What do you mean by that?"

"The Council never summoned Elswyth to the tournaments to see how many levels she can master."

"No, their rules blocked an ex-slave's wife from admittance," Elswyth said brusquely. "Years passed before they'd even allow me to leave Enfield House to visit other sahirs."

"After you became a widow—" Nathan prompted gently.

"Some of the challenge crystals always clouded with grief and anger every time I tried to lift them. Since you cannot wield full power unless they are perfectly clear, I was disqualified." Pain shimmered through her voice and reluctant admiration for her masters.

Like an *Argos* quest, sahirs had a limited number of crystals—or weapons—to use in each tourney. If a sahir survived a round against other sahirs or preset spells with at least one crystal and his life, then he moved on to the next round, just like a warrior moving on to the next quest in *Argos*. But if he shattered all of his crystals, then he would only be given magickal assignments at the level associated with the highest round he had survived.

The process allowed the Shadow Council to know roughly which sahirs were most powerful, while losing the fewest sahirs.

"I never went to the tourneys," Astrid said quietly. "World War I started before I was old enough to gain admission. My marriage to Gerard, a British sahir, disqualified me from both the British and American sessions."

"They haven't asked you to do so?" Elswyth asked sharply.

Astrid shook her head. "The Cold War made my ability to work with the British an advantage to both sides and kept me too busy."

"And my story is much like yours, Elswyth," Nathan said, his deep voice huskier than usual. "Grief and rage clouded the crystals. They'll not see me there any time soon."

"You can still get things done, even if you're not formally rated." Astrid pulled Belgian chocolates out of the cupboard, set them on a plate, and skimmed them across to her friends. Distractions were definitely needed.

"You were very reckless once before and lived through it. But there was nobody around to rate you for power, based on the results."

"Not on our side anyway," Elswyth corrected him dryly. "The Nazis might have known, if they were aware the torpedo was aimed—and warded?—by magick."

Astrid nodded slightly, remembering the layered spells she'd felt that morning. She caught herself up quickly before she could betray too much.

"So?" She smacked the coffeemaker again and sent another cup on its way. If she needed chemicals to help deceive Elswyth, then only the very best would do.

"You're breaking the rules again, but this time the Council can monitor you." Elswyth carried the argument forward.

"You mean they're giving me enough rope to see if I either die or become a highly rated sahir?" Astrid's jaw dropped.

Holy shit, that sounded exactly like what those ruthless bastards on the Council would do. Even to somebody who'd been one of their top agents for almost a century.

"Exactly."

"If this cop calls you back, don't see him again, Astrid. It's not worth taking the risk," advised her protégé and partner, the Boston banker.

Astrid shoved a clean cup under the dripping spigot.

How could she tell her friends that Jake Hammond was a

kubri, more vital and irresistible to making magick than honey was to bees?

She hoped the kubri recruiters would reel him in far better this time than when they'd originally given him the ear cuff, however long ago that was. Of course, they'd have to find gaps in a homicide cop's appallingly overcrowded schedule to contact and seduce him.

Her very workaholic, homicide cop. Astrid refused to shudder.

Because if her link to him through this investigation was the only way to add a new kubri to the community, then sheer survival for all sahirs dictated she'd have to see him again.

Maybe she'd get lucky and he'd find the murdered woman's killer quickly. Very quickly.

The next day, Astrid curled up on the sofa in a decadently luxurious peignoir and clicked the remote control at her brand-new TV.

Somehow a full day spent deep in the details of guarding lethally minded traitors had felt more like shoveling mud out of a swamp than building walls to protect innocent citizens. She'd twice needed to refocus her magick on the task at hand, lest she cast a scrying spell on Jake Hammond's whereabouts.

But maybe a brutal gym workout the minute she returned home, followed by a pint of triple chocolate ice cream, would make her sleep well.

She switched rapidly past a multitude of ancient sitcoms, filled with unhappy, badly dressed actors spouting snappy dialogue about domestic trauma. Maybe someday there'd be a game about unhappy families. Until then, she'd never met a show that matched the life she'd led or what her friends had survived.

Thoroughly bored, Astrid brought up an independent show about tracking ghosts to fill her big-screen TV, while the news played in a small window. Maybe something interesting would pop up that would send her back overseas, where life was more honest.

"Tonight's lead story, a plea from the Belhaven murder victim's mother," the local anchorman announced, his blue eyes bright with interest under his thin gray hair.

Despite all logic and discipline, Astrid sat up. She zapped the local news into the wide screen and banished the ghost show.

Maybe she'd catch a glimpse of Jake . . .

"My baby," a black woman intoned. Her voice quavered on the third syllable and then snapped back into rigid control.

The note drove into Astrid's gut like a knife. She tried to close her eyes but could only stare helplessly at the glowing wall.

Three younger women huddled around her on a sofa as if their shared love could somehow blur unbearable pain into something survivable. Tears streaked their faces and the youngest clutched a wad of tissue, her fancy manicure chipped and scratched.

"Melinda was always the best girl." The woman held a formal portrait on her lap. Somehow the photographer had reached beyond such pictures' usual institutional dreariness to capture a beautiful woman's laughter and strength, plus a solid resemblance to the other ladies on the TV screen. "She worked hard and she was never in trouble. She put off college so she could help her younger brothers and sisters get through."

Once again, Astrid heard Melinda's dying scream of rage and flame-edged agony rip through her skull.

"If this could happen to her, who never did anything wrong, then it could happen to your daughter." Melinda's mother's voice broke into a shuddering sob. "Please, if you know anything about what happened to her, please call the police. Anything at all."

Astrid doubled herself up into a ball and buried her face against her knees.

CHAPTER EIGHT

A door opened in the overcrowded room's back corner and allowed a brief ray of light to wash out the monitors.

Jake gritted his teeth against a useless protest. Everyone here knew who had money and who didn't. It didn't pay to piss off the folks who might be able to help later. Besides, he too would have rushed over the minute he heard there was a break.

"What have you got for us, Hammond?" Fisher demanded. The FBI agent's voice was hoarser than it had been at the Belhaven police station.

"Good morning, Murphy. Fisher." Jake lengthened his drawl to emphasize Southern gentility and pushed back from the long table to welcome the two agents.

As befitted a regional traffic control center, the small lab was packed with monitors showing every aspect of Northern Virginia's notoriously foul traffic, from video of cars and trucks whizzing past to charts bubbling and popping like demons as statistics changed.

Two walls contained panels of small monitors, while a pair of large monitors occupied the central wall. The room glowed like a witch's cave, lit only by the screens' lambent phosphors.

Murphy coughed briefly and a smile flickered across her face. "Good to see you again, Hammond."

She held out her hand and Jake shook it, again impressed by

her grip. He nodded toward the other man in the room. "This is Hamilton, who's running the cameras for me. We've worked together before."

Hamilton, a wiry guy who could be any age from thirty to sixty, lifted a hand in the back corner without looking at anyone. Then he returned to pounding on the keyboard and muttering under his breath.

Fisher raised an eyebrow at Jake, who gave him his best confident shrug.

"Coffee?" Jake offered. "Makings are in the corner."

"Thanks." The two Feds draped their dripping raincoats over the coatrack and headed for one of a cop's major food groups.

"Williams's fiancé has a solid alibi," Murphy offered under her breath and briskly stirred cream into her coffee.

"Are you sure?" Jake's first breath of hope wouldn't be so easily denied.

"Coroner's pretty damn sure she was killed the day of that last big snowstorm, right?"

Jake nodded. His stomach didn't like where this was going, any more than it appreciated the traffic center's coffee.

"He's a trauma surgeon in the District. His hospital called in everyone that day. So we've got him on time cards and visual monitors for the full period in question." Her tone was far too matter of fact, as if she didn't like these facts, either.

"Any gaps?" Criminals always found holes to worm through.

"Fifteen minutes at most. Not enough to drive from the Capitol to the crime scene in good weather, let alone during a major snow." Fisher's eyes were bitter pools in the eerie light. "Sorry, man. We'll keep pushing, but . . ."

He shrugged.

Jake nodded, equally hard-edged. The likeliest suspect for Melinda's killer had the best alibi he'd ever heard. Not impossible to break—there was no such thing as impossible—but pretty damn close.

"You got a photo of him?" he asked, just to shut that last

door. Astrid might be able to rule him in or out, even though the killer had been wearing that mask.

Murphy's eyebrows shot up.

"Think your eyewitness can ID him?" She mouthed the most optimistic explanation for his request.

Jake shrugged, deliberately noncommittal. The fewer people who knew about Astrid's involvement in the case, the better for the case—and her. He wasn't about to say anything more in front of the traffic center dude.

Murphy and Fisher both gave him looks that yelled they knew better than to ask anything more. Hell, they'd undoubtedly been tight-lipped a few times themselves.

"Sure, although you've probably seen him before," Murphy said loudly. "Lucius Tyler Johnson, better known as L.T. Johnson or 'Lightning' Johnson."

"The famous Gamecocks running back who had the big NFL career." Jake whistled. Well, that explained where Melinda's ring came from. A fiancé with that background would buy his lady the best diamond he could find.

"Up until the church bus accident killed most of his family, that is. After that, he finished out his NFL contract, went to med school, and wound up in the District," summarized Fisher. "Always kept himself clean with no whiff of anything illegal."

Jake's intuition yelled for a stop: Lightning Johnson was a dead end in this case. Disappointment soured his gut.

Even so, he'd ask Astrid to glance at the picture.

"What are *you* working on?" Murphy sauntered toward the largest bank of monitors.

Every monitor ran a continuous loop, showing a different view of the same section of the Capital Beltway at the snowstorm's beginning. Cars and trucks whizzed through five lanes in each direction, while snow slowly obscured the pavement and eventually the camera lens. One held steady on a long-distance shot, from tree level, of a muddy car.

"Zoom in on the sedan, please, Hamilton," Jake asked.

He'd already seen it, but maybe a review for the Feds would help him, too.

Two clicks later and the sedan's very blurry image popped up on the big central screen.

"Maryland plates?" exclaimed Fisher. "Is that Williams's rental car?"

"Yup. It was ticketed on the day of the snowstorm." Jake crossed his arms and almost wished he was back working traffic detail. Resolving crime with a multipart form made everything so much simpler, not to mention more profitable for Belhaven.

"Why the hell didn't we know about it right away?" demanded Fisher.

"See where it's parked, off to the roadside? It got plowed in by the big snowplows."

Hamilton obligingly popped up later images, all time stamped, showing mountains of snow and ice being heaped over the sedan by enormous yellow plows driving past.

"It was days before the county towed it"—profitably—"and the rental company claimed it. Was it a long-term rental?"

"Yes," agreed Murphy cautiously. "What does that have to do with it?"

"At that point, the car rental company notified the renter— *Ms. Williams*—that they'd repossessed the car. They will continue to charge her for the rental until they hear from her or until the lease runs out, whichever comes first. Since she's dead—"

"They never heard from her," Fisher said. "Crap."

"The car effectively vanished—and the rental company's making money." Murphy sounded like a woman, always looking for sales.

"It's what the lease agreement calls for." There were some pieces of paperwork Jake was willing to fight or subvert. There were others he simply lived with, like car rental agreements. Starting out in traffic detail, when he'd wanted to be a homicide cop, had taught him a lot about the difference. "It was eventually towed to an impound lot, where we found it. Everything inside was untouched."

"Everything?" Murphy cocked her head at him. "Briefcase, computer, suitcase? Info on the current real estate deal?"

"Everything," Jake reaffirmed. "Even her purse was there. She hadn't even taken her keys."

"Crazy," Murphy muttered.

He couldn't have said it better himself.

"Why are you looking at these moments in time?" Fisher tapped time stamps on two different monitors. "They're before the car got ticketed."

"Williams's mother's appeal last night for witnesses?"

"So?" Murphy blinked at him before enlightenment lit her eyes. "You got a useful tip already?"

"A driver was passed by the speeding Ms. Williams."

"He's sure he saw her?" queried Fisher sharply.

"Very. He's an NCIS investigator who was on his way home who can describe her car. He's still upset about her speed." There was more than one way to identify a victim and Jake was in no position to look a gift horse in the mouth. "We'll put out another call for witnesses, narrowing the time frame, of course."

"Go on," said Murphy and gulped coffee, as if preparing for battle.

The second large-screen monitor snapped into life.

"Later, he saw her stopped by the roadside next to an unmarked police car, talking to a plainclothes officer."

"Any ticket filed?"

"None on record."

"What?!"

"We searched all local jurisdictions and both states. There's nothing for this car or Ms. Williams." A fact that sent cold waves rippling across his skin faster than the sound of bullets being fired.

"Description of the man?" Murphy's question would have pulled answers from a grave.

"Witness was looking at Williams, not him."

"God damn it, did he notice anything at all?"

Time had taught Jake not to predict eyewitnesses' vagaries, even when he'd honed his cursing skills on them. Even so, this lapse hurt more than most, no matter how stunning Ms. Wiliams's curves had been.

"Best guess is white, average height, average weight, possibly thirty or forty. Maybe fifty." Jake's drawl thickened, the way it always did when he was stressed.

"That describes half the men in America's jails!" Fisher exclaimed and kicked the table leg hard enough to jostle any unattended coffee cups.

"Pretty much. But our witness did note the time, since he was trying to make it home for dinner."

An image of two sedans, with two people standing before them, popped up on the second monitor. Cars and trucks hovered nearby, ready to dash into motion, while scattered gray blobs blurred the pavement and sky in snow's first dusting.

"Here's the first shot where the car is pulled over," Hamilton announced.

"Hey, the second car is there, too." Fisher bolted around the table to Hamilton's workstation. "It looks big enough to be a Crown Vic."

"Virginia State troopers avoid obvious cop cars for their unmarkeds," Murphy remarked in a tone that would have made a college professor rethink an exam question.

Jake traced the car's tiny outline on the monitor with his finger. He couldn't tell whether it was foreign or domestic, or even guess if it sat two or four people.

His gut settled solidly between his ribs, content that this was Melinda Williams's killer. Then again, his brain needed to be sure she was there.

"Enhance it for me, please, Hamilton?" he asked. "I'd like to get a better look."

"Yeah, I want to see this rat's face." Fisher braced a hand on Hamilton's chair back and leaned over his shoulder.

"Or his license plate, since he was the last to see her alive." Murphy's breath almost fogged the big monitor.

Keys clacked rapidly and the mouse's small arrow darted over the image. Then a small circle whirled around the arrowhead and Hamilton watched, his hands poised over the keyboard.

Jake drank his last drops of coffee and tried not to think about how long this was taking. He'd seen demos before of the traffic center's wonder systems. They'd always whizzed through bringing up license plates.

Maybe he'd text Astrid later and see if she could join him in *Argos*. Hell, maybe Astrid could confirm that this guy was the same guy she'd seen.

The monitor shimmered for an instant and settled back into the same picture, leaving Melinda Williams and her killer each approximately the same size as Jake's thumb.

Jake's gut began a long, slow roll toward the floor.

"Shit, what's wrong?" Hamilton's fingers flew over the controls. "You should have been able to see what kind of clothes the guy was wearing. I know it'll work this time."

The monitor went black—and came back exactly the same.

Shit, shit, shit. Jake's intuition gave him a mule kick.

"Let me try." He dropped into the seat next to Hamilton.

"Yeah, why not? Maybe it's some kind of weird boundary condition, and you'll luck out with your selection." Hamilton gave a frustrated shrug and surrendered the keyboard and joystick.

Jake shook out his hands, then accepted the new controls. His intuition screamed that he must hold the joystick just so. Okay, he could accept that; he'd listened to his instincts for years as a homicide cop.

Next step, mark a patch of image.

Listen to your intuition, man. It's driving the boat now.

He half-closed his eyes until the monitor was a blur and clicked when the joystick sang under his hand.

"You're good with that thing," Hamilton said grudgingly. "Have you used one before?"

Jake shrugged in what he hoped was a competent fashion and accepted the commit option. If only this worked . . .

The monitor blinked. Something felt right up there, as if a bad guy's picture was coming to life.

Jake focused intently on it, willing the computer to bring the bastard forward.

The screen shimmered again—and suddenly a blinding headache smashed into Jake. He fell back into his chair and instinctively threw an arm up to protect his eyes.

The big monitor blinked once, twice, then settled into the same indistinguishable vision of two tiny people beside two boxy cars.

Jake wrapped his arms around his stomach and willed himself not to puke his guts out. His intuition hadn't yelled at him so loudly since he'd charged into a drug lord's hideout to serve an arrest warrant.

Fisher stared at him, then got up to pour a fresh cup of coffee, the beat cop's answer to every problem.

"Maybe there's something wrong with our software," Hamilton said, sounding totally unconvinced.

"Maybe," echoed Murphy. "If you give us a copy of the tape, I'll have our labs work on it."

Jake levered himself carefully out of the chair and accepted the hot beverage from Fisher.

He had no idea how to tell Murphy their software wouldn't work any better on this tape than Hamilton's had.

The Viper hummed happily. Very satisfactory bank balances, calculated by his numerous computers, were reflected in his tall glass of beer.

The only question now was where to put the extra money from that last job. Not Switzerland, of course; he already had enough in that boring place for three or four lush retirements.

Perhaps Dubai, where the lengthy flight times were matched by a fluid acceptance of bribery.

Or maybe someplace riskier, to make up for the last job's utter boredom. Really, it had hardly been worth his time—except for the price tag.

Big Ben's chime sounded. Even after all these years and so many jobs, the Viper's pulse kicked hard.

He rubbed the glass of beer across his face to calm himself, savoring the cool chill. It was heaven, this flash of uncertainty at the very beginning, because it came so seldom.

Then he pressed a single key on one very secure Macintosh and a single message popped up on the monitor.

It was double-encoded, with the first code being the highest grade commercial code. The second code had been invented for Viper by a brilliant academic, who'd died immediately after assuring Viper even the U.S. military couldn't easily crack his darling. Clients never directly received it, of course, only access to a Web site that encrypted their message.

If he agreed to talk, an additional two-part code would be used, in which he had half of the key and the client held the other half.

Nobody had ever complained. The Viper's track record spoke for itself: one hundred percent satisfaction and complete discretion. He never blackmailed but he always demanded full payment—in advance.

Incoming message from France, said the balloon.

Well, now, what was going on over there these days that might interest him? It was probably well known he spent much of his time in the States these days.

The Viper finished his beer, poured a fresh glass, and brought up the dialogue screen.

Three comrades—*Comrades? How quaint*—need rescue from U.S. government.

A few keystrokes banished his beloved bank accounts for the moment and brought up the latest news.

A-ha! Headlines screamed about terrorists arrested abroad and extradited back to the United States. The countries involved made Viper's breath quicken.

What do you want me to do? he asked bluntly. It never paid to beat around the bush. Most clients were stupidly terrified that his conversations might be tapped.

Rescue.

The money involved immediately made his cock harden.

Very expensive, he warned reluctantly, and not my specialty. It may not be possible. He had to maintain his reputation for telling clients the truth, even if it meant the hit would go elsewhere.

If not rescue, then death. They must not talk.

Viper could almost see the unhappy shrug at the other end.
He closed his eyes for a moment and willed his cock to go back down. He needed at least some self-control during this type of negotiations.
Then he named a sum.

No, not possible!
Find somebody else.

There was a long silence during which the line stayed open.
Viper unzipped his fly and began to slowly stroke himself. Difficult negotiations were always the most enjoyable, especially when the other side started to waver.
Very well. We pay your price, the new client said sullenly.

Deposit the money here. He gave them the account number and name of the Swiss bank he used for this purpose, one where he never allowed funds to linger more than a day or two. I will tell you later where to pick up your comrades.

Viper fondled his balls, fat and aching the way his coffers would be in a few days. Christ, how he loved this part of negotiations.

Fifty percent bonus if they're alive, the client added abruptly.

Fifty percent? Why, that would be— His hips slammed forward in his chair, the golden sum tantalizing as any orgasm.

It's a deal, he typed, his fingers more unsteady on the keyboard than they'd ever been on a rifle.

Agreed. His new client vanished.

Fifty percent.

Viper pumped his cock, heat rising hot and fast, searing his brain.

Fifty fucking percent bonus!

He shot his load into his hand, numbers blasting his brain into the stratosphere like an artillery bombardment.

He came to, with his head thrown back and his trousers somewhere around his knees. He didn't care, not with a fifty-fucking-percent bonus on the way.

The news photo blinked at him and sanity stirred.

The new job would be a bitch, to say the least. Going up against the FBI, U.S. marshals, and every cop in Virginia would make a lesser talent back off.

But he could do it.

He'd need help. Not too many hired hands, of course. Those idiots talked, even when they were good enough to do what they were told without asking questions.

Gear, too, starting with the best guns.

And maybe that set of license plates Mr. Big had given him. He'd sworn everyone seeing a vehicle wearing those plates would think it was a real cop car.

It worked, too. Viper would have sworn somebody'd notice a red sports car beside a cop making a traffic arrest. But nobody had put out an APB on the Mustang, even after that gal's mother groveled all over TV. He'd gotten away free and clear, just like Mr. Big promised.

Viper smiled, shiny and bright like the money about to flow into his account.

He'd use those plates again, despite Mr. Big's warnings about not reusing his gear for anybody else. After all, what Mr. Big didn't know wouldn't hurt him.

CHAPTER NINE

Astrid took another long, disbelieving look at the kitchen table. A midnight supper's leftovers should not turn her heart into taffy and make her dive into dangerous conversational waters.

Dinner hadn't even been fancy, just pizza. Okay, he'd provided a cheese pizza specifically for her, plus a green salad. None of her family's menfolk had ever produced anything edible at mealtime; they'd always simply showed up, expecting to be fed. They thought about women only if their stomachs weren't satisfied and then dealt out hell.

All her old caution, etched deeper into her bones at Oslo, yelled at her not be anywhere near Jake Hammond. But the hope in his voice when he mentioned a possible clue had made her beg off an evening planning session with a half dozen other Shadow Guard members. Maybe if he had a good lead, she could bow out of his life for good—an unfortunately dismaying prospect.

Distracted brown eyes set amid harsh crows'-feet lured her gaze and set her fingers itching to caress.

Folly, pure folly. Friendship with him was acceptable, especially through cyberspace. A vibrant intellectual discussion was acceptable, albeit risky. But a repeat of their highly combustible physical relationship, especially when she didn't have any of the protective wards carried by a kubri recruiter? Intolerable.

He peeled another pepperoni slice off the cold crust, rolled it into a tube, and nibbled on the crimson-striped meat. A glass of imported lager glinted pale gold against the kitchen's brick wall.

What had exhausted a kubri enough to ignore an excellent beer for ten minutes and barely nibble his pizza? She'd infused him with a Niagara Falls of magick two days ago. It should have lasted him for at least a month.

She ignored her silk cashmere cardigan's delicate sleeves and leaned her elbows on the table to study him carefully. Could he still be starved for magick? Horrifying thought, for a kubri with his potential.

Or was it worse to consider his investigation might face wards strong enough to drain his magick, even without face-to-face contact?

She grimaced internally. Wiping out his magick should be impossible. Only Shadow Guards and their equivalents from other countries were powerful enough to work at a distance. No, it was far more likely Jake was starved for magickal attention. She could give him that.

She restarted the conversation at its ostensible purpose—Jake's current investigation.

"Do you think the picture's the real deal? An actual shot of the killer?" she asked.

"Maybe. Or maybe not." He waggled his fingers at the food cooling between them. "Do you want any more of this?"

"No, thank you. I'm already full." She shook her head, rueful laughter lifting her mood. How many times had he stalled an *Argos* game for his so-called food of the gods?

"Hey, I picked up some gelato, too," he offered, the last two slices of a gourmet, meat lovers' delight clutched in his big paw.

"Gelato?" Despite her best Shadow Guard instincts, which

urged a quick return to Georgetown, she rechecked the restaurant's name. Hmm, not desserts to quickly turn down.

"Interested?" A fine rasp roughened his drawl.

She met his dark eyes and, for the first time, allowed herself to drop her guard. She considered him directly, sahir to kubri.

Exhaustion muddied his skin and stubbornness tightened his jaw. His T-shirt had the well-worn aura of a knight's undergarment, which had been chafed far too often in a mix of armor and sweat. Yet his last feeble attempt at a joke still lifted the corners of his mouth.

She impulsively laid her hand over his and his kubri ear cuff immediately sprang into sight, released from the invisibility spell she'd set before.

His expression promptly softened and he gripped her fingers. His uneaten pizza dropped back into the box.

"Yes, I'm interested," she said softly, warmth purring through her veins. The first, faint musical chords of magick starting to gather, sounded in her ears. "In gelato—and other things, too."

"Like playing *Argos*?" Jake teased.

She snickered and curled her fingers through his, savoring every brush of skin over skin. Any and every willing contact between kubri and sahir was to be cherished—but this felt better than those she'd shared before in an aerie.

"Or why you said *maybe* to whether you'd have the killer's photo," she gasped, trying to stay grounded for a few moments longer.

His grip tightened until his rough calluses abraded her finer skin. Anger and unease lined his face until he looked ready to shatter anything close at hand.

Without thinking, she sent a surge of reassurance mixed with magick to him.

His nostrils flared and he swayed back, as if bowed by a great wind. To her shock and delight, his shields dropped, revealing his aura as pitted and dark.

A chill washed Astrid's bones. A kubri should never look so bereft.

She had nothing to give him, since her day's labors had sapped her resources. Sahirs could never harbor power for very long.

Maybe something else would work.

She planted her feet firmly and sent down tendrils deep into the house's roots. This was not her best skill but perhaps it would answer to desperate need.

Then she whispered an old, old spell.

Magick flew out of the old house's foundations, through its walls, and into her, brighter than a star's burning heart. She'd reached for a candle and lit a supernova.

Astrid's heart skipped a beat. Could he survive this?

But the magick gave her no chance to protect him. Before she could even consider throwing up wards, it dived into Jake like an incoming tide's first wave.

Jake shuddered and wrapped both hands around Astrid's. He held on to her like a drowning man in a hurricane, his knuckles white.

Wind sucked her breath away and pressed hard on her ribs. She clutched him tighter than a cowboy had ever gripped a bucking bronc's reins.

Slowly color returned to his cheeks and filled in his aura. Magick gradually settled back into the walls and earth, like fireworks fading into smoke.

Astrid dared to cast a wary eye over their reflections in the window but saw only two disheveled people. She quickly cast a housekeeping charm to clean them up before Jake could wonder why they looked as if they'd been outside in a gale, rather than than cozily indoors.

Not that her brain relaxed. Far too much power had answered her request for aid. Either Jake's house sat on an immense ley line, which tapped a previously unknown local power source, or else Jake was so powerful that rebalancing him made his ancestral home give everything it had.

Astrid wasn't sure which explanation she liked least. Washington, D.C.'s ley lines were a national treasure, over which wars had been fought. No local ley lines should still remain unmapped. But houses and gardens rarely poured out their entire storehouse of magick.

Jake gulped down his beer with the air of somebody imbibing liquid gold.

"The killer's photo comes from a traffic cam." He studied the bottom of his glass and decided not to add anything more.

Astrid considered him, more and more unsettled that he thought only one beer was enough for the evening. For one thing, he'd need more than that to wash down the amount of pizza he'd consumed.

"Traffic cam?" she questioned softly, grateful Jake was at least talking to her.

"This one's a state-of-the-art beastie out on the Beltway." He held the glass up and swirled the golden dregs around to form a brilliant kaleidoscope. "Records ten lanes of traffic with no problem."

She waited patiently to hear his true concern and watched him with all of her senses, both physical and magickal. If he didn't want to say anything more, she'd assume he needed to keep his investigation sacrosanct for its future courtroom appearance.

"Right now, all we have is the long shot where you can't tell a person from a bear."

"That's a start," said Astrid with sincerity. If somebody or something else had seen the killer, then she could disappear from the investigation. That would be a relief, no matter what it did for her chances of seeing Jake again. "What else?"

"Nothing." Jake shoved his chair back so hard it bunched the kitchen carpet. "We can't magnify the image."

"What?" She gaped at him. That was impossible, given the million ways to pull off looking deeper into a photo.

"It won't work, no matter who or what tries. The Beltway camera system won't zoom in. FBI systems suffer software errors if you ask them to magnify. Ours just babble hex code and demand a reboot." His voice was harsh enough to sharpen steel.

"Holy shit," she muttered. A photo that couldn't be magnified stank of magick.

But she'd worry about what to do with the picture later. Jake was more important right now.

His aura was so smudged. No wonder, since that kind of frustration must be destroying him from the inside. "What will you try next?"

"The FBI is still looking into it."

"But you're not very hopeful."

"Not really." His broad shoulders were rigidly erect in front of the coffeemaker, where nothing was turned on. "If nothing else, it will take extra time. We need to try something else."

"Like what?" She made her question as gentle as possible. If he didn't want to be more specific with a civilian, he could always change the subject.

"Look deeper at the obvious suspects, of course." He turned to face her and leaned back against the counter. "She had a half dozen siblings, who are all married, plus a dozen or more cousins."

Astrid whistled softly, remembering the enormous families of her childhood. "Lots of room there for misunderstandings to ripen into hatred and feuds."

"Yeah. Everybody denies it so far, but you never know until you check them out thoroughly, especially the spouses."

"The killer seemed like a pro. How he held her and especially how he wielded the knife." Astrid started to be more specific, then stopped abruptly. She flushed, biting her tongue like a Sunday School student caught reciting the wrong hymn.

Jake didn't notice, thank God, since he was staring at his wine cellar as if it held the murderer's identity in addition to fine beverages.

"I'd bet on that, though I can't prove it." He pounded his palms on the granite counter, then shoved himself away. "I can at least rule out money problems for Ms. Williams. She had no big debts—but no real savings either until she moved in with her fiancé."

"So she was clean."

"Just a boring bureaucrat, except for her tendency to pick up speeding tickets."

Jake started to clean up and Astrid joined him, working silently together as if this was another *Argos* quest. Too efficiently together.

"What about Melinda—Miss Williams's—job? Have you checked that out?"

The garbage disposal roared happily. It could shred useless items, unlike Astrid—or Jake.

"That's the FBI's job, since she was a federal employee."

"Shit."

Jake shrugged. "They're my partners in this investigation."

"Are they treating you like a partner?" Astrid demanded. She was suddenly, fiercely—stupidly!—angry on his behalf. She spent too much time with the Feds not to know just how arrogant and self-centered they could be.

"Usually."

His wry tone stopped her an instant before she exploded.

"Usually?" She considered the implications. "You're very lucky."

"Don't I know it." He snorted and grabbed a coffee mug from the top shelf. "Do you want anything else to drink?"

She wanted to kiss that proud, unhappy, stiff back and whisper that everything would be all right. A vagrant heat tiptoed through her blood and brushed her most delicate skin, until it simmered like a banked campfire.

Surely she could ease him a little, without exposing what she truly was.

"Coffee would be fine, if that's what you're drinking."

"I'd like to ask around at Miss Williams's job," he told the coffeemaker a few minutes later. "Start out by checking into her coworkers."

"The obvious questions, the same ones you'd ask no matter where somebody worked." Astrid wrapped her arms around his waist and snuggled her face against his back. Sahirs couldn't infuse kubris with magick very easily, except through direct physical contact.

"Yeah. GSA doesn't have many scandals."

Laughter bubbled up through Astrid until she quivered. Trust her experienced homicide cop to be disgruntled by an absence of crime.

Jake spun and caught her into his arms. Astrid's heartbeat exploded in delight, then settled into a fast, sweeping dance, which stole her breath.

"It's not that funny," he protested, although a small tremor at the corner of his mouth belied his words. "Stuff has disappeared from their huge warehouses."

Astrid pursed her lips and nodded slowly, determined to string together a sober conversation. He'd shown no signs tonight he wanted more than friendship, so she must have moved too fast the other night. Although men's dicks usually did most of their thinking . . . It was probably safer to go for a slow seduction.

"All those enormous warehouses, filled with tens—or hundreds?—of millions of dollars of government goods." What examples would impress Jake? All that interested her right now was the chance to unbutton his crisp, long-sleeved, cotton shirt. She swallowed hard against the urge to rub herself over him like a cat.

"Nice, juicy stuff to steal and sell for big bucks. Like, maybe, the Ark of the Covenant?" she offered, remembering one of Hollywood's wilder suggestions.

Jake choked and waved her suggestion off. "Think bigger. Computer parts, for starters."

"Really?" She cocked her head to consider the notion, rather impressed. Her body shifted with the movement, rotating her hip against his.

Suddenly she was tucked much more completely into the

crook of his arm. Rich masculine scents enfolded her, evoking his hard-edged work and his ancient house. His strong chest rose and fell quickly until his stiff cotton shirt teased her breasts through her thin sweater more thoroughly than his mouth could have.

Some lucky woman would one day have him for more than a fuck buddy. All Astrid could do was rebuild his strength and snatch a few memories.

She rubbed his arm and dared to give herself the luxury of relaxing against him. She enjoyed standing astride his leg far too much to move away easily. But that didn't mean she wanted to talk about her odd feelings of contentment.

"I always thought of GSA as being more inclined to drown the world in catalogs of stuff to buy, or pages of turgid prose on how the government should spend its money."

"Uncle Sam's Sears Roebuck?" He rubbed the small of her back just above her belt and small fireflies dove into her spine. She was very wet between her legs.

"Something like that," she agreed. She'd spent decades serving her country and had always been very happy that the Shadow Guard looked after its own, not Uncle Sam's minions.

More important, her ability to form long sentences was disappearing, the longer she snuggled against Jake.

"No matter what GSA locks up for Uncle Sam, I think Ms. Williams worked for a different group." Jake kneaded Astrid's shoulders lightly. Her eyelids slid shut, the better to enjoy his touch. Unfortunately, it also allowed his sinfully rich voice to pour through her like a mint julep. "The folks who looked after buildings."

"That's different." Astrid blearily considered the appeal of the broad chest so close to hers and sighed. All she wanted to do was unbutton his very crisp shirt and give her starved senses the delight of exploring his bare flesh.

If she opened his shirt now, she wouldn't speak again for a very long time. "Has that bunch at the GSA had any big scandals?"

"Not lately."

He widened his stance until she slid down his leg. The harsh fabric of his jeans caught her clit through her trousers at exactly the right angle—and she burned rich and slow, like the flame under a pot of chocolate sauce. More cream flowed down her thighs and every fiber hummed with lust.

He dragged her back into a standing position, his eyes dark with anticipation.

She spread her fingers over his heart to steady herself and hunted for a coherent thought.

"Maybe she was a recent transfer and you could focus on her old group."

"Williams had a degree in business and one in architecture." Jake kissed, then nibbled on Astrid's palm. She trembled, tremors unrelated to murder and investigations running through her spine. "She hadn't done much with the architecture degree, except help remodel her sister's house."

"But she used it on the job to help oversee contractors for federal buildings," Astrid said slowly, fumbling her way past Jake's accelerated heartbeat to thoughts of the case. "That's commitment."

"Good way to get ahead, too," said Jake, more cynically. He nuzzled the top of Astrid's head.

"Yes," Astrid agreed, far too breathlessly. "But you can kill two birds with one stone."

"True." Jake pulled her closer to him. "Like right now."

He kissed her and sanity fled. Sheer, silky pleasure swept through her every time their tongues entwined. The taste of his mouth, the sharp clack of his teeth—everything about him was somehow new and wondrous and different from anybody she'd ever kissed before. Nothing existed beyond his hand in her hair urging her closer and his lips' harsh pressure, which somehow incited her mouth's desperate race to join him.

She couldn't snatch enough of him too soon to satisfy her greedy senses. She stretched her leg over his hip and tried to wiggle closer. His chest rose and fell against hers, pumping his heartbeat into her. He shoved his hand down the back of her pants and yanked her closer, up his leg until he shamelessly rolled his hips under her.

Motes of magick swirled around them, like tiny dragonflies, drawn close by Jake's pleasure.

"Ah, Jake." Astrid whimpered and tried to reach that tempting, red-hot bar lurking behind his fly. So close and yet so far when he still held both of her hands.

He abruptly released her hands and yanked her sweater over her head. Astrid blinked in surprise, then smiled in anticipation when he dropped his head and nuzzled her breast through her silk camisole. Lust heated and centered under his mouth into a slow, fiery crescent between her nipple and womb.

His fingers tightened on her hips—and the magickal motes thickened around them until the kitchen was a distant memory. But who cared about where two humans stood, when pleasure thrummed so strongly through a girl's veins?

Astrid moaned again and rubbed herself over his leg, fierce as any tigress marking her mate.

"You're still dressed," she muttered, irritated beyond measure.

He gave a harsh bark of laughter, which the top of her head stifled.

She tugged his shirt out of his jeans and pulled it open, too eager to worry about upsetting delicate farasha sensibilities with an unusual show of strength. His lack of undershirt made her sigh in pleasure. Ah, what delicious opportunities his nudity presented.

In that instant, Jake peeled her camisole over her head and captured her breasts in his callused hands.

"Jake." His name was more gasp than word. Her head fell back and her fingers gripped his shoulders. She kneaded his shoulders for strength and pleasure—and magick rippled to meet her, invoked by his pleasure and the link between them.

"You are so magnificent." She kissed the strong muscles girding his chest, the ancient bullet scar below his collarbone, the tattoo on his upper arm, the flat male nipple that needed so little encouragement to tighten—and make him shudder.

She lingered to lick and kiss it, swirl her tongue over it or flick it like a light switch to brighten more and more magickal motes. Then she turned her attentions to the other one.

"Astrid, for the love of God!" Jake grabbed her head between his palms. "You wretch, my turn now."

Her eyes widened at his commanding tone. But he wasn't looking at her face. Instead his gaze lingered lower down, where her nipples promptly perked into aching buds.

He rubbed his thumbs over them—and Astrid whimpered a wordless, desperate plea.

He bent and suckled her breast, first one, then the other, until she became a creature of pure sensation, living in a world where nothing existed except him and hunger for more of his touch. Lust pulsed through her, sweeping between her breasts and her womb, firing her lungs to breathe air colored by the scent of his musk, heating her skin against his and the magnificent hot shaft locked away inside his jeans.

"Astrid." Jake's tone was more feral than civilized. It thrummed through her bones and she quivered in response. More cream heated her core.

"Face the counter." His fingers bit into her hips and he turned her around.

A granite counter. It was made of natural stone, so she'd be grounded. Perfect.

Astrid's eagerness raged brighter, like magma in sight of the caldera.

She leaned forward across the beautiful golden rock. Jake fondled her, teasing her eager flesh as if only passion existed, not clothing. He removed her trousers easily and she kicked them off, glad she hadn't worn boots.

His hand cupped her pussy from behind and his fingers teased her clit. Astrid keened and arched her back, driving herself down on those talented digits.

"Oh yes, do that some more!"

Thought didn't matter, magick didn't matter, his needs as a kubri didn't matter—only gaining the orgasm that lurked so appallingly close and yet not quite close enough.

One finger slipped inside her and she humped it eagerly.

Somewhere foil ripped, but who cared? She had more important things to think about, if she ever managed to think again.

"Astrid, honey." His cock's broad tip nudged her ass, neatly sheathed in a condom.

She whined deep in her throat and thrust back against him. "Please . . ."

He slipped into her pussy. She shifted slightly, then instinct found the best possible angle, and she shoved back onto him.

"Astrid." He growled and thrust again and again. She moaned in pure satisfaction, her body deliciously stretched by his hot length.

He rode her hard and fast, braced by her shoulders. Both her back and legs were mantled and abraded by his heavy muscular frame. She was surrounded, both inside and out, enveloped in kubri. She keened her pleasure and drew him closer, her internal muscles gripping him close and her cream pouring hotly around him.

Magickal motes danced without, within them both until eyesight became unnecessary on the road to pleasure. Ecstasy gathered closer and closer, tighter and tighter, like a tornado racing across the prairie.

Then he nipped her shoulder.

Climax exploded through her in a glittering cascade of magick. It blew through her bones and tore apart her flesh, shattering her and remaking her a dozen times over. Astrid howled, more than delighted at the sahir-kubri connection, and let herself fly.

Jake growled something and then jerked against her. His cum jetted into her, hot and rich despite the condom's veil.

Magickal motes dived and swooped into them, more intoxicating than the finest alcohol.

Astrid gasped and helplessly tumbled into her second orgasm, every cell transformed by magick—and Jake's pleasure.

It seemed like a very long time before she lifted her head. Farashas would demand a week's sleep after orgasms like that. Yet she wanted to run a marathon.

How could she explain this to Jake? And what if he'd seen any magick?

She stretched cautiously, uneasily aware she lacked a certain big cop anywhere near her chilled body.

A wary survey soon established his location—sound asleep on the kitchen floor.

Astrid began to giggle.

CHAPTER TEN

The courthouse garage's dank smell rolled past Jake, leavened with motor oil and traces of gasoline. A few hours ago, he'd feasted on the best aromas in the world—aroused woman and fresh pizza.

But Astrid had left before he woke up, leaving only a brief, irritating note behind.

Grr. "Hope to see you again," my ass! At dawn, he wanted nothing more than to be back in bed with his lover, not freezing his balls off for the FBI.

He stomped down hard and his boot sent a satisfying *whomp!* through the concrete den. A very precise pivot turned him to face the few tendrils of light drifting down the ramp.

His sergeant raised an eyebrow at him but said nothing, not with so many FBI agents and U.S. marshals around.

"Two minutes to showtime," Murphy announced in Jake's ear. She sounded a good deal more content than she ever had discussing Melinda Williams's murder. Smart lady but still not one he'd choose to back him on a raid.

Sirens bayed in the distance like sheepdogs herding their flocks.

"Accident at the Beltway exit to Route One north," Fisher added unexpectedly from the helicopter. "Less traffic than expected entering the city."

His laconic, street-smart tones made an ice-cold wave lift

the hairs off Jake's neck. A pattern like that could open up an escape route for bad guys.

Don't be stupid, Jake.

All the Feds here would make even make a bronze statue jump at shadows. Washington's metro area had the second or third worst traffic in the country, depending on who did the measurement. It kicked Belhaven in the teeth every morning and afternoon. Jake had learned early how to dodge the worst choke holds.

Even if there was a real threat, cops out there would deal with it.

He forced the image back. He had a job to do down here, in this half-lit cavern, before he could go back to hunting Melinda Williams's killer.

He broke the line and began to pace. Hell, it might have looked strange if he didn't survey his men, given that he was Belhaven's senior cop present. At least down here: the chief and the lieutenant were up above, soaking their bones in what passed for March sunshine and listening to nervous cops on the radio.

This corner of the garage was normally reserved for the judges. Special lanes on the levels above allowed those senior members of the bar to drive here surely and swiftly, no matter how heavy the traffic. Blatant signs and vivid stripes warned all comers not to approach any of these precious parking spaces. A well-lit lobby led to a high-speed elevator, which whisked the judges upstairs to play critical roles in each court-room drama.

The garage's floor was usually icy from water tracked in during the day that froze at night. But this morning, they'd poured enough salt and chemicals to dry out an iceberg.

"One minute to showtime." Murphy's voice had lost some of its crisp arrogance. Maybe she'd started to remember that no plan survives first contact with the enemy, even if it comes from the FBI.

Jake snickered privately and refrained from tugging at his

godawful black uniform. No matter how unfamiliar it was, it did fit perfectly under his Kevlar vest. More important, it allowed him easy access to all of his gear.

Showtime should last only a few seconds, just long enough for the terrorist to be escorted from his vehicle to the elevator.

All the elements that made life easier for judges also made transferring a prisoner slick as shoving a cleaned and trussed goose into an oven. All an expert had to do was point the bad boy at the entrance and press the up button.

That was the plan, anyway.

All vehicles had been taken out of this section of the garage, leaving a clear field of fire for the cops stationed behind the barricades. The streets outside had been cleared and blocked off, the lights synchronized, so the convoy would have a swift drive here from the high-security prison. Helicopters circled overhead, on the alert against the smallest mishap. The entire courthouse had been checked multiple times by bomb-sniffing dogs. It wouldn't open for regular business until after the terrorist's arraignment was completed.

All the risk should be outside where any attacker would have a variety of attack vectors and escape routes. Jake could recite a dozen options in his sleep. His mouth was too dry to name one.

A large contingent of Belhaven cops guarded the damn building, together with enough FBI agents and U.S. marshals to police an entire presidential inauguration. They'd even taken the entire homicide and vice squads, who'd have to change clothes before they went back onto the streets.

Sirens howled again, clear as wolves rushing a caribou to its doom.

"Thirty seconds to showtime." Murphy roughened before she steadied her voice. "Do we have go?"

Jake's pulse quickened, then steadied into a slow, deliberate thud.

The convoy was only a few blocks away. No signs of trouble on the streets or in the skies.

Jake glanced at the chief U.S. marshal, who had the responsibility of deciding whether or not to continue.

"It's a go," the wiry Asian said firmly, calm as if he closed his fist around a computer joystick instead of a risky prisoner transfer.

Any other response and the convoy would have veered off and hurtled through Belhaven toward a different sanctuary.

"Roger that," said Murphy. "Fifteen seconds ETA."

High above, metal groaned and surged into motion, sullen as an *Argos* troll hauled out from under a bridge.

"Spartan entering the garage," Murphy announced. She finally sounded as calm as her seniority demanded.

Why not? Her job would be over at the bottom of the ramp.

Jake's stomach flopped back into place. This should be straightforward, dammit. All he had to do was hustle that worthless piece of treacherous trash into the elevator.

He dropped his hand and unsnapped his holster. Any of the duty sergeants would flay his skin off, if they saw him. But he'd rather have his gun ready for instantaneous use, even if he risked theft in an extremely close-quarters fight.

Headlights sliced the ramp's gloom, faster than knives in a gangland attack. Heavy vehicles thudded across the concrete floors overhead.

A fast sweep with his eyes reassured Jake that everyone was in position. Two quick paces took him to the lobby's edge, beside the FBI agent and the marshal.

The convoy burst into sight, moving far faster than the posted speed limit. Tires whined like hornets and their lights flashed blindingly bright.

Two big Cadillac Escalades shrieked to a stop beside the lobby and the others flung themselves into a protective semicircle. Doors slammed open and operators jumped out. The central vehicles' windows stayed locked and dark.

The perimeter was deep enough within seconds to make the Secret Service's presidential detail jealous.

"Good to see you." Murphy flashed a brief smile at the cops waiting in front of the elevator.

Jake nodded and waited, his stomach tauter than during his first raid as a rookie.

Murphy knocked on the lead Cadillac Escalade's side window. "Ready when you are."

The door opened and a civilian stepped out. Her black dress coat, black pants suit, and high-heeled black boots befitted a judge's dinner party far more than an FBI shindig. Her cold, calm expression warned that she wielded both words and guns to kill.

Yet her diamond jewelry and coronet of blond braids were achingly familiar to Jake's hands.

"Astrid?" he mouthed. *She* was riding shotgun on the most dangerous criminal in America?

Her head snapped around, fast as a wolf hearing ice crackle in the forest. Her gaze traveled over him, assessing every detail of his gear, and a woman's hunger flashed through her expression.

Then her incredible green eyes locked onto his, brilliant as emeralds and unfathomable as the Potomac's depths.

"Ready?" Murphy asked.

A scruffy man climbed clumsily down behind Astrid. Every move forward was a robotic dance where he fought to jerk his limbs forward and two agents guided his cuffed and manacled joints.

He didn't look like somebody who'd blown up a day care center at a government lab. But the truly dangerous ones never looked like they were worth a second glance.

"Let me go," the rat snarled at his handlers when he reached the ground. He tried to pull away but they tightened their grip, with little more care than they would have shown poison ivy.

Murphy's lip curled. Astrid never looked at the prisoner, only Jake.

"Time to get this show on the road," Murphy said brusquely.

Astrid shot a swift glance around the cavern, and lingered briefly on the lobby and the elevator. Maybe she was thinking about the private conference rooms upstairs.

God knows when he'd see her again. He'd checked in this morning but found nothing new on the Williams investigation. The FBI was still taking their own sweet time and his inquiries were going nowhere.

Texting was okay but nothing like holding Astrid in his arms. He needed a better excuse than gaming or the investigation to see her privately.

"Hammond comes with us," Astrid announced, nodded at him, and turned for the elevator, firm as a Supreme Court justice handing down the law.

She must want to talk to him while the prisoner was arraigned in the courtroom.

Yes! Jake's heart leaped into his throat to follow her before his feet moved into action.

The two handlers yanked the rat into motion.

"But—" Murphy gobbled hard enough to sound like a turkey and astonished jealousy darkened her eyes. She must want the chance to appear in court during a big media event. "If she needs extra firepower, I or one of my agents can do the job."

"If Carlsen wants the cop, then he's going. Besides, we don't need him down here any longer," the senior U.S. marshal retorted. "We'll leave through a different exit."

Jake took up position behind the rat with his two handlers, and did his best to look indifferent to the argument. This close to Astrid, he could smell her unique perfume, soft and strong as springtime flowers.

"Ready?" asked the marshal inside the elevator cab. "Time's a' wastin'."

"Ready," answered Astrid firmly and waited beside the open door.

Jake took two long strides and entered the elevator first.

The two handlers escorted the rat into the conveyance and Astrid took up position last.

Murphy's face wore a professional mask through which blazing brown eyes burned.

The doors slid shut like the rudest of gestures and Jake could have applauded.

Numbers slid silently across the overhead display like rattlesnakes rising from their den.

One . . .

Judge Berkeley must be waiting in the courtroom by now. He was probably pissed as hell he'd had to use the staff elevator today, instead of this one.

Two, three . . .

The terrorist rocked on his heels. He and his handlers were equally silent, with all three heads tilted up to stare at the countdown. Even the marshal by the door had his head canted back to watch the numbers run past.

Four, five . . .

Astrid shifted slightly. She glanced over her right shoulder, past the rat, at Jake. A faint frown line furrowed her brow.

What the hell? Was she having second thoughts about a private chat with him?

The elevator lurched to a stop. The display flickered five, then six like a baffled drunk.

Oh, shit, not again! Was there an elevator in this building that hadn't broken down in the past year?

Something grated quietly within the elevator cab. A cold whisper rolled over Jake's skin.

Time slowed.

"What's wrong?" the prisoner whined. "If you're going to make me climb a dozen flights just to prove how tough you are, I'll call my lawyer. That's inhumane!"

"Don't worry, we're all in this together." The marshal's shoulders were very stiff, as if he wanted to forcibly silence the yammering fool but wouldn't allow himself that luxury. He opened up the control panel. "Help will be here in no time."

The chill touched Jake more directly, this time from overhead. He craned his head back but was too late.

A very soft pop sounded and the lead marshal's knees buckled. He collapsed onto the carpet and the control panel door fluttered over his head like newspaper obituary pages.

Time stopped. The world became a tunnel, centered on a very small gap in the ceiling through which a silenced pistol protruded like a cannon.

The other two handlers dived onto the prisoner and knocked him onto the floor.

Jake dropped too, anything to get away from that damned elevator wall, which drew bullets like flypaper drew vermin.

Another splat and one of the guards grunted, the bone-deep sob of a strong man hurt bad. Blood spewed across the wall brighter than any signs leading to a trauma center.

Astrid was still upright, backed into the corner and staring at the pistol as if hypnotized. Jake couldn't reach her, not without crawling over the prisoner.

Jake's heart careened into his mouth. He had to do his job first, God help him, not take care of his girl.

"Finally!" the terrorist yelled. "Get me out of here, you idiot."

The other guard drew his gun and somehow shouldered the rat deeper into the floor, silencing his demands. His partner wasn't moving at all.

The remaining guard and Jake fired again and again at their attacker. The sound blasted their ears and shook the cab's thin walls like a giant's fists.

Yet more shots came down from the ceiling, more merciless than spearfishing trapped fish in a lagoon.

The last marshal's gun fell silent, half-hidden on the floor beneath its owner's bloody head. Astrid was wringing her hands.

Jake cursed under his breath and wished the damn cavalry would arrive.

Astrid lifted her hands and shoved something invisible toward the damn hole.

What the hell was she trying to do?

The assassin's next few shots zipped into the elevator shaft, not the cab. A man cursed overhead but not in any language Jake recognized.

Astrid chanted something, looking as deadly as her barbarian counterpart, and made a complicated gesture.

A web of purple lightning enveloped the enemy's gun.

Magick? Stage magicians needed time and effort to pull off tricks like that. They'd never try it while they were being shot at, let alone when people were dying.

The weapon turned incandescently bright and the man yelped in pain.

The pistol disappeared—but Jake didn't dare draw a deep breath.

Another gun appeared and this one was no quieter than Jake's.

His finger tightened on the trigger, but Astrid acted first.

"Begone, you bastard, and never enter these premises again, lest you die!" she yelled. Bone-deep certainty that she'd be obeyed laced her voice. Another gesture sent purple lightning to wrap itself around the man's hand and pistol again.

Magick. Oh shit.

Jake's stomach was an appalled knot somewhere near his knees. But his gun hand was rock steady.

The assassin screamed and yanked his gun away. The panel slammed shut and feet pounded briefly on the ceiling.

Jake dared to shoot a glance at Astrid.

She slowly released her attention from overhead and turned it to him. "He's gone."

"Great." For fifty cents, he'd chase the bastard. Yeah, and if he did that, three lawmen would lose their best chance at first aid.

The terrorist was blubbering like a well-spanked three-year-old under his two guards' bodies.

Astrid dropped to her knees beside the heap, her expression sober.

"Three officers down!" Jake yelled into his shoulder radio, grateful to his tactical uniform for making it handy. "South elevator, fifth floor."

He could dimly hear boots pounding through the corridor but it never hurt to make things official. He'd bet the marshal by the control panel was dead, though. The fellow had never moved or spoken after the attack began. Plus, the stench coming from that corner told its own unmistakable tale.

She lightly touched her fingers to the back of the rat's hand.

"Sleep," she ordered in a tone the good nuns at Blessed Sacrament School would have approved.

The vermin promptly went limp and blessedly silent.

Holy crap. Had she worked magick once again to pull that off?

Jake didn't work vice squad, so his eyes weren't trained to spot every flicker. But he should be able to spot any sleight-of-hand from this close.

"Are you a sorceress or did you just pop him some drugs?" he demanded.

"Sahir—what you would call a sorceress."

Jake stared at her. What exactly was she admitting to?

She yanked the first guard's Kevlar vest open and slid her hand over his left shoulder. Blood still spewed from his wound, but she made no move to bandage him. Her attitude sang of listening.

Jake crawled over to the second guard. He had a nasty bullet wound alongside his head and lots of blood loss. The guy was still out cold, which suggested a possible concussion in Jake's very inexpert opinion. *Come on, Jake, remember First Aid 101.* How the hell could he treat this?

Fists drummed on the door.

"Hammond? Can you hear us?" Chief Andrews yelled.

"Loud and clear." Thank God the cavalry was here.

"The bad guys locked down every elevator door in the building."

Shit. The son-of-a-bitch assassin had made sure nobody would find out what he'd done or be able to quickly follow him. God bless modern technology: the courthouse designers had made sure that simply tugging the doors open wouldn't work here.

"We're going to have to either cut you out or come in from the roof."

To the sixth floor of a twenty-five-story building? "Can't think of a better way to have fun, sir."

"Knew you'd feel that way, sergeant." There was a brief pause, filled with indistinct muttering on the other side.

"You said three officers down, Hammond?" the chief asked.

"One is dead, sir, and one is critical." *Goddamn the sneaky bastard who did this.*

Astrid hummed a chant and the first guard's breathing eased a little.

"We'll do our best to hurry, Hammond. I'll let you know what our plans are."

"Roger that, sir."

He studied Astrid warily. It might be the lighting, but she looked more drawn than she had in the garage. Maybe magick—if there was such a thing!—knocked the hell out of its user in real life, the way it did in *Argos.*

Jake took his helmet off and laid it on the floor. He didn't need an extra headache-inducer for the next hour. Then he began to strip down to his T-shirt.

"How is he?" he asked her gently. Her fancy wool coat and trousers were soaked in blood.

"Dying. I give him five minutes at the most." She stroked his forehead with her free hand, her expression very pensive. "Did you know he's about to get married? They're rushing the ceremony so his pregnant fiancée will have insurance coverage."

"I'm sorry." He stopped ripping up his T-shirt for bandages and lightly squeezed her shoulder to offer comfort.

For a moment, something sparked between them. Fireflies trailed across his arm to her throat and then vanished.

"What the hell was that?" Jake demanded. "Static electricity? That could kill us in here; we've got no place to go to get away from it!"

"Not electricity." Astrid sat back on her haunches and eyed him like a housewife studying a display of gourmet chocolates.

Jake frowned at her. What the hell was she up to now?

"Will you help me save his life?" she asked bluntly.

"Even if the two of us strip, we probably don't have enough clothes to bandage both of them," Jake returned, equally blunt. "Not when he's losing that much blood."

"Not first aid." She shook her head. "Magick."

"I don't believe in it." No way he'd trust anything he hadn't personally seen or touched. "If you need a credulous dupe—"

"I need a kubri and that's you."

"What the hell are you talking about?"

The first guard's breath rattled in his throat.

"Give me your hand!"

Jake's hand locked around hers before his brain caught up.

"Now think about your home or another piece of Virginia that you love."

"Huh?"

"Come on, Hammond, picture someplace that's magickal for you. Where you always go to find refuge and comfort." Her hand tightened on his hard enough to hold fast in a hurricane. "I need that magick to save this man's life."

Her eyes blazed at him, fierce and green. Lights swirled within her iris, brighter than gemstones.

His heart shifted and warily opened a door.

"St. Anne's," Jake murmured. The Hammond family's first

parish church in Virginia, the place where his parents were buried. "The churchyard always has something in bloom. In springtime, the dogwoods look like candles lighting the way."

His mouth curved, remembering all the hunting and fishing trips down to the Northern Neck with his father. The summertime trips to the church fair to help clean up the grounds and buy local produce. All his visits as a grown man, when he'd discuss difficult investigations with a silent headstone—and pray his brother didn't fill the plot next door too damn soon.

His family had peopled that cemetery for four centuries. They'd been buried in that land for far longer, thanks to marrying into the local tribes.

Astrid brushed her lips across his hand and Jake smiled faintly.

He could see all of it now—the trees' delicate blossoms veiling the churchyard, the soft green grass waving over the ancient graves, the warm red brick, the soft white gravestones, and the ironwork's tracery like a door between worlds. Nothing had seriously changed St. Anne's—not the British, nor the Yankees, not even the two centuries since the new building was erected.

He could feel its strength, surging into his bones like the walls rising from the rich soil to protect the flowers.

The first guard wheezed beside Jake's knee.

"Hmm?" Jake questioned, still caught in his memories of St. Anne's.

"Look into my eyes, Jake," Astrid commanded harshly.

Jake opened his eyes cautiously—and blinked.

Her irises blazed with light, more iridescent than any kaleidoscope. Was she real or was this a dream?

Pinwheels of flashing color rotated around the tiny compartment, until it seemed like the inside of a genie's jewel box.

"Now hold onto me tightly, no matter what happens."

Jake shot her a disgusted look. Did she honestly think any so-called hocus-pocus could frighten a homicide cop?

Her mouth was a thin line above a taut jaw. For the first

time that day, she looked nervously determined, rather than confident.

"Ready whenever you are." Jake flipped her a casual, two-fingered salute. Hell, if she'd scared off the attacker, then just maybe they could pull this off, too.

Her lips settled into a cockier grin and she winked at him.

Jake settled down to give Death another damn good run for its money. He'd rather fight the bastard on this side of the grave, while the victim was still alive, than afterward when it became murder.

Astrid's free hand rotated into a different position atop the first guard's heart until her index finger pointed upward. She chanted something in a language Jake didn't understand.

The lights brightened into a continuous glow and caught at Jake, like a pack of cops at a planning meeting who looked to their leader for confidence.

Hell, he could do this.

In the afternoon, the sunset lit St. Anne's churchyard in gold and crimson until dogwood blossoms became fiery jewels . . .

The lights around Jake strengthened and settled into a steady gleam, vibrant as his flashlight.

Astrid's voice deepened until it sang through Jake's bones.

The glow tightened around Astrid and Jake, a soft woolen blanket shining against firelight.

Astrid chanted again, this time singing something whose rhythm hinted of spring.

The band of light began to pulse outward in a steady dance, ever obedient to Astrid's voice. It lingered over the first guard and penetrated through his clothing until Jake could see his bones. He too glowed like Astrid and Jake by the time the light moved on to the second guard.

The glow moved over this marshal like a ballroom dancer, in a far more lighthearted series of steps.

Astrid ended her song with a series of rhythmic claps. The unearthly glow promptly blinked out, blacking out the elevator.

Jake gasped and slumped back against the elevator wall. He'd spent days in the gym that took less out of him—but no workout ever left him with a goofy grin on his face like this one.

"Jake?" Astrid sounded hesitant. Exhausted, too.

"Yeah, honey? You doing okay?"

"I'm fine. Tired, but not too much." The elevator lights crackled then came back online, one by one. "How about you?"

"Couldn't be better, especially after I have some coffee." He levered himself onto his knees—nobody designed elevators for somebody his size—and checked out the second guard. The fellow stirred and grumbled under his hand but didn't quite wake up. His bullet wound was now a scratch across his temple, complete with small scab.

Jake would bet that any potential concussion was probably ancient history.

Astrid slid her hand out from under the first guard's Kevlar vest.

"How's he doing?" Jake nodded at the dude.

"Fine. Perfect, in fact." Her smile broke open like sunrise on the first day of spring. "He'll live to see his son born."

"Awesome." Jake didn't give a damn about the rat's condition, wherever he was under that bloody heap. "Now would you mind telling me exactly how the hell you pulled all of this off?"

"Ah—" Her expression shuttered faster than SWAT tactical helmets during a bad raid.

Jake waited grimly to see if she'd try to make him undergo a memory wipe or whatever sorceresses called it.

Fists pounded on the door again.

"Hammond?"

Shit.

"Yes, chief?" Jake kept his voice more professional than his thoughts.

"We've got the top elevator guy here. He says he can take

you up to the sixth floor and cut you out. Just give us a couple of minutes, no more."

"Great." Not enough time or privacy to get any answers out of Astrid.

"We have to talk." He shot his best interrogation glare at her. It was unlikely to have much effect, if half of *Argos*'s rules were true about sorceresses.

Or sahirs, or whatever she called herself.

She looked straight back down her nose at him, haughty as any high-born elf. No barbarian could have pulled off such an ice-cold survey.

Then she knocked his world's remnants around his ears.

"Yes, of course. You need to know, if you're to catch these bastards."

Bastards? There was more than *one*?

Now didn't that make the rat rustling at his feet look like a piece of cake, instead of a five-year manhunt's prize?

CHAPTER ELEVEN

The last two joggers hurtled past Jake, apparently on their way to dry clothes and warm food. An elderly Labrador and its aged master hustled up the path. Wind hurled waves against the parapet but a few rays of sunshine still dueled the racing black clouds.

At least for the next hour.

The forecasters swore this storm wouldn't strip any incipient cherry blossoms from the trees. They'd also fired off enough foul weather warnings to blanket a weather map for the next twenty-four hours.

Nobody with any sense visited Patriots' Park when a storm was coming in. Located just north and upriver from the munitions factory where Melinda Williams's body had washed ashore, the entire place would be underwater long before the factory's great clock struck the turn of the tide.

Which was exactly why Jake had agreed to meet Astrid here.

He could understand why she wouldn't visit the station. But his house? That refusal felt like a bullet to his gut.

He'd offered Duffy's, but she preferred an open space. So they settled on this, someplace even the gulls were deserting in droves.

He shoved his hands deeper into his coat pockets.

At least two of the three marshals were alive and well.

The terrorist rat was fine, too, and chattering faster than any social networking site about all his connections. He'd apparently decided whoever sent all those bullets ricocheting inside the elevator didn't give a damn about his health. Now his only hope for a long life was to make friends with the federal government—and good luck to him.

Crap, how much blood could one woman get on her clothes and still keep her head?

Jake kicked a pebble into the grass and wished he could arrest somebody for loitering. Or vandalizing. Or something, anything, just so he could pretend he was setting the world straight.

"Hi."

He spun around.

She watched him from a few steps away, the wind whipping stray locks of hair around her face like a veil—or her avatar's war garb. She was dressed in the same casual jeans and boots she'd worn last night. But he couldn't penetrate her expression any better than he had in the elevator.

How had she arrived so silently? Okay, there was a Metro station a few blocks away, but he should have heard her walking in. On the other hand, did he really want to ask that question yet?

"Hey there." He joined her quickly but didn't touch her, not this time. "How do you feel?"

"A little tired." She lifted one shoulder in a shrug. "Mostly I'm glad the two marshals survived—and the first didn't feel anything when he was taken down."

"Amen. That's always the best way to go." He brooded for a moment, then said his usual quick prayer for his own passing. After eighteen years as a cop, he had very strong opinions about how and when he'd like to meet his Maker.

He glanced over and Astrid met his gaze silently, composed as a Roman battle monument.

"Will you tell me the truth today?" he asked abruptly.

"If you let me put you under compulsion to keep it a secret," she answered calmly.

"Put me under compulsion?" His jaw dropped. "You talk like casting spells is an everyday matter!"

"It is." She waited, relentless as his Sig's ability to deal out bullets until somebody died.

"What if you tell me you've committed crimes?"

She blinked at him, then threw back her head and laughed. The sound rang through the skies like bells. Despite anything his old patrol sergeant ever told him about dames and their ability to lie, Jake found himself grinning.

"Jake." She wiped tears of glee from her eyes and tried again. "Sergeant Hammond, I give you my word that I don't do crimes."

"Great." His lungs started breathing normally again instead of hovering somewhere between guffaws and stentorian barks to obey the law.

"At least not according to American law."

"Not according to . . ." That was a huge hole. "What about other countries?"

"Take my word for it that you'll never extradite me." She took another step forward, then looked back over her shoulder when he didn't follow. "Are you coming?"

"Crap, you make it sound like there's a whole underground world out there." He matched her stride and took the next corner. He wouldn't falter the next time, dammit, no matter what nonsense she spouted.

"There is."

"Riiight." *Like pigs flew and mountains walked.*

"They can, if we pour enough power into the spell."

"What the hell are you talking about?"

"Pigs flying and mountains walking. You shouted your thoughts."

"Jesus H. Christ." Jake ground his teeth and swore he'd do better. He was a skilled interrogator; he could pull answers from her, no matter what she was.

When his heartbeat stopped hammering his skull, he shoved his wrist at her. "Okay, let's get this compulsion thing over with."

"I already have."

"What the fuck?"

"You mentally agreed and were calm enough to accept the spell. So I've performed it." Her voice was gentler when she spoke again. "I would have immediately reversed it, of course, if you'd objected when you spoke again."

"Thank you," he said stiffly. Good God, what kind of prissy jackass did she think he was? He wasn't afraid of anything Astrid could do to him. At least, not much.

The river raged past them, angry enough to silence the tour boats. Two men chatted on the riverbank, but the waves' white froth clouded their forms. One had long black braids and carried a bow slung over his shoulder. The other wore a low-brimmed, long-billed cap and leaned on his rifle, as if to make sure he'd always know where the weapon stood.

Jake frowned and peered a little more closely at the two strangers. Reenactors would have to be certifiably insane to come out in this weather, even if a miracle birthed an event that elicited both an Indian from John Smith's Jamestown and a soldier from Civil War Belhaven.

"Do you see that guy in the leather?" he demanded. "I've got to call him in."

"Why?" Astrid's question was sharper than the temperature.

"Drunk and disorderly, public nuisance—something!" Jake reached for his phone. "Nobody sane would be out here wearing so little."

"You're worried about him."

"Of course I am. Nobody goes to the ER with pneumonia while I'm watching." He shot her a disgusted look, his thumb flying across the keys. Damn, sometimes he woke up from nightmares twitching in the same pattern. "The other guy will be okay. Those Civil War reenactors always have modern long johns under their old-fashioned duds."

"Excellent logic—but you might want to make sure he's still here before you finish the call."

Her chilly tones warned him more clearly than a loud shriek

could have. She nodded toward the Potomac and Jake slowly turned to look.

Another wind gust hurled foam across the park and Jake blinked. When his vision cleared, the two strangers were gone—if indeed they'd ever been there. There hadn't been time for them to run to the park's edge or disappear into any foliage. They could have dived into the river, but either he or Astrid would have seen them do that.

Ghosts could vanish like that.

Bullshit! There was no such thing as a ghost. He didn't do spectral apparitions, or whatever the hell the popular word was. No, they'd just been something cooked up by the light and the mist.

Astrid coughed firmly, bringing his attention back to her. A muscle twitched in her jaw, but she was otherwise the composed warrior who'd stepped into the police garage that morning.

"Farashas—what we call people without magick," she said quietly, staring at the water as if watching a flotilla, "have such an imperfect knowledge of sorcerers, wizards, and so on."

"You can't write off all those stories so easily." Dammit, he knew testimony. There were too many accounts of magick for all of it to be wrong.

She glanced sideways at him.

"Exaggerations and lies." She dismissed centuries of storytelling with a brief flick of her fingers.

"All of it?" Her emphasis stripped his one escape from the job into no more than drops of black ink on a white page. All those childhood books kept in his library for constant rereading meant nothing? "That's impossible."

"*Argos* has some of it right: They only allow a few classes of player to wield spells, while the other players must make do with mortal weapons." She studied him from lambent green eyes.

"So if everybody else in the world only knew about magick from rumors and a few unavoidable glimpses—"

She shrugged and turned away from the wind. Her hands

framed her head for a moment. When she tucked them back into her pockets, another braided coronet restrained her hair.

"How the hell did you do that?" Jake roared and walked backward, staring at her.

She caught his elbow and forced him to turn around.

"Magick," she said succinctly.

"To arrange your hair?" His breath was poised like a first-year cop's evaluation report—sometimes up, sometimes down, and always scaring the hell out of his heart.

"Yes. It's actually a very easy spell." She yanked him into step with her.

"There truly is magick." His tongue was thick enough to choke him.

"Yes, but we don't use it the way your legends say."

"Could you make my hair long?"

She snapped her fingers and a black strand whipped across his lips.

"Jesus Christ, don't do that to me!" He closed his eyes. He didn't want to know how long it had grown.

She chuckled and snapped her fingers again.

Strands tickled his earlobes again, in a silent reminder that he needed to get his shaggy locks cut. He shivered and promised himself at least two beers, the minute he walked into his home again.

"Any other tests?"

"No! I believe you." He'd been a homicide cop for years. He knew how to sift evidence and match theory to facts, even when a sane man would have said something was impossible.

His stomach was doing slow somersaults, like a drunken astronaut in a new galaxy.

Think about this news, Hammond. What difference does it make?

"Am I a farasha?" He stumbled over the word. He didn't need magick, although such a life could be as dangerous and exhausting as *Argos* said.

"No, you're a kubri." Gold flecks floated in her eyes, luminous as candlelight. Christ, he could watch them for hours.

Kubri? Was that better than a farasha?

"I'm a sahir, a wielder of magick. There are multiple levels and networks of sahirs, but that's all you need to know for now."

Had he missed something by looking into her eyes? Could she hypnotize him?

"Okay." Jake would not tap his toe on the pavement or drum his fingers. He was a professional who didn't obviously display impatience, even when he wanted to yell. "If you're a sahir, then why is it important that I'm a kubri?"

"Kubris draw raw magickal power from the earth and the cosmos, then feed it to sahirs."

Raw magickal power? That could be useful. "Can a kubri wield magick?"

"No, only sahirs."

"Damn." He'd have to work through her and he couldn't control her for shit.

Her beautiful mouth twitched.

"So you need people like me to obtain the most power?"

"Correct."

"What if there aren't any kubris around?" How much did she need him?

"We recharge our power through sex with a willing partner, which is less emotionally intense—or effective, or transfer it from another sahir." The frown lines deepened between her brows before she went on.

"There are few kubris available, Jake. I'm only telling you this because we will try to recruit you." Her green eyes met his without evasion.

"Recruit for what?"

"To have frequent sex with sahirs. The best sex of your life." She caressed the words until they implied more pleasure than any *1001 Nights* sultan had ever enjoyed.

He couldn't object to that, could he? On the other hand, it didn't sound like Astrid was the only sahir he'd be bedding.

Stupid to feel possessive about a woman he'd only spent two nights with.

"We'll keep you healthy, too, of course," she added, her voice still seductive.

"Protect me as a cop?" That could be an advantage. Maybe he'd transfer over to SWAT—or maybe not.

"Not that part, unless you resign and live full-time in an aerie, with sahirs. Most kubris choose to do that," she added.

Quit—and live in a dormitory? No way!

"Not this one! Give up being a cop, my ass. Who the hell would speak for the dead and find their killers?" He glared at her, the Founders' Oak tree rising tall and solid behind him. Planted when Belhaven was born, it had stood witness to the tumultuous centuries since.

"You don't know who we are and what we do," Astrid countered. "Or how you'd help by strengthening us. Do you have any idea how much it meant to have a kubri right there when that man was dying? I'd never have saved his life without you."

"You're joking." He crossed his arms over his chest. He wouldn't back down for any high-flying nonsense designed solely to get his attention.

Then he hesitated, the ground under his feet suddenly more unstable than the waves. Astrid—or Andromache—never wasted time during a game on bullshit.

"Not a bit. That required immense power, since he was within seconds of death." The muscles in her throat rippled before she went on. "You were incredible, Jake. Thank you."

Her tone was so simple that it compelled belief.

Ice ran through his veins and his knees weakened. He needed to sit down and rethink his world.

He rubbed his sleeve across his face to wipe the sweat from his forehead.

"How did you do the rest of it?" he mumbled, keeping his

eyes hidden. He couldn't look into her glowing green gaze and think straight.

"I warded the elevator cab against the shooter. After that, his gun locked up on him."

Wards. Holy hell, he was standing here, looking at Washington, D.C., and talking about *magickal wards.*

But did anything else describe what had happened? The assassin had yanked his hand out of the elevator, then run away as if that web of purple lightning burned him.

"How did you heal the marshal?" Maybe the next question would put a hole in her explanation.

"My talent is battle magick, not healing, so I probably overdid that."

Delicate Astrid wielded battle magick?

"I linked to you, summoned power through you—"

"The memories of St. Anne's?" They'd felt like the anchor his father always promised.

"Yes. Do you mind?"

"No, not a bit." He chewed on his lip and went with his gut. He had to be going nuts. "Did you create a specific picture of what you wanted his body to do?"

"Not at all." She shook her head like a girl presented with too many options at the ice cream parlor. "I told you, I'm not a healer. If I were, I'd have knit it together just enough to last until the EMTs could take over. That way, nobody would suspect magick."

Oh crap, this was making too much sense. He could hear all the other cops and hospital staff talking now. But she hadn't been there to listen.

"Instead, everybody thinks we're the luckiest dudes on the planet because so many bullets whizzed around that elevator and we only took scratches."

"Exactly."

"Shit, you honsestly are the real thing." How could he use this news to solve the Melinda Williams investigation?

"Told you so." She tugged her heavy quilted coat closer. "But you can't mention it to anybody, remember?"

The last ledge holding his stomach up slid aside and it plummeted from his knees into the muddy ground.

Crap.

She started to walk back up the hill toward the city. And parking or taxis or Metro—or however she planned to leave town.

Heat stirred back into his blood.

He couldn't let her go. If she could work magick for the FBI, then she could do a good deed for him, too.

"If you're such a powerful sahir . . ." he shouted.

He stumbled a little over the last word but who the hell cared when everything was at stake?

She glanced back at him, her green eyes wide with shock. "What are you talking about?"

"If you're such a powerful sahir, then tell me who killed Melinda Williams." He planted his feet wide and his fists on his hips, the same way he'd stand while dressing down an arrogant rookie.

She spun around. "That's not how it works."

"Then explain it to me." He beckoned with a single finger.

She took a single step closer, then stopped to glare at him.

"Finding her murderer is your problem, not mine. I look after my country."

"What good is that if you don't help the little people?"

"The needs of the many outweigh the needs of the few."

"Bullshit. There won't be any *many* if you don't help the few."

"You need honor and a framework for the many to live within, else the beasts will trample the weak."

"I cannot turn my back when I see injustice."

"That is your job; mine lies elsewhere."

Jesus H. Christ, he wanted to wring her beautiful, stubborn neck—then haul her back into his bed.

"You could help me track the killer." He softened his voice to his best interrogation room purr.

"Have you heard anything I said?"

"I said help, okay? Not do everything yourself."

"Why should I trust you?"

"Six years of gaming together?" Jake suggested.

She hesitated, then offered a small concession. "Good start."

"How about a bet?"

"You haven't got anything worth playing for."

"Sex—with me." He put his only asset on the line. If she powered her magick through sex and the best came with kubris like him, then maybe—just maybe—he could make her fine brain stop thinking while she was in bed with him. Then she'd agree to anything, like helping his investigation.

Lust danced behind her eyes.

Shit, it had worked. His cock twitched happily.

"Go on," she said.

"You said it's emotionally tight when sahirs and kubris have sex, right?"

"Correct." Her mouth thinned for a moment. "Go on."

"We spend one full night together at my place. Each of us tries to drown the other's senses with sex until somebody cries, 'Uncle!' Afterward, the one who wins gets the other's help for a week."

She considered him, her thoughts no more discernible than the river's currents.

"You won't enjoy it if I win," she warned him. "You'll have to work for my goals, plus spend your nights with me."

"I'll take the chance. It's the only way I've got to break the case."

"I can understand that." A wry smile twisted her lips. "Very well, you have a bet. I'll come to your house tonight."

Jake blew her a kiss and reassured his gut that such a gamble would work.

CHAPTER TWELVE

The portal outlined its triangular frame in a shower of brilliant sparks, like fireworks burning through space and time to claim territory. Astrid quickly stepped through and shut the door before the void could claim her long, black angora coat.

A chill breeze brushed her ankles, but she dismissed it with the same haughty runes that wiped out the portal. She was here to win a new kubri for the Guard, dammit, not hesitate over warnings sent by Elswyth about the Council's squeamishness.

If the inquisitors hauled her in, she'd assure them she'd always met the spirit of the Shadow Council's laws—even if not the letter.

She spun, checking the shadows behind Jake's house for observers. Knowing his workaholic habits from his pattern of logging in to *Argos* over the years, she'd arrived here long before he could have come home.

His backyard was little more than a small brick pad, topped by a barbecue grill. Billowing shrubs, which probably flowered in warmer weather, blocked his neighbor's view but allowed him to see the Potomac River. Even with early spring's quarter-inch, pale green leaves, they provided more than enough cover to keep her arrival undetected.

Perfect. Now to go fight for her prize: A week with Jake as her kubri . . .

Her breath hitched and steam hung for an instant in the chill air. What decadent visions that thought created! A kubri's stamina mixed with a sahir's fire. Jake bent over her, his cock deep inside her, and his thumb rubbing her jaw in a silent request to begin yet again. Jake stretched out beneath her, his eyes wide with joy, as yet another orgasm shook them both. Jake lying half over, half under her, while his big hand toyed with her clit until magick raced like fire through her veins . . .

The sorceress Medea would have fought the goddess Athena for him.

Astrid shook herself until silk slithered across her breasts and her hair whipped her neck like tiny knives.

She was here for the Guard, not herself, remember? Thinking any other way would leave her so distracted she'd lose the bet and maybe start remembering all the reasons why getting involved again was dangerous.

Heck, why not? She'd try the simple approach first.

Very, very carefully, Astrid whispered a simple request, then blew sparks over the doorknob.

It glided easily in her hand, slick as cream sliding down her leg under her lover's tongue.

She hissed through her teeth—*Dear God, not a plea for attention!*—and yanked the solid panel toward her.

A split second later, the blessed darkness indoors closed around her. Light glimmered briefly off a glass panel and disappeared into well-polished wood. She'd found her way to the library, which she'd glimpsed before from the kitchen.

Her pulse stuttered then steadied and a single bead of sweat crept down her brow.

Confidence, tonight was all about confidence.

A metal rod nudged her chin.

"Welcome to my parlor," purred Jake. Hunger and masculine anticipation roughened his voice.

Astrid froze in place. The gun's sights nicked the underside of her throat and her heartbeat lurched abruptly. Jake wouldn't, couldn't shoot her, not when the barrel pointed across her neck.

He clicked something inside his pocket. The desk lamp came slowly alive, resembling the oil lantern it had once been, and revealed her adversary.

Jake wore full SWAT gear, down to the assault rifle cradled in his arm. Blacker than the room's shadows, it emphasized all of his masculine advantages, including shoulders broad enough to block out the skies when he catapulted his lover into orgasm. Thighs long and strong enough to set multiple deadly weapons glinting when he moved—and power hours of ecstasy for his partner.

What a damn unfair advantage, compared to her black coat, which revealed nothing.

Her idiotic body immediately lit like a beeswax candle. Even the fact that he'd put his M4's safety on meant nothing. Hell, she'd come here to win, not the other way around.

"How polite of you to arrive early." Jake ran his hand possessively down her hip.

Heat rippled through her skin and centered under his palm.

"Let me go," she demanded. At least she hadn't squeaked, no matter how much his proximity affected her breathing.

He had the effrontery to chuckle.

"Or what? You'll turn me into a frog?"

"Yes!" she snapped. Her hands lifted into the spell's first rune. Green and croaking would suit him very well.

The rifle tightened against her throat and pushed her back against the wall, inches from the door into the living room. Her breasts rose and fell rapidly, until her coat and silk tank top teased her nipples like a skilful lover.

"What good will victory do you then, Astrid, if you gain it by magick?" he asked very quietly. Ruthless logic cut through his words like a knife. "What will it mean to you? Would you expect me to honor the bargain?"

She snapped her teeth together before her first, angry answer could brand her a liar. Of course, she'd prefer to win quickly—but it wouldn't be a fair fight if she used magick and he had none.

"No," she whispered. Her body tightened and cream warmed her thighs at the first submission she'd freely given any man other than Gerard.

"Very good, Astrid." Approval warmed Jake's eyes for an instant and his gun caressed her throat. She closed her eyes and fine tremors racked her body. She wanted to faint, she wanted to leap on him, she wanted to beg for more . . .

"Take off your coat." He stepped back a pace and took away all contact. She could have whimpered but instead straightened her shoulders.

She undid the buttons slowly, one at a time, starting from the bottom. By God, she'd do her best to tease out any lascivious thoughts lurking behind his expressionless mask.

The sight of her stiletto heeled, knee-high boots, which looked like wide, black leather bands wrapped around her calves, made his hands flex on his rifle and his tongue sweep across his lips.

She paused, but he waved her on imperiously.

Drat.

A few more buttons revealed her bare thighs and her skirt's hem, only a few inches below her hips.

His throat tightened but a tortured, raw sound of pure need escaped him.

Anticipation ran through her, fast as her lust. Her fingers lingered on her coat's soft black wool, as if too nervous to open the next button.

He shoved his hand into his pocket again and clicked the controls. A single spotlight flashed into being and the library beyond suddenly came alive. Books covered every wall in a living pageant of police work. A large armchair crouched before a littered desk in one corner. But there was no other seating, no other signs of life beyond the cop who owned this house.

A soft pool of light illuminated Astrid, which allowed him to see everything and her to glimpse only a little.

His chest rose and fell more rapidly under his black vest. His golden ear cuff twined its way around his ear, delicate as a lover's kiss and ready to help him draw power.

Perhaps he'd let her have a small taste now, nothing too big . . .

"Jake," she whispered, "may I—"

"Continue." The word was so guttural it barely sounded like language. He jerked his gun upwards to emphasize how she needed to behave. Light flashed along its barrel and bounced off his vest's silver patch.

Dark eyes watched her, eager as the light yet more tightly leashed than the rifle.

Her knees weakened. If her magick was an unfair advantage, then so was his damn badge. "Ah, Jake . . ."

She forced her fingers to work the next button, and the next, and the next.

Finally she flung the coat's panels open and let him see her own weapons. Black suede vest, purple silk tank, and black miniskirt—the last tight enough to reveal every detail of what lay underneath.

His expression hardened to allow no clue to his thoughts yet his eyes roamed over her as if he wanted to either memorize her or grab her. They swept her over and over again, always coming back to the line running from the deep vee of bare skin between her breasts.

Her body heated like a candle under his gaze. Her breasts tightened until the fragile cloth thrummed across her chest.

"Interested, are you?" he asked, very softly.

"Maybe." She cursed her treacherous voice for turning husky. This would be easier if she could pretend some indifference. After all, she was usually very casual when she recharged at the aerie. Surely this required no emotional commitment.

He barked a short laugh, his eyes dark enough to drown sanity.

"Perhaps I should give you something else to think about."
He fished something narrow and long out of his pocket. "Take
your coat off and toss it aside."

What did he plan? She couldn't see what he held.

"Move it along, Astrid." The crack of his words, sinfully attractive as any leather flogger's first slap, compelled obedience.

She shrugged her coat off first one shoulder, then the other.
Its satin lining lingered over her leather vest like a lover's
hands, then fell to the floor.

Jake's pulse drummed in his temple but he said nothing.

She kicked the soft, shapeless mass aside. It swirled like a
flying carpet into the living room, where a dull thud marked
its resting place. She didn't care where it fell, only that Jake's
gaze now memorized every inch of silk and skin covering her.

Suddenly the micro miniskirt and delicate silk tank were far
too much clothing for her overheated body to endure. She
stretched and her vest slipped away from her throat, baring
her collarbone.

"Turn around."

She blinked at him, too startled to move rapidly. What on
earth was he planning?

"You heard me." His tone was now a crisp order, not a
suitor's plea. "Put your hands behind your back, Carlsen. You
won't find it pleasant if I do it."

She faced the wall before any clear thoughts entered her
head. Hot, sweet cream eased onto her thighs and begged for
him.

She closed her eyes and silently fought for self-control. Anything not to leap on him. Dammit, she had to win this bet, if
she was to take him back to the aerie.

His hot mouth nuzzled the nape of her neck until she
moaned and leaned toward the wet incitement to hedonism,
sparks flying through her veins like tracers.

"Jake, I thought . . ." She tried to remember something log-
ical, something about his next step.

"Don't think." He kneaded her hip through the thin, stretchy fabric and every stroke sent tremors through her pussy. "Just give me your hand."

She extended it to him behind her back, too blissful to worry about his intentions. He scraped his teeth lightly over her nape and she shuddered in pleasure, fires burning brighter in her core. She never noticed when her other hand fell into his.

But when the stiff, narrow bands locked around her wrists with a *zzzip!,* she jerked away from him. "What the hell are you doing, Jake?"

"Tying you up so you can't cause any trouble." He steadied her by the shoulders and turned her back to face him. His hands and voice were equally implacable, equally soft—and equally attractive.

She shivered, trapped and held by his barbaric fearlessness. Even his quilted vest emphasized it, thanks to its ammunition pouches.

"I agreed to . . ." she stammered. Surely she needed to say something, just for a chance at claiming him. For a hope of not risking too much. She wet her lips and tried again with a far too fragmented brain. "Our bet was . . ."

"Stay where you are."

"What?" She blinked at him, baffled. Why on earth would he want her to stand in front of a bookcase, midway between a corner and an open door? What was he planning now?

"Obey me, Astrid." That damn tone again.

A pulsating wave of lust poured from her breasts through her lungs and down her spine. She was wet, aching with it, scenting the air with it.

She closed her eyes and nodded. Dammit, why did she have to be a badge bunny for this one cop?

"And keep your eyes open!"

Shit. She whimpered but obeyed, unable to protest her inability to hide from his attractions.

"Good girl." His smile was half feral when he set aside his rifle.

Maybe he'd shuck his pants fast and they'd fuck right away.

"I'm sure you know, Astrid, that well-made police gear needs to be properly looked after." He unlatched the bottom clasp on his vest. "This exercise has its points but—"

Exercise? She was about to go insane!

He undid the next two clasps equally slowly. Her ragged breathing was the room's only sound.

Oh, hell. His vest was still zipped, dammit, so she couldn't see a thing.

He rubbed his chest and his fingers circled his pecs. Her nipples tightened hungrily.

"Perhaps . . ."

He toyed with the vest's zipper. She watched him greedily, unable to breathe.

"I should . . ." He dragged the zipper leisurely down halfway, displaying more of his snug black T-shirt.

She moaned in frustration. Her eyelids were so heavy, they ached, yet she could have watched him for days.

"Or perhaps pay attention here." Jake cupped his crotch and blatantly outlined his straining cock. "Do you think my officers would approve of so much stress?"

"Probably not," Astrid managed to say. Her hips rocked back and forth, swaying to a beat older than time, the same rhythm that powered the heat rippling through her veins.

He unzipped his vest and flung it into the living room. He unbuckled his heavy belt and his pants gaped slightly. Fulfillment lay behind them but she couldn't reach it. She couldn't even see her goal clearly.

"Oh, fuck, Jake." Astrid writhed and rubbed her thighs together. "Can't you . . . Can't we . . ."

She stopped, a sahir too blind with lust to form words, even though they formed her magick's tools.

"Hungry, Astrid?" Jake asked softly. He cupped her mound through her thin skirt.

She leaned into his big hand and whimpered hopefully. "Please, please."

His big hand slid between her legs and past her thong. She ground herself down on his finger, too hungry to care about anything other than him and her own satisfaction.

"Interested in this cop?" he asked. His voice was so deep, it rumbled like a tactical assault vehicle rather than purred like a cat.

"Infinitely," she assured him.

He stripped her fragile silk stockings down her thighs.

Good, now he was getting serious. Magickal fireflies dived through his jewelry and into him.

His mouth crushed hers, brutally possessive. She answered him eagerly, ecstasy starting to sing a siren song in her veins. But he broke the kiss off before the harsh contact could trigger her climax.

She staggered but couldn't find the strength to protest.

He peeled his T-shirt off and dropped it to the floor.

Heaven help her, all those beautiful muscles . . .

She started to step closer but he growled, deep and low. "Stand fast, woman."

She obediently froze, her knees wobbly. She'd get down on her knees to beg if he did much more.

Surely his cock was larger behind his quilted trousers. Her fingers flexed, eager to sample its size, and her pussy rippled.

"Pretty lady," he breathed against her hair and rubbed himself over her hip, sinuous as a cougar.

"You're mad," she groaned and thrust herself back at him. If she found the right stroke, she might be able to come.

"Silly girl." He kissed the top of her head and shoved his hand down the back of her skirt. It was so tight that the fabric drew him closer until his fingers were inside the cleft of her ass.

"Damn thong," he grumbled and ripped it off from under her skirt.

She wriggled harder, anything to encourage him. "Oh yes, Jake, just like that." Her eyes closed to focus on the delicious surge of lust down her spine and into her pussy.

"That's my baby." He kissed her so marvelously, she barely noticed when his hand left her ass.

She was drowning in sensation—his chest rubbing against hers, his nipples somehow abrading the silk until they were imprinted on her skin. His trousers' matte perfection, rougher than satin but finer than sand, which caged her thighs and made her cream sizzle. And, oh, the thrust and sweep of his tongue into her mouth in a delicious promise of more intimate delights to come.

"Jake." Words, every sahir's lifeblood, faded before the need to hold and encourage him.

He lifted her up slightly and sat down in the big armchair, with her astride his lap. An instant later, he snipped off the plastic tie around her wrists.

Astrid barely glanced at her free hands. Instead she put them into action and wrapped her arms around his neck.

He chuckled, harshly triumphant as a returning soldier, and deepened his kiss. She sank into it, finally able to enjoy him without hindrance. She ran her hands through his unruly shock of black hair, and golden dragonflies danced over his ear cuff.

Yes, oh yes, magick was pouring into him through his kubri connection to the earth.

"Vest off," he muttered and tugged the fragile scrap of leather down first one arm then the other.

Her balance changed with his every move. Her very short skirt slid up. For the first time, she was able to feel his very aroused cock and the surety of forthcoming climax.

She wiggled slightly to confirm it, then again to find the best possible spot for present enjoyment. His cock against her clit, his balls against her ass if she leaned at just the right angle . . .

"Astrid, dammit, don't start that yet." His clenched tones sounded like he was gritting his teeth, but she didn't look.

She was much more interested in how his cock had surged to meet her—and how much wetter she'd become. She rocked against him, long, hot waves pulsing from her breasts and down her spine.

He started to lift her arms again to remove her silk tank top. But she was too absorbed in rolling herself over and over again across his crotch to lift her hands from his shoulders. Oh, the sparks shooting up her spine every time her clit rubbed against his stomach.

Nothing mattered more than uniting herself with the energy he was raising up.

Nothing mattered more than uniting herself with Jake.

"Astrid, for the love of God, you're torturing me." He clasped her hips.

"You know"—her breath caught in her throat when his cockhead nudged her pussy—"how to fix that."

Her eyelids were too heavy to lift. She was a being of pure sensation, pure magick catching power from the cosmos.

"Astrid!" He wrapped his arm around her waist and hastily lifted his hips out of the chair. A clumsy shove, aided by her magick, sent his trousers down his legs.

He landed back in his chair with a thud and her kneeling above him.

"Now," she announced firmly and clasped his face in her hands.

"Anything I want?"

She stared at him. She was so needy that orgasm threatened to rip her guts out if she didn't satisfy it.

"You got it." She pushed madness back far enough to summon two more words. "What else?"

"A condom . . ."

Ah, yes, he'd be happier with that key element of farasha lifestyle than an explanation of sahir reproduction. Astrid snapped her fingers and sheathed him in the latest high-tech version, one used at the aerie between houseguests.

She caressed his head and let his magick flow through her bones, up through his spine, across her hands, down into her pussy where it met his balls . . .

"Holy fuck, Astrid." Both of his hands locked down on her waist.

She arched her back, millimeters away from capturing and riding him.

He squeezed tight and forced her to stop.

"Anything I want, right, Astrid?" He dragged the words out of his heaving chest. "For one week, you work for me."

Her eyes flew open. His aura surrounded him, golden as the sun and blinding as the desperation pulsing between her legs. His ear cuff was incandescent.

Certainty tugged at her.

She nodded. "Agreed."

His fingers bit into her. He raised her slightly and speared her on his cock.

"Damn, you're beautiful, Astrid."

She howled happily and pushed down. He surged upward to meet her and her hungry muscles grabbed him. *Yes, oh yes.*

Again and again, closer and closer, sparks circled and dove through them until fire wove deeper and deeper into her bones, etching the path for climax to follow.

Suddenly the last remaining scrap of silk shifted across her ribs and up to her throat. Jake's warm, wet mouth captured her breast. He swirled his tongue over her nipple and her breath lurched to a hopeful stop.

She hung suspended, every particle, every bit of magick waiting for his next move.

He suckled hard—and she exploded into rapture, tumbling through the stars like a newborn sun. Her body shattered, dissolved, remade itself from magick etched with his blood and passion.

"Jake!" Her fingers dug deep into his shoulders in gratitude and joy.

"Oh, fuck." He jolted under her and flung his head back, his expression an astonished rictus of ecstasy. Hot, wet pulses bombarded her sweetly, then disappeared into the condom.

She turned her face into his shoulder and breathed in his

sweat, the one fluid she could openly indulge in. Their breathing and heartbeats tumbled over and over each other until at last they slowed to a decorous walk.

Had he noticed the change in his aura?

"Bed," Jake said in the same matter-of-fact tone his chief would use to announce a shift change. He stood up, still holding her, and pulled her skirt over her head. He flung it across the room where it caught on a bookshelf and hung like a battle flag, a warrior's symbol of triumph.

Astrid choked at its blatancy and her body's immediate surge of arousal in response.

Jake glanced over his shoulder and grinned. "Quite a mess, isn't it?"

"The living room is worse," Astrid said faintly. Good God, how had they managed to fling so much clothing so far? "We should hang everything up."

"Like this?" He abruptly pulled her purple silk tank top over her head and tossed it onto the newel post.

"Jake!"

"Are you backing out now, Carlsen?" He raised an eyebrow at her in challenge.

"Not a damn bit, Hammond." *No matter what hell you dig up, we'll at least have tonight.*

CHAPTER THIRTEEN

Jake tied off the latest condom and leaned out of bed, pleased he'd had the foresight to hide a small trash can inside the nightstand. He'd never done it before, not that he'd brought anybody back here since college. But he didn't want to spend an unnecessary second away from Astrid, nor did he want her to be offended.

She muttered something and shifted onto the sheets away from him, totally relaxed. His aching cock immediately twitched and asserted its eagerness to explore her backside, echoing her insouciance.

How many times had they fucked in the last six hours? Four—or was it six? How many orgasms had she enjoyed? More than that! Yet she looked fresh and happy, like an Olympic athlete ready to stride into the stadium.

Jealousy flashed through him, fiercer than a gun's muzzle flash across a darkened alley. Who'd taught her that, her dead husband? How could he compete with a ghost?

Not well, he admitted reluctantly, then shied away from why he'd want to challenge a specter for anything.

She stretched, extending every limb like a sated cat lolling on a windowsill. Her hair whipped over her head in a golden veil and settled onto the pillow, smooth and fine as his grandmother's lace curtains.

Astrid must have used her magick to clean up the wild tendrils he'd enjoyed a few minutes ago.

Magick.

"Can you make it to the station by eleven a.m. tomorrow morning, Astrid?" Jake asked.

"What?" Astrid rolled onto one elbow and stared at him. The bedclothes were still jumbled around their ankles, thanks to the last round of sex. Her sweat-streaked, naked body gleamed like an offering to *Argos*'s gods under the nightlight's distant glow. Glowing like a pearl, her skin was touched with rose and amethyst from his nibbles. She didn't look entirely real except for the growing fire in her emerald eyes.

Had they ever flashed at him before? Truly flashed, like fireworks or an old-fashioned gun, which needed fire to set off the gunpowder?

No, that had to be impossible, just like the golden lights he'd seen spinning around him when they had sex.

"Why are you asking me *right now* about eleven a.m. tomorrow?" Astrid said carefully, clipping her words as if she were handloading a shotgun.

Jake refused to wince. He had the advantage, after all: he'd won their bet.

"That will give me a few hours to clear my desk, then go through my files and figure out the best place to utilize your services."

"Utilize my services?" Her breasts heaved, bringing her nipples up toward his mouth.

He kept his gaze steady on her face. If he looked down, he might remember just how responsive they'd been an hour ago and how she'd pulled his head closer to encourage him.

"Jake, it isn't even one a.m.," she pointed out. She jerked her thumb at his high-tech alarm clock, which blazed the time brightly enough to compete with the sun and monitored every governmental radio channel, to boot.

"Murder investigations are damn important," he shot back.

Umbrage pushed heat toward his skin and into his voice but he beat it back. He needed to make Astrid, more than anybody else, understand. "Murders happen every hour of the day and night. They need to be solved fast before the killer escapes."

"Jake." Astrid laughed as if she couldn't find words, the sound sharp as water erupting from a hot skillet. "Jake, when was the last time you went for twelve hours without thinking about your job?"

"What does that have to do with this?" He gaped at her, genuinely astonished.

"Come on, Jake, you can tell me." Her voice softened to an irresistible lure.

"Not since I became a homicide cop. So what?" He'd never admitted this much to the departmental shrink.

"It's the middle of the night, you have a naked woman in your bed who's very willing to have sex with you—and you want to talk about *your job*?" She ran her fingers lightly up his thigh and rested her hand on the old bullet wound in his hip. "Does this strike you as maybe a little odd?"

"Not really." He shrugged but kept watching her, torn between irritation and the urge to claim her. Better not mention how often the other sergeants teased him about always being online to the station. "Most homicide cops stay very busy."

"No family—"

"Got a brother in the Army," he countered quickly. At least, the last he'd heard. Logan's job didn't encourage writing about his schedule.

"Good! Having family is vital." Her smile was bright enough to blind him. She leaned forward and kissed him on the cheek. But the way her breasts brushed against him hardly let him relax.

"Your house is set up so you can eat, sleep, and do cop business. There isn't room for anything else here."

"Oh yes, there is." He stroked her jawbone with a single finger, just the way she liked. "I keep all my gaming systems in the attic."

"Locked away in high-topped trunks?" Her eyes tilted into opalescent green slits of pleasure, like a purring cat, but she didn't lean her hips against him, dammit.

"Nope, out in the open, monitor after monitor." He nuzzled the thrumming pulse in her throat and she shivered. "Lots of high-powered systems to play risky games with, like *Argos*."

"Games that will wait for you to come to them," she pointed out, but the edge was gone from her voice. Her leg slipped between his, silky smooth compared to his hair-roughened, scarred limb.

He cupped her ass and savored how her feminine curves rippled along his front. Who cared what they argued about when it ended like this?

"Yeah, of course they'll wait—but this won't." He lowered his head to kiss her again. As he hoped, she responded like a gasoline-soaked rag to a cigarette. Conversation stopped, to be replaced by the purely enjoyable sensations of a woman wrapping herself around him and hurling herself into his kiss.

"Eleven a.m. tomorrow, right?" he murmured a few minutes later when he lifted his head.

She shut her eyes and laughed, all good nature this time. "You truly don't think about anything except cops, gaming, and sex, do you, Jake?"

Her long fingers stroked his lower back, near his tailbone. How did she know that played havoc with his ass—and cock?

"Why should I?" he countered lazily and rolled a little closer.

Two months ago, he'd have agreed with her. No way in hell he'd tell her that his favorite troika had become a quartet, with her as the fourth member.

His fingertips teased wetness from between her thighs, musky and irresistible as before. His brain promptly skittered south.

"You might try it," she murmured. "It could sharpen your edge. But I'll be there when you say, no matter what."

She blew a kiss across his cheek, soft as a cherry blossom's first blush. Then her mouth opened for him and he claimed her eagerly.

Better to think about the fun here and now than worry about getting involved with a broad who wasn't telling him everything she knew. Even if she was his oldest friend and only ally.

Jake shot another glance around the bedroom, just for form's sake. Years of overhearing gossip at the station assured him that this was not the moment to strut, no matter what he thought. Astrid was using the master bathroom to clean up, something no mere male interfered with.

"No, honey, I can't see anything of yours up here." Despite his best efforts, the mirror showed an enormous smirk on his face. Damn, but he'd had a great time last night, as evidenced by his bed's utter wreckage—and their clothing's disappearance.

Shit, he'd better wipe it out of his voice before she got pissed. He cleared his throat then used the same, soft drawl he'd use to placate his favorite barista. "I'll check downstairs to see what I can find."

Astrid shut off the running water and gave a very unladylike snort. "If anything survived to be found."

Jake's grin broadened. How did he get lucky enough to find a fuck buddy like her?

He laughed at himself and finished tucking himself carefully into his trousers. His cock went comfortably, even though it should be demanding a long day attired in nothing more than sweatpants.

He was neither bruised nor sore, despite a night when sexual excesses had outnumbered hours of sleep. He'd drowsed for no more than a few minutes at any time, yet he felt more than ready to take on his qualifying exam at the firing range. A full day of bracing heavy guns against their kickback and concentrating on ever-changing targets' fine details would be a delicious challenge. But not today.

There was no clothing on the upstairs landing. If he remembered right—damn, what memories!—he'd been the only one still sporting any clothing at that point. Mainly because his boots, unlike hers, wouldn't let him remove the other stuff very quickly. The last item of hers he'd removed was that purple top when . . .

Jake halted in mid-stride, halfway down the stairs. Black hair, cut shorter than his, stirred against the leather sofa. His grandmother's much-darned quilt barely concealed the man's form sleeping underneath, folded like an origami bird to fit onto the narrow space. Two stockinged feet rejected the sofa's strict confines and hung over the edge in mute refusal to conform.

A tanned face was shoved into a pillow, like a small boy collapsed into a sudden nap.

Jake's heart flew into his throat.

Little brother Logan was home. At least for a short while, he was alive and safe.

"Hey there, big bro." Logan's hand emerged from under the pillow and waved. No point in asking yet how long he'd stay this time.

"Welcome home." This time, Jake welcomed the shit-kicking grin to his voice. He vaulted downstairs, using the newel post.

Logan unfolded himself from the sofa and met him in a bear hug. He was heavily tanned—not surprising for a Special Forces sniper—but solid muscle clutched Jake, not concealed flinches or hidden wheezes from sickness or injury.

They pounded on each other happily, hard enough to leave bruises. It was a few minutes before they broke apart to share words.

"You're looking good, Logan." He had dark circles under his eyes and the long-distance stare of somebody fresh from combat. His rumpled uniform reeked of scents that Jake could only guess at and didn't want to learn the origin of.

Dammit, he had to take some leave to spend time with his brother. But how?

"Get in late last night?" Jake asked, careful to keep things casual. "Glad you made it long before that guess in your last email."

"After midnight. Didn't want to wake you after I saw *that*." Logan jerked his head at Astrid's purple top, brilliant as a tropical bird atop the coffee table.

Jake felt the old, slow burn from his teenage years climb into his cheeks. He and Astrid hadn't left it there, nor any of their clothing. No, the silk had landed on the damn newel post.

Fifteen years of living in different worlds vanished under Logan's knowing gaze. He grinned and gave Jake the thumbs-up.

For an instant, they were teenagers again, covering up each other's wild antics.

"Lucky guy," Logan said softly. "Didn't think you'd ever bring a girl here, especially not somebody who'd spend the night."

"She's a good friend." Jake shrugged, unable to explain his relationship with Astrid any further. Guildie? Sahir? Material witness in a murder? Better not say anything more.

"Anyway, I folded all of the clothing and put it there." Logan scratched his back through his suspiciously new army-green T-shirt.

"Thanks."

"Like to see her wearing that skirt," Logan added.

"Hell, no!" Why had he said that? Was he getting possessive? This was his brother talking, not a stranger.

"Got you that time, didn't I?"

"Pig." He'd fallen into another of Logan's traps. At least it eased the tight lines around his brother's mouth.

"I won't poach." Logan playfully punched him in the arm, his eyes dancing. "Just been a while seen I've seen a woman in anything so feminine."

"Maybe. If you ask nice." Jake drew himself up, mimicking their father's railroad engineer hauteur.

"Nice? You should want to show her off, if you ask me!"

"Jake?" Astrid's clear voice cut through the start of a new mock battle. What was she doing here? How had she gotten dressed?

Both men spun to face her.

She wore a neatly tailored jacket, a crisp wool skirt that barely reached her knees, and a ruffled silk blouse which refused to let him glimpse her breasts. She was a vision of femininity that he needed to somehow let walk out of his house, when every instinct screamed "drag her back to bed."

"Wow," Logan breathed.

Her mouth didn't quite twitch.

Jake definitely wanted to wall her off from his brother. Instead, he slipped his hand under her elbow. Time to stake out his claim—and make sure his FBI lady knew how much his rumpled sibling was worth.

"Astrid, this is my brother, Master Sergeant Logan Hammond. Logan, this is Astrid Carlsen from the Bureau."

Logan's eyes narrowed briefly at the last word, proving he'd registered the reference to her employer.

"The pleasure is all mine, Miss Astrid." Logan's drawl became even slower, the way it always did when he was under stress. "My brother sure is a lucky man."

"It's an honor to meet you, Logan." She nodded politely, her eyes never flickering below his face. "I'm very glad you made it home safely and I wish you a great reunion with Jake."

"Thanks, ma'am. Now, if you'll excuse me, I hear a bathroom calling my name." Logan disappeared up the stairs as if chased by J. Edgar Hoover.

"As I said before, you're very lucky in your family," Astrid said softly. "He's a fine man."

"Yes, he's the best." *Especially if you overlooked some of his more memorable teenage scrapes.* "I'm sure your family—"

Her expression closed into an icy mask, more suitable for an enemy's graveside than recalling fond memories. "All of them are dead, Jake."

He'd investigated far too many homicides to ask any more questions if he didn't need to. The worst loss was probably her husband. He sure as hell wasn't going to ask her about that. Grief cut everyone in different ways, few of them pretty.

"My condolences on your loss." He sure fumbled his sympathies for somebody who'd met a wealth of grieving widows.

"It's okay; it was a long time ago." He doubted it was okay, judging by her tone. Hopefully, the scar was buried deep enough to let her think about other men.

She picked up her coat. He helped her into it, his hands lingering on her when he helped her fasten the buttons.

"I'll ask my FBI supervisor for leave, which shouldn't take long," she said briskly. "Once I have that, I'll let you know when we can start working together."

"Thanks. Can I drive you back home?"

"No, I'll take Metro. You should spend time with your brother." She kissed her fingers then laid them on his lips. "I'll text you later, okay?"

"Gotcha." The old anticipation of texting Andromache ripped into him again.

She started to turn away but he caught her back to him and kissed her. When the only thing holding his wits together was the pressure of his zipper against his cock, he released her.

He was damn glad to find her flushed and breathless.

"Wretch," she whispered softly. Green and gold sparks whirled through her eyes, like living motes of laughter and lust.

"See ya later, Astrid," he said, certain now she'd come back.

"Until then."

A whirl of brisk morning air gusted through the living room behind her and chilled his bare chest and toes, together with any tendency to hover by the window.

"Nice girl," Logan commented from where he sat on the stairs. He'd washed his face but still wore his uniform.

"Thanks." Jake leaned against the wall and looked over at him. He had a few minutes left before he absolutely had to leave the house. Even if he was late, telling the lieutenant that his brother was back from deployment would automatically buy him extra time. Every second with Logan was valuable.

"Food in the fridge is edible; Señora Ramirez replaces it every week when she cleans," he announced to block one ancient source of arguments.

"What—no science projects?" Logan headed for the kitchen.

"Nope, and no extra work for her, either, to clean it out." Jake grimaced involuntarily at some of the lectures he'd received from his mother's cleaning lady. "She comes every Thursday and won't open any closed door."

"Sounds good. Glad you kept her on all these years."

"What else could I do?" He hesitated for an instant, then added one of their old jokes. "Why should I keep up with things? After all, Mom made you do the chores, since you were the one who always screwed up."

"Like hell!" Logan lowered the carton of milk and rubbed his forearm across his mouth to remove his mustache. "You can't boil water!"

"Which is why Señora Ramirez had a job after the folks died."

"Bullshit. You mean the good old motherly touch for the high school boy, that the social services folks demanded to see when you were my guardian." Logan shook his head. "Get real: you just wanted an excuse to keep her on when I enlisted after graduation."

He took another long swig of the ice-cold milk.

"For the times like now when you show up unexpectedly." Jake leaned back against his wine cellar and crossed his arms over his chest. Maybe Logan wouldn't spot the latest additions in this area too soon.

"And to keep the food safe and the dirt out." Logan ran a hand over his very bristly jaw. "Maybe I'll order in something. Vietnamese soup, maybe."

"Lots of menus by the kitchen computer."

"I noticed. Still use the same password for it?"

"Yup."

"Awesome." Logan yawned wide enough to swallow a whale.

"Is this investigation as big as the papers say?" he asked without looking.

Jake blew out a breath.

"My gut thinks so," he admitted.

"That's real bad, big bro." Blue eyes, so like their mother's, opened to regard him intently. "Neither of our guts has ever been wrong."

"No, they haven't." He met Logan's gaze steadily. "I haven't always been able to do anything about it, though."

"Who has?"

They laughed together bitterly.

"I'm going back to bed, Jake. I've got a few weeks' leave—"

"Hallelujah!"

"Yes, pretty much." Their eyes danced together. "After that, I'm stateside, probably for some kind of R&D stuff."

"Working with deep thinkers?" Logan, condemned to be polite to folks who wrote papers, instead of being in action?

"Yeah, I ran into some in the 'Stans." He waved his hand vaguely, but Jake wasn't about to press for details. Logan's world was notoriously close-mouthed to the point of penalties being etched in blood.

"After that episode"—*Episode? Adventure, more like. Shit, Hollywood probably couldn't match the story!*—"the Pentagon believes I'm one of the few who can talk to this bunch. So here I am, at least for a little while."

"Pentagon desk job? You're lucky." Jake tried to sound convincing.

Poor guy, he probably didn't have any choice. Jake had one when he left the streets, not that he'd enjoyed taking the sergeant's exam.

"Yeah, maybe." Logan hunched his shoulders and turned away. "I can at least run in the Tidewater 10K. Isn't that next week or the week after?"

"Something like that." Jake fumbled for something positive to say. "The station has several teams running in it, to raise funds for Enfield House, the battered women's shelter."

"Great cause." Logan reached for the banister like an old friend. "For my money, the Tidewater's one of the best races for meeting up with old special ops buddies."

"Great idea." Logan's friends would be good for him. "Well, I think I'd better get ready for work."

"Are you going to take the car?"

"Yes."

Logan's face shuttered faster than a holding cell door on Saturday night.

"There's a BMW motorcycle in the garage," Jake said softly. Like hell, he'd keep the kid tied down. "Not a Harley, but—"

"Can't keep your hands off German vehicles?" Logan's drooping eyelids couldn't hide the sparkle in his eyes. "Guess I'll have to forgive you, since it's a motorcycle. Thanks, bro."

Jake tipped his head in acknowledgment and kept going.

"Your pickup's two blocks away at Old Man Lafferty's place. Keys are in the usual place."

"You didn't put it in storage?"

"Why spend the money? Lafferty had room after he sold his wife's minivan after their divorce."

"Isn't he the one who bikes everywhere?"

"Got him in one. He fit your kayak onto the rack below his and helped me wash and wax it, too."

"Awesome." Logan swayed, a half smile dancing around his mouth. "Say thanks for me, won't you?"

Jake could have shouted hallelujah. Instead he simply nodded soberly, as if reliving the thick yellow gunk he'd plastered onto his brother's boat—and much of his own skin.

"You won't stop by a grocery store on the way home and buy stuff so I can cook your dinner?" His brother eyed him suspiciously from halfway up the stairs.

"No, not unless you beg."

"Beg? I'm pouring myself into the sack, big bro! Then I'm going to have some cold beer, a good meal, and a good lay—"

"If you can find the latter," Jake cut in.

Logan flipped him off without missing a beat.

"After that, I'll call an old buddy and spend some quiet time enjoying the water. You heard me—water, the strange stuff that isn't found anywhere in a desert."

And which answers a scientist's questions, like a well-behaved inanimate object should do.

Jake envied his brother's straightforward quest, so very different from a homicide investigation. But maybe he'd get lucky, too. Perhaps the lab tests would have come back by now on Melinda Williams's car and give him some leads.

CHAPTER FOURTEEN

Jake smacked the *Send* key, then shot a jaundiced eye at his in-box's counter. Two solid hours of paperwork and e-mail had done little to reduce the overflowing number of demands for his attention. Only a masochistic idiot—or a power-hungry fool—hungered to perform police paperwork. He'd never quite forgiven himself for joining the competitors for this job, even if it had kept Cosby out of the seat.

No flashes from his telephone to announce a breakthrough on the Williams case, or anything else on his plate. Nothing but biting his nails, kicking red tape, and booting another request for help into thin air whenever he thought it might work.

He could send another e-mail to the lab—and get his ears chewed off.

He drummed his fingers on the table. He should have picked up some peanut brittle if he truly wanted a bribe. Maybe at lunch.

But Astrid should call soon. He grinned, warmed by anticipation for more than the case.

"Jake." A boxy female sat down beside his desk with more emphasis than grace. "I need to talk to you. Don't bother standing up; neither of us has time."

"Good to see you, Lieutenant." Jake rapidly locked down his computer.

She shot him a filthy look from underneath Belhaven's cheapest haircut.

"Magdalena," he corrected quickly. She tolerated formality from nobody.

Her clothing was immaculately clean, thanks to the early hour and her lab coat, and virulently polyester. It had probably originated at a store more frequented by the town's indigents than its cops. Unlike other women, she never talked about shopping, only family and work.

"Care for some coffee? Or would you prefer tea? We just added some new decaffeinated green to our stash," he added, remembering recent gossip.

"No, not now, I've got to see the district attorney in a few minutes. But I wanted to get this to you right away." She shoved a folder across his crowded desk.

"The Williams case?" He grabbed the anonymous rectangle. "Anything interesting?"

"I personally did all the work."

"What the hell?" Belhaven spent a fortune on its CSI, and nobody ran a tighter squad than Lieutenant Baldwin. She had plenty of grunts to do the dirty jobs.

She kicked his door shut with her heel and leaned forward.

"The car's a complete loss so far; nothing there except the victim."

"Looked like the perp was wearing gloves, according to the traffic cam." Jake lowered his voice to match hers.

"Well, if you saw that much, it's more than anybody else did, even with computer assistance. The FBI couldn't blow that video up."

Jake frowned and tried to think back to the traffic control center. Williams had been standing . . .

Magdalena cut into his thoughts.

"No sign of the victim on the mask. Heck, there's no sign of anything on its outside—it's just a plain wool ski mask."

"*Plain* wool ski mask?" Jake felt as if he was feeling his way through a fog, where every word only made the mist deeper and deeper.

"Yes, a solid black wool ski mask. Pure, virgin wool with absolutely no trace of any other products or markings."

"But I thought . . ." he stopped. Hadn't there been Nazi insignia on it? Had he described that on the evidence report or simply let Reeves in the evidence locker write it up?

"That's the way it came in, Jake, just like the tag says. Now the good stuff"—she thumped the table—"is all inside the mask."

"Good stuff?" Hope, quick and bright like the scent of a day's first true meal, stirred inside him.

"Yup. Lots and lots of skin and blood cells, plus a few hairs."

"Enough to type?"

She snickered. "More than enough to let every court between here and the U.S. Supreme Court retest!"

Hope bloomed into full glorious life, richer than a Thanksgiving dinner.

"Have you run the DNA yet?" he asked.

"Who do you think I am, a magician?"

Astrid could do it.

Jake yanked himself back to reality. "You've pulled off wilder feats," he wheedled.

"Maybe." Magdalena's freckled, homely face crinkled into a smile. "And maybe not. But I did call in a few favors. Quick look hasn't found a match so far."

"Damn." Hope faded but refused to disappear. DNA tests took longer than birthing a brat, as the chief said. Maybe a hit would turn up.

"At least you can be sure that it's the killer's, since it's all on the inside."

"Cool. That is truly cool." He leaned back in his chair and shared a grin with one of his best friends in the department.

"Gotta get going now; I have to talk to the DA about the

Tunner case." Magdalena shoved her chair back and stood up. Her success rate in courtrooms was equaled only by that in budget battles.

"By the way, why did you do all the work?" Jake reached the door before she did but didn't turn the knob.

"My staff got headaches every time they worked with it." For the first time, Magdalena frowned. "We tested it for every chemical we could think of."

"That's why you know it's pure wool." *What the hell happened?*

"Exactly. It's as organic as it could be, but we still had to use the isolation chamber."

"Shit, that's too bad."

"We needed the practice. Damn thing was so tightly knitted that it was tricky sampling the wool itself. But you learn to manage."

"Are you okay now?"

"Yeah, I'm fine. I came on late, so I only worked in the isolation chamber." She shot him a no-nonsense look and he quickly opened the door. "The mask is locked up again in the vault, workload's off the charts, and everything's back to normal. What could be better?"

"Nothing at all."

Except knowing for sure whether magick had been used on that mask.

Viper stepped into his living room with sweat pouring from his brow. A few seconds allowed him to mop his face and reassure himself that nobody had disturbed any of his tells. Nobody ever had messed up his lair, but a wise man never took that for granted if he wanted to live long and prosper.

And Viper intended to live very long indeed.

Shower, news, stocks, food—in more or less that order. Then he'd see about new clients.

A lesser man would kill that cop who'd wrecked the last hit.

But not him. At least, not unless he could figure out a way to do so that wouldn't trigger any suspicion.

After all, murdering cops was the fastest way to shorten one's life—and one's enjoyment of retirement.

He smiled, his good humor restored, and buried his face more deeply in the towel to scrub himself clean.

His cell phone rang and he automatically flicked it open.

Realization attacked him an instant later. His gut cringed, faster and colder than being brushed by a cobra's poison in an equatorial jungle.

The *prepaid* cell phone had rung, the one he'd purchased yesterday that only he knew about. He'd bought it to place calls for his business, not to receive calls.

Whoever it was knew he'd answered.

He gritted his teeth and glared at the display, ready to brazen out his presence.

"Yes?" he snarled.

"You are a fool," the all-too-familiar voice barked in those hateful, almost guttural tones.

Viper's gut knotted, worse than any time he'd awaited the French Foreign Legion's unpredictable and always unpleasant discipline.

"Mr. Big," he stammered.

How did he find me?

Control yourself, you fool, he reminded himself. *You have completed his jobs so far.*

But the last three assassins who took Mr. Big's money and didn't complete their tasks all died within a month.

"You lost the mask," Mr. Big commented, remorseless as a grenade. "Or should I say, you threw it away?"

"Sir, you didn't say anything about what I was supposed to do with it," Viper protested desperately. *Merde,* now his brow dripped as if he was still running.

"Did I give you permission to dispose of my property?" The icy tones cut with a scalpel's bitter precision, able to separate bone from flesh before a man stopped screaming.

"No, sir—but I couldn't breathe inside the wool," Viper blurted.

A brutal hand clamped around his throat. He choked for air and clawed at the invisible attacker, but found nothing to fight.

A heavy silence fell, broken only by his lifeblood drumming in his ears.

"An allergy attack?" Mr. Big seemed transfixed by a new vision of torment, like a cat contemplating a bird's broken wing.

"Yes, sir," Viper wheezed. His vision blurred.

"Very well. You are forgiven—this time."

The hand vanished and fresh air rushed back into Viper's lungs. He gulped it down greedily until the stars slowly faded from the room's edges.

Rage swelled against the unknown bastard but he fought it back. He had the money, after all, plenty of it from Mr. Big's first—and so far only—hit.

Looked like this was when he'd break his rule about going against clients after the hit was over.

"Remember that lesson before you dare to fail me twice." Mr. Big's harsh voice underlined how much stronger the next treatment would be. "I will call you when I need you again. And, worm—don't bother to get a new phone: it irritates me."

An empty line's vicious buzz told Viper exactly how alone he was.

CHAPTER FIFTEEN

A strid leaned back against the car seat and considered her companion's face, silhouetted against the bright spring sunshine. So far he hadn't said a word about their destination, just stuffed her in his big Mercedes and headed across the river like a man on a mission.

If Jake wanted to play all-knowing homicide dick—in multiple senses of that word—and not tell her where or what they were going to do, so be it.

Maybe some innocuous conversation would loosen his tongue.

"Wow, the cherry trees are just starting to bud up here," she commented. "Good thing the last storm didn't harm them."

Her antisocial partner grunted.

She rolled her eyes. It was the oldest and safest conversational topic in D.C. at this time of year. Everybody who'd seen cherry blossoms come alive became protective of them.

What was he worried about? Taking a week off had come together easily; her FBI boss had been delighted she was finally heeding his suggestions about getting some balance back in her life. (As if he knew what her world truly consisted of!) She hadn't told the Shadow Guard's captain; that unpleasant duty wasn't absolutely required. Yet.

"Do you need anything special to work your magick?" Jake

asked abruptly. He cut the wheel over and shot down a narrow road into a subdivision.

"What kind of magick?" Guarding the two of them? His Mercedes was very protective of him, so casting wards over it would take little effort.

"Spotting things." He shot out of the little side street onto a major road, inches ahead of an enormous tractor trailer.

"Like seeing?" She blinked and tried to envision what he could possibly mean.

"Can you tell whether somebody is inherently good or bad?" Under a policeman's stern eye and strict hand signals, the old car decorously turned into a church driveway.

The church was a big, classically simple structure built of golden brick. Its belfry caught the light and reflected it, as if strengthening the prayers of the single deep bell steadily tolling at the top.

Cars covered the parking lot, most of them organized into the frozen cavalcade of a future procession. A black hearse, polished like a jewel box, and a half dozen equally impressive limousines framed the path inside.

Astrid rolled down the window and sniffed, to cautiously taste the area. A chill, unwelcome finger touched her spine.

She promptly flung her hand up and snapped wards into place around her and Jake.

The subtle disturbance withdrew like a disappointed eel, leaving no trace behind. Had it been a magickal probe or her own unwelcome memories, come to unsettle her? How had it reached past Jake's car's own innate strength, dammit?

In any case, she'd leave the wards up. They cost little energy to maintain, unless there was an attack.

"Why are we here, Jake?" she asked, any relaxation gone from her voice.

"This is Melinda Williams's funeral."

A few women glanced at them, their anguish protected behind immense black hats.

"What do you want from me, Jake?"

"Murderers like to visit these affairs. If he's here, I want you to tell me."

She chewed on the inside of her cheek.

"You do realize her murder involved magick," she said bluntly.

"Yeah," he said finally. He'd probably prefer to visit the dentist for an entire day than have this conversation. "You do whatever you have to, in order to find him."

"Even if it means magick."

"Even if it means waving long sticks of wood, chanting strings of funny words, and hurling thunderbolts like the second coming of Merlin! I don't care, I just want the damn killer." He folded his arms and glared at her.

That opened the door to a great many options, even though the church sanctuary itself would limit some of them. Still, she would be doing good with no intent to cause harm so she should be okay.

"I don't read any killers here," she warned him. "Nobody linked to her by violence and blood, at least not from inside the car. And nobody that I saw in my vision."

The grooves deepened beside his mouth.

"You can try again inside the church, where you're closer to folks." He jerked the door latch open.

She blew out a breath. Then she took another and another to compose and cleanse herself. Finally she passed her hands over her body and voilà! She had a new outfit, suitable for a funeral instead of everyday office work.

Jake raised an eyebrow at her quick change but said nothing when he opened her door.

"I set wards on both of us," she said under her breath, when she stood next to him, the car windows tightly closed behind her.

"Wards? You mean, like protection?" He searched her expression, visible despite her fashionable black hat. One hundred and thirty years after leaving that Nebraska farm, she still enjoyed those frivolous trifles.

"Exactly."

"There must be a bad guy here, if you're nervous. Where? Can we reach him fast?" Light brightened his eyes faster than a smile could reach his lips and he reached for his radio.

"Maybe and no."

"Shit." He rubbed his hands on his legs. "Well, there should be better hunting inside. Let's go."

"In a minute."

Every mourner filing into the church wore grief like a shroud, sometimes dark enough to obscure every feature, sometimes merely a veil wrapped around the shoulders. But it was always there, even for the children, black as the night-dark depths of Oslofjord where the German battle cruiser lay.

She'd never attended a funeral where she'd have to walk unprotected amid so much sorrow, let alone deliberately delve into it.

She staggered—and Jake's hand caught her elbow.

He exhaled sharply as if he'd been struck in the chest. An instant later, his grip tightened and magick surged back into her, warm as the sun's rays.

"Are you okay? If not, I'll have somebody drive you back to Belhaven."

"How big a team do you have?"

"Both we and the FBI each brought a full surveillance team."

What a relief it would be to walk away—and what cowardice. The alternative was to let Jake and his farasha brethren hunt for a magickally armed killer. Sending puppies against a lion would be a more even fight.

She was the only one here who could do this. Plus, she had a fledgling kubri to help her through.

"I'll be okay." She gave him her best cocky smile.

"Of course you will be." She'd be happier if he sounded like he believed it.

She slipped her prism out of her shirt and it instantly unfolded to meet her need. It was a perfect pyramid, as big as her thumb and more perfectly clear than any diamond ever found. For a moment, it hung free from its gold chain and spun rainbows of infinite possibilities over her and Jake.

She'd never taken a kubri into a scrying spell before. Oh, she'd participated with them before. But somebody else had always been responsible for the precious kubri's health.

She'd rather kill herself than let anything happen to Jake. But he'd never accept that path.

"Hold on," she said softly.

"Sure thing." He braced himself, as if he stood ready to be inspected by an unpleasant taskmaster.

She hummed and a spark lit deep within the prism.

She hummed again and the spark built brighter until it filled its invisible cage.

She shaped the ancient spell silently and cast it with the most powerful protection runes she knew. If this rebounded on anyone, she prayed it would only be her, not Jake.

The spark burst into flame and leaped out of the crystal. It flared over her and Jake in an instant, brighter than the dawn yet soft as a hearth fire. Then it faded back into her prism and vanished.

Astrid inhaled, then slowly released a cleansing breath.

She opened her eyes and the entire world was luminescent, as if lit by great lanterns from inside. Every blade of grass, every tree trunk, even the church's bricks glowed like a great artist's vision. The hearse's sleeping engine was threaded with flame, eager to carry its passenger forward to the next stage of life.

At least there'd been no backlash from another sahir's wards.

Just how much power did Jake have? She'd never seen so much in a scrying spell before when linked to only one other person.

Jake looked at her warily and Astrid shrugged, unwilling yet to confirm her full ability.

She turned back toward the pathway to the church. A covey of women walked along it, chatting with the ease of old friends. Their ages were as varied as their clothing, although all had tried to be formal. A few paid attention to style but most favored durability, especially in their coats.

"Their auras aren't as soaked in grief as the others," Astrid murmured. "There's more jealousy here and some catty remarks about the departed's fiancé being up for grabs."

"Holy shit," Jake muttered under his breath.

"What's the problem?" She shot a quizzical glance at him. "Did your radio suddenly make nasty noises in your ear?"

"Nah." A hand wave dismissed any unexpected problems from his team. "Are you sure you haven't read any FBI reports on this case?"

"Jake." She wouldn't shake him in public, satisfying though that might be. "It's not my job, remember?"

"Then how did you know that those gals are Melinda Williams's coworkers?"

"Really." She studied their departing figures until every aspect of how they moved sank into her consciousness. "There's no murder in them. Not hard-core, deliberate planning, anyway. The little, skinny one wouldn't lift a finger to stop it. But she believes she'll get everything she desires sooner or later, without having to work too hard."

"Typical female. No money to hire a hit man."

"Too much effort to plan it."

"Is that your opinion?" He glanced down at her, one eyebrow rising.

"Don't you agree?"

"Far too often." He slipped her arm through his. "Let's go inside and take our seats. You need to be comfortable."

He meant she needed a good view. She'd have settled for someplace with good ventilation and a little distance from the people who kept crowding in.

The church's interior was as simple as the finest haute couture, like a Chanel suit's elegant lines that continued to impress decades later. Tiny details in the masonry spoke of love and craftsmanship, where every brick was a gift of love. Stained-glass windows, too high to be readily damaged from outside, captured the light from above and gave it to the congregation, like protection or flowers.

Even Astrid, who was usually uncomfortable in any religious institution, relaxed in this building.

She sat beside Jake at the edge of the balcony's front row, where they could see but not be readily seen. The rest of the pew was so stuffed with people that there wasn't room for another fold of cloth, nor another person's coat. The other rows were the same. People muttered and sniffled and flipped through the program, or simply stared at the larger gathering below.

After all, this group represented the visitors on the edge of the tragedy—neither entirely there, nor entirely forgotten. But certainly not as important as the rustling, black-hatted, uniformed covey of mourners filing respectfully into the seats below.

They'd long since filled the polished wooden pews that circled the great sanctuary. Now the white-gloved ushers sought to widen gaps and insert one, or perhaps two, more into a spot barely suitable for a large cat. Chairs appeared through a hidden door like Ali Baba's treasure and slotted into place under the new arrivals.

Marines sat in a solid phalanx beside the garden door. Some of them were so old that a cane steadied their pace or a wheelchair gave them ease. Some were young and tanned but hardeyed and bitter mouthed. But all wore what medals they could and the same uniform as Melinda's father.

Black hats rustled and fluttered throughout the congregation like butterflies. Old women—and younger ones, too—had brought out their most spectacular millinery to pay homage to the beautiful lady in the picture above the casket.

Grief—blacker, deeper than the ocean's darkest depths—wrapped them all.

Nausea surged into Astrid's throat again. She clenched her teeth together and grimly fought it back.

She hadn't felt this sick since she'd hunted Nazis through the Parisian catacombs before D-day.

Focus, Astrid, focus. You're the best scryer in the Guard . . .

Some people weren't here to grieve, only to accompany the mourners. She filtered them out first.

She wiped the children out of her search next, which was harder. Their thoughts and emotions were so undisciplined and randomly powerful that they could be overwhelming.

"Anything?" Jake whispered.

"Not yet." She gritted her teeth against a curse.

She scanned the throng, one by one, hunting for the never forgotten profile she'd seen by the river. The man who'd sent a young woman into that casket.

Nothing, nothing, nothing. Certainly not his personal evil and complete lack of anything innately magickal.

She leaned over to Jake. "He's not here."

"Are you sure?"

"No line of blood and violence between that casket and anyone in this room. Not even a whiff." Maybe he'd show up at the graveside where the cops could physically apprehend him. Maybe.

Jake rumbled discontentedly and shot an apologetic look at the casket.

Grief surged through the crowd. Astrid blinked and glanced back down.

The family entered the church, a long, rolling wave of young and old, all clad in black, both physically and mentally.

Dear heavens, how they'd loved her.

Astrid dug her fingernails into her palms and tested their emotions, one by one.

"Well?" Jake demanded. He didn't need to finish the question: *Were any of Melinda Williams's family members involved in her death?*

"Unlikely," she answered. She felt as if small spikes were digging into her skull. "I'd bet against a connection."

His shoulders relaxed. An instant later, his hand squeezed hers. "Fiancé."

A tall man, his expression too rigidly controlled to be called handsome, strode down the aisle with an athlete's grace. He stopped in front of the white casket and bowed his head. His shoulders were hunched tighter than if a thousand barbs sank poison into his flesh.

An immense vortex opened up.

Astrid flinched, overwhelmed by pain, and quickly etched a silent rune to block it.

He turned away and stumbled on the carpet. Melinda's mother caught him in her arms, as if he were a teenager. Shared understanding flashed between them, more powerful than a song, and she handed him a handkerchief before guiding him to the front pew.

Melinda's father, gallant but gaunt in his Marine uniform, squeezed the newcomer on the shoulder, then gave him a hymnal.

The three sat down together and centered the great room's mourning.

"Not him," Astrid reported to Jake.

"Sure?"

"He doesn't know how to kill." Astrid sought the right words. Telepathic links were often more convenient, since they conveyed a wider range of emotion more easily than speech. "At least not someone he loves."

"Thought not." Jake settled back against the pew and flipped open his hymnal with an experienced hand.

She flicked a glance at him. Would he notice that she hadn't relaxed yet? Never mind; she still had work to do.

Her head was pounding like the combined drum sets at a rock festival. It shouldn't be this hard to read grief, even when it was extremely strong and came from many people.

Someone was hiding among the mourners, someone who didn't want to be seen by a sahir. But she was a member of the Shadow Guard, one of the strongest hunters. Who could hide from her?

Could she find him, despite this headache? Or was the pain making her imagine things?

She closed her eyes and concentrated. Sorrow from hundreds of voices washed over her. A thousand different visions of loss filled her mind and she shuddered. She wrapped her arms around her stomach and fought forward.

No Melinda at Christmas, or graduation. No wedding, no babies with Melinda . . .

She bit her lip and staggered on, searching through the room with the same grim concentration she'd once brought to the struggle for women's suffrage. The fight that had landed her in jail with a tube down her throat and brought her to the sahirs' attention.

The headache tried to rip her skull off, worse than dueling other sahirs in school when nobody knew how to focus their energy.

"Are you okay?" Jake whispered. His big, warm hand closed over hers—and the pain faded to an endurable agony.

She whimpered deep in her throat for a moment before she could answer. "I'll be fine."

Maybe so much grief had just made her relive her own sorrows too well. Besides, nothing had tested her wards.

She took a deep breath, then another, and focused on cleansing her energy.

Jake frowned at her. The organ started to play doleful chords and the mourners stood up. The baleful aura began to fade, tempered by the congregation's focused love.

Astrid rose and hoped nobody would notice if she didn't sing.

"We'll leave now," Jake muttered. His fingers wrapped around her wrist like handcuffs.

"Jake!" She yanked her arm away from him but couldn't free it. Dammit, had he already been infused with enough magick that counterthreats wouldn't penetrate his hide?

"Excuse me?" A man's voice broke their absorption.

Both of them stared at the newcomer and Jake's hand fell away.

"May I sit there?" The gentleman indicated the seat on the

other side of Jake, who quickly nodded. Eagerness flashed through his eyes for an instant.

"Sorry," the fellow apologized as he stepped over Astrid's feet. "I had to work late at the office."

"No problem." She did her best to become invisible and shifted her scrying spell to eavesdropping.

"John Curtis."

"Jake Hammond." They shook hands in the awkward, abbreviated stroke of two large men in cramped quarters.

"I was Melinda's boss."

Astrid nodded silently and clutched her stomach under her suit. He'd carried that news on his aura like a Times Square billboard.

"Come see me sometime when you're in D.C., okay?"

Jake's jaw dropped almost to his lap.

"They"—Curtis cast a significant look at the obvious FBI agents by the rear door—"said I could talk to you about her boyfriend."

"Glad to." Jake nodded, his brow furrowed.

But only the FBI was supposed to discuss her job, since she was a federal employee. Why was Melinda's boss bypassing them in the investigation?

"Don't mind helping the *police* in any way I can." He glared at the FBI agents for a moment, then shook out his program. "My father's a retired detective in Georgia."

"Always good to help family," Jake intoned, hiding his puzzlement.

The organ wound up with a flourish and the hymnals thudded shut. People began folding themselves back into the pews like origami, complicated to execute but orderly to behold.

"Great." Curtis sat down, looking innocent as only three hundred pounds of very well-dressed adult male can. The Cheshire Cat would have been proud.

Astrid wished she could find an easy route to hunt the magick lurking somewhere in this room.

CHAPTER SIXTEEN

"Come on." Jake wrapped his arm around Astrid and urged her into his living room. Damn, but she fitted comfortably against him. He could get used to feeling her there very easily.

"Why are we here?" She looked a little dazed, eyeing his leather furniture as if she'd expected a fancy spa. She'd been far more alert an hour ago at Duffy's, when the team had unwound after the funeral. "I thought you'd drop me off at Metro."

"Come on: do you honestly think I'd let you take the train home after a long day's work? You need some pampering." He gently removed her black wool coat from her hand and tossed it over the sofa. He'd hang it up properly later, after he'd taken care of her.

"I need to go home and recharge." She leaned her forehead against his chest for a moment.

"Recharge?" That sounded like electricity. Or *Argos*, after a mage went through all his spells. Shit, that's when mages got killed.

"Magick. There must have been a thousand people at the service."

"You scanned them all, poor darling." Shit, how many field generators would he need to power metal detectors to check that many suspects?

He kissed the top of her head and savored the light, sweet scent that was so vividly Astrid. It was somewhere between spring's first flowers and fresh-cut hay, yet all woman. Perfect.

"The aerie where I live has partners who can provide me with sex to recharge my magick." She flexed her shoulders to start moving away from him.

Sex partners? She'd do that with others just to get more magick?

Something deep inside roared for the first time in his life. Like hell she'd go anywhere else!

"No way!"

"Jake, what are you talking about?" She blinked up at him. Her green eyes held only pale shadows of their usual brilliance. "I truly have to leave. Now."

He reined himself back in, startled by his own vehemence.

These were deeper waters than he'd ever experienced before. He'd worried about one of his cops, who was close to burnout. He'd sat with a wife more than once—even a husband—while their spouse fought for life in a hospital bed. He'd held a policeman's widow upright at a funeral, too.

But his own heart had never been threatened before, not like this. Not like the red surge that threatened his eyesight when she mentioned another man in her bed.

Cool it, Jake. Think about Astrid first; your own craziness can wait.

"You said that kubris"—he stumbled over the strange word—"bring power to sahirs."

"Correct." Her expression turned guarded.

"I'm a kubri, right? I helped you to make magick today."

He'd save a better description for later. Talking about a big-ass diamond which unfolded itself like paper, shot beams brighter than a bank of searchlights, then disappeared like a card trick up a magician's sleeve was not something writing police reports had prepared him for.

"That you did." Her gaze became a little warmer. "You did very well."

"Then I can help you now. What's more, I'm here and you don't have to go anywhere else." He kissed her hand in a fancy move he'd seen a few times on late night TV.

Her fingers cupped his bristly cheek for an instant before falling away. He caught her hand and held it close. Damned if he'd let even that much of her slip away!

"Jake, I'm a very powerful sahir." She spoke gently, as if to a baby.

"Of course, you are." Like he'd be stupid enough to think some numbskull sahir could scan so many people! That would be like asking a rookie cop to thoroughly pat down a city council meeting without offending anybody. Yeah, like that'd happen.

"Recharging me quickly will take a lot of power."

"Honey, you don't jump-start a tractor trailer truck with a single AA battery, either." He spread his hands wide. This was basic logic that any dude totally understood. Why was she wasting time?

"Kubris are conduits into the Earth's power source and different kubris can channel it better."

"You're saying kubris have different bandwidth, like the difference between an overhead power line and the wire within your house." Now the hesitation in her eyes started to make sense.

"Something like that. Some are like the big cross-country lines, which can power an entire region. Some are more like an old-fashioned copper line, cranky and slow, but still better than nothing. All are valuable to sahirs."

"Fine." Jake kissed the inside of her wrist and privately grinned when a slow shiver ran up her arm. "You've got all of me to play with."

"Jake, a sahir can burn out any of those kubris, just like the power grid can short out!"

"As in, kill?" He stopped in his tracks, with one foot on the stairs.

"As in dead, burned to ashes. I can't let that happen to you, guildie." Astrid—Andromache, his best friend—looked back at him with both feet still firmly in the living room. But she hadn't pulled her hand free from his grasp and a few sparks floated in her eyes.

Anticipation heated his blood.

"Yeah, but what a way to go, baby." He tugged her closer. "Pity they couldn't put it in *Argos*, lest they scare the kiddies. But we'll have fun making up our own rules, right?"

"You're crazy." She leaned into him, warm and soft against his wool suit and starched shirt.

"Maybe." He probably was loony but not for reasons he wanted to examine.

He kissed her on the mouth and savored how she answered him. Every thrust and sweep of her tongue was so experienced and yet she was so enthusiastic in his arms. And how her hips swiveled to meet his when the first slow beats of lust pulsed between his lungs and his crotch . . .

Shit, why the hell were they standing here when they could be in the bedroom?

"Come on." He tempered the words' urgency with a kiss to her temple. Hell, her pulse was beating fast and hard there, too.

Perfect.

A quick glance at the second bedroom reassured him that his brother was fast asleep inside. The door was shut, in the traditional warning to all passersby. Anybody who entered did so at their own peril: Logan had never appreciated being disturbed from his slumbers, a trait the army had only exacerbated.

But Jake's door was open and the lights flashed on in welcome.

Inside, Astrid turned to face him, her breasts rising and falling under her soft black-and-white dress.

Jake gathered her close and kissed her again. Every inch of

her caressed him, from her beautiful breasts swelling against his chest, to her thighs notched around his. Even how her back glided past his fingers and flexed under his palms.

His breathing kicked up faster, like revving up for a high-speed chase. They could do what they wanted, now that he'd closed the door.

What did she have on under this silky dress? It didn't feel like the undies she'd worn before. Would she have to do something special to remove them?

His cock hardened hopefully.

"You're wearing stockings, aren't you?"

"We were at church. You're wearing a tie." She made an urgent little noise in her throat and he dropped more kisses along her cheek. The sooner he reached her throat, the better.

"I can take that bit of silk off faster than you can remove those stockings," he pointed out and lightly dragged his teeth over her ear.

She shuddered. Thinking wasn't going very well for him when she wriggled like that.

"And isn't that a bra, too?" he managed. No wonder his hands were so focused on her sweet ass.

His experience with unfastening upper-half stuff was limited. He usually followed women back to their place after picking them up in a bar, banged them to mutual satisfaction, and went home, never to see them again. With that modus operandi, the ladies wanted to get down to business as fast as he did.

Astrid was very different.

"As I mentioned, dude, we were at church." She tilted her head sideways and he nibbled his way down her throat. God bless the designer for making a dress that opened like a necklace in front. There were no ugly folds of cloth to pull down from his darling's neck, even though the design stopped short of letting him dive straight for her breasts.

As she said, they'd been at church.

"Your shirt and tie clasp are rubbing the hell out of my

skin," she crooned, sultrier than any late-night jazz singer. Her hands kneaded his shoulders, her fingernails digging into him like a little cat. Every prick shafted hunger straight down his spine into his cock.

He pulled his head away and stared at his TV's expressionless screen. Shit, he sounded like he'd just run five miles in full SWAT kit.

"Make you a deal," he gasped, too desperate to wait until sentences came easily. "You strip down to your underwear and I'll strip down to mine. Then we take the next step together. Deal?"

"Deal." She released herself from his arms. His hands twitched and his fingers curled to hold her again.

"Better get started, big guy." A knowing smile teased her mouth.

He dug a finger into the knot in his tie, as if that would assuage the pressure in his cock, then yanked the damn contraption off.

"Good start," she purred. She teased her dress's skirt upward on her thighs. It was a black-and-white print, which any sane man could look at straight. But it made her slender and young and vibrant.

He stared, his eyes almost ready to fall on the floor and crawl to her. "Don't you have to unbutton something?"

"Did you feel any buttons?" She dragged the cloth higher on one side, confusing his eyes until they didn't know where the silk should end. His cock had no such doubt: It simply wanted to lunge. Now.

"No buttons on your dress." He dumped his jacket onto the chair and started ripping off his shirt. What idiot had put so many buttons on men's dress clothing? Maybe next time he should think about a turtleneck in the winter.

"Or a zipper?" he suggested, just to restore some balance. Hell, the damn things were all over his stuff, from his trousers to his police gear.

"Sorry." She leisurely peeled the clingy scrap of cloth up her torso. He stopped to watch, his pulse pounding in his ears.

It stroked over her hips, wrapped her waist, embraced her breasts until it finally left her throat with the same reluctance he'd show.

She swung it slowly around her finger, her tongue teasing her lips. All of his blood dove south in a single huge rush.

Dear God almighty, she wore a simple black silk bra, equally simple black panties, which covered her from waist to thigh, and stockings. Garter straps disappeared under her panties and black high heeled shoes cradled her feet. She looked elegant and delectably sinful, like a box of candy ready to be unwrapped.

Holy fucking shit, garters? He'd never undressed a woman wearing garters.

"You've got plenty of buttons, though." She licked her lips. "It's cute. I like it."

"Shit." The damn things exploded like popcorn when he yanked his shirt off.

She blew him a kiss. Then she rested one hand on his bed and bent her leg up behind her to leisurely slide her shoe off. Her free hand caressed her foot, then intimately fingered herself in a graceful display of sensuality that stopped Jake's breath.

What would it be like, to have hedonism so ingrained in your blood that even the simplest things became a doorway to pleasure?

This wasn't the time to wonder whether dawn would shine more brightly, or whether it would simply bring another chance to do his duty.

He stripped cell phones and gun off his belt and onto the chest of drawers.

Astrid removed her second shoe the same way as the first, with equal grace and sensuality. Her panties gleamed damp between her legs, testifying to her hunger.

His leather belt sang like a fast-moving hornet when he

ripped it out of his pants. He didn't bother to empty his pockets before unfastening his trousers and shoving them down.

"Garters?" she asked, her voice slightly husky.

He glanced back at her. Her breasts were rising and falling rapidly in their silky cage. Good.

"Leave 'em. You buy them as lingerie, don't you?"

"True." She sauntered toward him, green sparks flickering in her eyes.

He reached up to remove his ear cuff but she caught his wrist.

"Not that."

He looked a question at her.

"I like it." She kissed the inside of his forearm. "It makes you barbaric."

Not the full answer, but who cared when heat rippled through his veins under her kiss?

"We're both in underwear. But you're still dressed from the waist up. Naughty girl." He shook his finger at her.

"Very bad." She lowered her head and peeped up at him through her eyelashes. Her musk scented the room. "Perhaps I should take my earrings off—or go for my panties first?"

"Wretch!" Her offer's brazen effrontery tightened his chest. His nipples were hard enough to use for spikes.

"If you'd prefer something else . . ." She rubbed herself against him like an eager cat. He slid his hand inside her panties and kissed her mouth. He took the kiss fast and deep, to hurl his own need into her.

He kissed her until the world tasted of her. She was tight and wet inside the silken straitjacket and her hot juices drenched his hand. She moaned and shoved herself down onto him, begging for more.

Oh yeah, honey.

He rolled his hips against her. The pressure of his briefs teased his desperate cock.

He needed a condom. He needed to be in her.

She needed more magick, whatever that took.

He managed—just this once in his life—to get a girl's bra off without fumbling the catch. Then he lifted darling Astrid onto the bed and eased her panties off.

All those golden curls between her legs, beaded in dew? He buried his face in her faster than any honeybee ever dived into a bank of roses. He lapped and licked and sent her hips pounding at his head. But he didn't let her climax, not yet.

He stripped his briefs off and knelt over her.

Fingers and tongue, maybe? She didn't look quite desperate enough for what he had in mind. Or maybe, if he could trust his unruly cock to be near her . . .

He retrieved a condom, covered himself faster than ever before, and joined her.

She whimpered and clawed at his back. Any thought of simply rubbing himself over her sped into the night faster than a racing motorcycle escaped a police cruiser.

The tip of his cock slipped into her.

The heat in his blood melted into musk and fired his lust higher. His balls were hotter than star shells, ready for the Fourth of July.

Gold stardust danced behind his eyes.

"Jake, please." Her sheath melted around him.

"Honey." He wet his lips and tried for enough sanity to make a sentence. Never mind whether it made sense; just string the words together.

"Honey, do you see those sparks?"

"Yeah." Her knees came up around his hips.

His lungs seized.

"Is that what you need?" he gasped.

"Need you and your magick," she groaned and locked her heels into the small of his back.

His hips surged forward until he was completely inside her. His balls tucked up neatly against her and reveled in her hot dew.

Jake howled, shaken by a silken whirlpool of heat and lust.

It enveloped him both within and without, and ripped him into a being of pure satisfaction.

Light came alive around them, like candlelight glimpsed through lace.

He thrust and she locked herself around him in welcome. He pumped again, and they fell into a rhythm, older than time, beyond time. All that existed was Astrid, and pleasure, and the stars that heated in his veins to be shared with her through breath and cock.

Until finally the tide grew too hot, too high, too fast.

She scratched his ass—and the small bit of pain triggered something deeper. Climax blasted through him, faster than a supernova ever remade a galaxy. Joyous cloudbursts of light pinwheeled through his veins and shattered his bones, remaking his world.

He poured himself into Astrid again and again, rejoicing in her cries of delight, her muscles milking him, the sinews binding him to a single place and time.

He could not have said where and when that place was, only whom he was with, until his eyes opened long minutes later.

At least his bed still looked the same.

Astrid was a limp bundle in his arms, sweaty, and, he hoped, sated. She hadn't said a word. Heck, she hadn't moved a muscle, except the slightest of stretches when he eased out of her.

Jake frowned. His best friend had never let much go past without commenting on it. Had he hurt her?

"You okay, Astrid?"

"Yes, of course," she mumbled. She didn't sound very certain of it.

Jake snuck the used condom out from its hiding place under the covers and into the trash can. The oddest things disturbed women, and he didn't want even the smallest trifle to fluster her.

"Did you get enough magick?" That was more important than if he was a good fuck.

She chuckled, music dancing through the sound, until she sounded much more like his old friend. His heart lifted into the palm of her hand.

"I certainly did." She eased herself a little closer and laid her head on his shoulder. Wisps tumbled around her face like a golden coronet. "You're a very powerful kubri."

"Oh yeah? How did that happen?"

"How did you get this?" She stroked her finger up the long line of his jaw to his ear.

"Why do you ask?" He eyed her warily. He never talked about it. Hell, he almost never took it out of his dresser drawer, let alone wore it.

"It's the mark of a kubri. It both shows that you are one and helps sahirs link to you." Her voice was very gentle, as if she spoke about volcanoes to a toddler.

"Shit." He instinctively ran his thumb over it. "I've always thought it was a good-luck charm. Like it helped me to get laid, or figure out a crime."

Something shifted behind Astrid's eyes but her expression stayed warm and approving.

"It's a good focus tool," she agreed. "What do you think of it now?"

"It's tighter on my ear." He slid his nail under the edge. "It doesn't want to come off, dammit."

"The bond grows stronger every time you give power to a sahir." She hesitated for a moment before going on. "It also grows more transparent."

"Are you telling me I can't take it off?"

"Yes."

"They never mentioned that to me." Jake's head hit the pillows with a thump. "Of course, who asks questions during an orgy?"

"Orgy?" Shit, now Astrid sounded thrilled. She braced her forearms on his chest to look down at him. "Where was it held?"

"It was sixteen years ago, so I can't take you back there," he warned, more irritated than if a civilian had begged to ride along on a high-stakes SWAT raid.

"Of course not." She kissed the tip of his chin.

"When I was a college junior, I went to New Orleans with some friends for Mardi Gras. We met a couple who invited us home. Things got pretty hot and heavy." He shook his head, his eyes closed as memories rolled past. "My friends wandered back to the hotel one by one during the first night, but I stayed."

Astrid nibbled on his shoulder. "Like it?" she murmured.

"I never knew there were so many ways to have sex. All legal someplace, all fun." Fucking had been important. Food, too, a little. But not sleep. And he'd never been bruised for longer than a few minutes. Strange. But who cared when everything felt so good?

Blood eased back into his cock and Astrid fondled it like an old friend.

"I went back to the hotel after three days." Surely he'd been there longer, but that was what the clock said.

"Just before your friends started looking for you?"

"No." Guilt rasped his voice once again. He closed his eyes, counted to ten as the shrink had taught him, and tried again.

"The cops had been hunting me since midnight, almost eight hours. My parents were killed in a drive-by shooting and somebody needed to take charge."

"Take charge? You were in college."

"Old enough to identify their bodies and become my brother's guardian."

Astrid opened her mouth, caught his eye, than shut it before she could let loose any pity, thank God. More than enough tears had washed his path back then.

He stayed silent and tried to remember some good bits about those days.

Logan had been shocked into cleaning up his act. What else? Hmm . . .

"My condolences," Astrid said softly. "Was it a crappy introduction to police work?"

"Pretty much. It wouldn't have been an easy crime to solve anywhere. But that jurisdiction and the cop working the case—they weren't even interested in hunting for my folks' killers. Said it was my dad's fault because he'd been stupid enough to have a blowout on a major highway, then called for help from a bad neighborhood."

"Assholes!"

"Yeah, I cheered when the Justice Department ripped those so-called cops apart. They even solved a bunch of cold cases, including my parents."

"I'm sorry it took so long."

"It's okay. The killer's serving time on Death Row—and yes, I am sure they got the right guy."

"Is that why you're a cop? Or did you always want to be one?"

"Oh, hell, no! I planned to be a stockbroker and make real money for my folks, instead of just letting their savings sit in the bank."

"You switched majors after the shooting."

"You know me too well." He smiled at the blonde who saw through him so clearly. "Yeah, by the time I settled my folks' estate and got Logan out of high school, I finished a degree in criminal justice and passed the exams for Belhaven PD. Then I worked my way onto the homicide squad as fast as possible."

"You didn't give yourself much time for fun—or returning to New Orleans."

"No, I never went back." Because he was afraid as hell he'd never leave. Everything went wrong when a cop put pleasure first.

CHAPTER SEVENTEEN

Logan held his paddle in the water and stalled his kayak, keeping it within the forest's shade so he could observe. The sun shone quiet and soft over the marsh ahead. Crystal blue river water wove in and out of the ancient marshes and forests, in a dance older than time.

In the woods, a trio of woodpeckers competed for the title of Loudest Noisemaker, uncontested by any human. Off to Logan's left, an osprey regarded him suspiciously, then apparently decided the human didn't want to steal the branch in its beak. It flapped off, mottled plumage rippling in the wind, to build its nest.

A flock of red-winged blackbirds swooped onto the tall marsh grasses, making them dance faster than the gentle breeze had. A wing of plovers dove past his head and into the headland, ready to begin a hearty meal.

All so damn different from any desert or war.

He lifted his paddle, then dipped it again, letting the lightweight craft ease forward into the sunlight.

"Thanks for bringing me down here," Logan said. "You were right: there's nothing like it close to Washington."

"Any time, dude, any time. You know there's nothing I wouldn't do for one of the old squad." Brant Slater shot his 'yak forward to catch Logan's. When they were side by side, he held his hand up.

Logan snorted and mimed exchanging a high five. Brant was quite right, though. Those two years of hell together ten years ago in the Special Forces had forged a solid bond among the squad's survivors, no matter where they were now.

Gulls flew overhead, wheeling and dancing like magicians.

"It sure is peaceful through here." Logan eyed the large groves of trees rising beyond the marsh grass. "Good idea to launch from that Army post."

"Yeah, they don't use their boat dock for much of anything, since it's so close to the marsh."

"Not even crab fishing?" Logan asked, remembering childhood pleasures involving chicken necks and a long string.

"That's not official use," Brant said, in his most sanctimonious voice. "Remember I know all the land that the Pentagon has around Washington."

"Which is how you knew about the dock." Damn, it felt good to fall into the rhythm of paddling, here in this world where everything was peaceful and serene.

"Yup. And the nice little wildlife refuge just downriver, which makes sure all those ducks stay well fed."

"And happy." Logan sighed in contentment. He'd have to remember this place when duck-hunting season arrived.

A school of minnows flitted past, their silver bodies breaking in and out of the surface as they surged to escape larger fish.

A gap in the trees opened up, leaving the marsh exposed to the sun. Was that a grassy knoll behind the marsh? With low white buildings on it?

"You're looking good, Brant," Logan commented. His old pal had always enjoyed mealtime more than most, but now he looked as fit as when he'd gone through SF selection tests. His unlined face made Logan feel scuffed and worn around the edges. "Has your wife—uh, Mary—learned some new recipes?"

"No, I've been working out regularly." Brant's next stroke cut the water a little harder than necessary and splashed his hands. "Ladies like eye candy in the guy who's giving the briefings."

Logan glanced sideways but didn't say anything.

Nobody had seen Brant in a gym since the knee injury that ended his frontline career. He'd always chased skirts but he'd never worked particularly hard at it.

His true talent was politics. Whenever the team needed something done, Brant took care of it damn fast.

"Besides, it's good for my knee," Brant went on. "You got to watch your act when you want to move up from the A Ring to the E Ring, dude."

"Not me, man," Logan said with complete sincerity. "I'd rather count bald eagles."

"Or a sergeant's stripes."

"Yeah, that." It was a good life. He knew what he did had value, even if he was about to be shackled to a desk.

A little boy ran out onto the bluff above the marsh grasses and watched them. Surely he was old enough to be in school, especially since his clothing shouted money. Yet he stood there, sucking his thumb and staring at the strangers.

"At least I don't have to own a bunch of ties." Logan stretched to name more of his job's benefits.

"True." Brant frowned. "Plus, I got screwed when they shut down the government the day after the big March snowstorm so the plows would have room to work."

"Had you already arranged to take vacation?"

The boy was rocking back and forth like a much younger child in the middle of a storm, too scared to either run or take cover.

Logan hesitated and scanned the shoreline for a landing spot. Maybe the kid needed an adult's help.

"Yeah, we took the girls to Florida. But if I'd realized it would snow—"

"You could have stayed in the city and saved your vacation time. Happens to all of us, dude."

"Yeah, shit happens."

A young woman skidded to her knees beside the boy and hugged him close. A tall, dark-haired woman ran up behind her and came to a halt only a few feet away. She stood like a guardian angel, arms akimbo, her gaze searching every inch of her surroundings.

The younger woman spoke to the child urgently until he finally nodded and placed his hand in hers. She stood up and gathered him against her hip.

Even from this distance, Logan could see the darkening bruises on her face.

He hissed in a breath.

Then she and the boy vanished, running like the wind into the grass.

Logan stared at their guardian. *Look after them,* he demanded silently. Stupid thing to do. Did he think she could read his mind?

Her body rocked back, as if in surprise. An instant later, she bowed very slightly to him and disappeared. She hadn't even taken a step.

Logan closed his mouth and told himself any chill on his skin was solely because some water was tickling his wrists under his dry suit.

Yeah, right. He'd mastered staying dry in a sea kayak during winter years ago, especially during good weather.

But that was his story and he'd stick to it, no matter what his subconscious muttered.

"What do you think?" Brant asked.

"Huh?" Logan replayed the last few minutes in his mind. He'd learned how to record conversations going on around him long before puberty. It was a useful way to keep his own thoughts private.

This time, he didn't like his companion's ideas.

"You want to visit Mallows Bay at low tide? Are you nuts?"

"I promised Rebecca I'd take her over to see the ghost ships. This way, we can scout it out first."

"Brant, there are drowned ships there. You know, really big ones, not just boats." Their SF skipper had said sometimes you had to drag the obvious out into the open before Brant believed he couldn't get what he wanted. Besides, what the hell did this Rebecca have to make Brant take such a huge risk for her?

Deep shade edged the water again.

"Yeah, so what? We have to go in carefully, that's all. It's not very far."

"All those wooden World War I boats have rotted away, leaving big iron spikes sticking up. They could rip our 'yaks apart at low tide."

"Adds a little spice, just like the good old days."

A pair of bald eagles watched them, enthroned in their nest high atop a tree.

"You're doing this for some chick named Rebecca?" Logan asked. That phrase might make Brant identify her as his daughter. If not, then she was his girlfriend.

"Do you need a better reason?" Brant shot back, echoing one of the squad's oldest jokes.

"Hell, no!" Logan roared. It would be neither desert nor war. Did he truly need a better reason, no matter how stupid Brant's were? "Race you down the river."

Their paddles dug eagerly into the water, followed a moment later by their kayaks.

The eagles didn't move, but simply resettled themselves into their perch like knights on guard duty.

"Idiot!" Elswyth shook herself angrily. She'd let two of Enfield House's most vulnerable residents be seen by passersby.

Worse, she'd allowed a farasha to see her work magick—and then had not wiped away the memory.

Stupid, stupid, stupid.

She couldn't even tell herself she'd been entranced by his handsome form because she'd only seen him from the waist up.

At least she had one small consolation. He had a bit of magick in him, since he'd projected his request far enough to be heard by her. Clumsy, so emotional that she could barely make out the words, but enough to tell he cared about the mother and child.

Enough to protect his sanity from her counterblast.

*   *   *

Edmund Carter, formerly of Carter Station, raised a haughty eyebrow at his secretary. Even a Northerner should know better than to receive guests when her boss was due to arrive.

He was certain there were no appointments on his calendar. Everything before noon was dedicated to catching up on legal gossip and sipping coffee, from the comfort of his sole remaining Virginia refuge. After that, he'd have another long lunch with an old friend.

"Good morning, Miss Clay." He trod across the carpet and picked up his mail. The ugly furniture was all in her office, of course, including the requisite bare steel cabinets.

"Good morning, sir." Ah, proper humility. She hoped to make her job permanent, of course. No chance of it, but that wasn't entirely her fault.

She pushed two business cards forward with her fingernails, as if the bits of paper were dead cockroaches. "Miss Murphy and Mr. Fisher of the FBI would like to talk to you, sir."

Annoyed, Carter glanced up from a headline detailing new rules for judicial foreclosure—not, thank God, much of a Virginia issue—then looked down at her cheap desk.

A round, dark blue seal surrounded by gold flames leaped out at him.

He blanched, colder than he'd ever been in Aspen during the glory days.

Shit, not them. He only needed a couple more days to be free and rich again.

Somehow his fingers were steady when he picked up the loathsome pasteboard. But he was a Carter, born to the finest blood in the Old Dominion. He would face down the enemy and buy himself some time, just as his ancestors had on the great battlefields.

"Good morning, ma'am. Sir." He extended his hand and granted the interlopers the necessary good, firm shakes. He'd scrub thoroughly later to remove their underbred dirt. "What can we do for you here at Carter and Carter?"

Once the other Carter had stood for sons, the proud second and third generations. Now it stood for ex-wives and lost chances, damn them.

"We'd like to talk to you about your work with Miss Melinda Williams of GSA." The female agent studied him like a suburban bitch eyeing fresh meat in a grocery store locker, unsure whether to pounce or walk by.

The worst topic, of course.

"Certainly. Why don't you come into my office, where we can talk?" Thank God, his voice didn't shake. He waved toward his soon-to-be-violated inner sanctum.

"Sorry to drop in on you like this, without warning," the man said, his words more contrite than his tone. "We had a hard time making an appointment to see you, for either ourselves or our auditors."

Auditors?

"We're very busy here at Carter and Carter these days, now that there's only one partner to carry the burden of a long and well-established practice," Carter gave his excuses smoothly, glad for all the occasions they'd previously rolled off his tongue.

Money. How much did they want to know?

He hoped, his unwelcome guests wouldn't notice how few antiques graced his office. If they mentioned anything, he could always say that it allowed more space to admire each individual item's finer points. They'd never stoop to personal inquiries about his living arrangements, no matter how much less the humiliating condominium's rental cost than his previous fifty-acre estate outside Middleburg.

And surely it would take even the FBI time to find those bank accounts in the Cayman Islands.

Now that thought was so comforting it allowed him to face them with the same relaxed bonhomie he'd used to charm decades of property owners and their heirs.

Chapter Eighteen

"Thanks for taking time out of your busy schedule to see me, Hammond." Curtis hurried out from behind his overflowing desk to pump Jake's hand. "Would you like some coffee?"

"No, thanks, I'm fine."

"We're good, Emma." Curtis nodded to his secretary, who smiled at them and withdrew, closing the door to a remarkably ugly reception area.

"My table's pretty clear so let's sit down there." Curtis waved at a small round table wedged into the corner between two rows of steel file cabinets, topped by stacks of paper. A battered wooden credenza behind his desk was topped by more files, while ranks of framed certificates beamed from the wall.

"Damned ugly, isn't it?" Curtis said proudly.

Jake blinked, then finished putting his notebook on the table. "Sir?"

"This used to be a warehouse. It's famous as the ugliest federal office building in the District of Columbia."

"I wouldn't think there are many other contestants, sir." He'd worn a good suit to come here, but the linoleum-clad hallways made him feel overdressed.

"But it's clean and it does the job." Curtis smiled proudly at his sturdy desk, which was probably last in fashion before Jake had been born.

"It certainly does."

"GSA does a better job for our customers, of course."

"I'm sure you do."

"Melinda Williams was one of our best." Curtis folded his arms across his chest, his eyes looking somewhere beyond the pale green walls. A West Point ring gleamed on his right hand. "She came to us as an intern, fresh out of high school, and worked her way up. I could count on her for anything."

Jake made a sympathetic noise. His pen was eager to start writing volumes.

"Hell, I used to call her at two a.m. whenever a water main burst or we had an electrical fire. I remember one time a cafeteria crew had a grease fire the morning a general was due to inspect the entire building."

"And?"

"She always answered the phone no matter what the hour. No problem, not my girl. Showed up on-site, no matter where, and got the job done. I don't know how we'll manage without her."

"I'm sorry."

"She slowed down a bit over the past year, which is why I wanted to talk to you."

"Sir?" All of Jake's cop instincts quivered like a bloodhound who'd just caught a new trail's first whiff of scent.

"She received a promotion last year—not surprising really, considering everything she'd pulled off. But it came with a big price tag: She had to put together a brand-new test facility for the Pentagon."

"Where?" She'd been roaming around Virginia and North Carolina, not the wilds of Utah or even Mississippi, where those places were usually located. The Defense Department needed privacy to play with its toys.

"They want someplace close enough that Congress can run down to see it during their lunch hour."

Jake gaped at him, stunned by a vision which his property tax bill said was impossible. "That'd take acres. There's nothing like that to buy near here, even if you've got their kind of money."

"No, there isn't, which is why we needed a full-time project manager to pull it together."

"Lots of travel, but all of it local."

"Yes, and all during normal work hours. She started working forty hour weeks."

"No e-mails late at night?"

"None—and no signs of trouble with her fiancé. I introduced them, since we attend the same church."

Biased in their favor, of course, but also plenty of observations to back his opinion up. Damn.

"Positive?" Jake slid extra doubt into his voice.

"Absolutely," Curtis leaned forward, his hands pressing into the table as if he wanted to lock the ideas into Jake's mind. "Those two saw each other and *bam!* Nobody else mattered. They were both grownups and had seen enough of the world to know what they wanted."

"Really?"

"Ask anybody. First chance she had, Melinda became a nine-to-fiver. Went from eighty hours a week to forty." He sat back, his eyes glistening. "She told me she planned to have a baby the moment the wedding ring went on her finger."

"It's a big loss."

"The Pentagon has agreed to name at least one of the new buildings at their facility for her. It's not the same as having her around, but it'll keep her name going forward."

Curtis shook his head slowly and shuffled some folders.

An idea nibbled at Jake.

"Where was she looking for land? The original missing persons report went out in North Carolina."

"The Pentagon wants at least a hundred acres. Plus, water access makes zoning and terrorist-proofing much easier."

"Ouch. Sends the cost way up, too."

"Oh yeah. Hence, North Carolina." He shrugged and his rueful gaze met Jake's. "I mentioned this to the FBI, of course."

"Of course," Jake murmured and kept writing.

"They seemed bored, since the *Washington Post* has already reported on it."

"Nothing new there."

"Not hardly. Anyway, Melinda also looked at a spot south of here, on the Northern Neck."

"Close to the Potomac?"

"Mmhmm." He dug through one of the folders and unearthed a scrap of paper. "It's next to a World War I military installation, someplace that should have been scrapped years ago."

"Amazing how many spots like that there are." Jake noted the address without ever picking the scrap up.

"Isn't it?" Curtis shoved it back into the file.

"What was the last time you saw Melinda, with or without her fiancé?"

"We last saw them together at church. He always tried to arrange his schedule so he could sing, although he didn't always make choir practice." A wistful smile teased Curtis's mouth. "Some of us are talking about making up a barbershop quartet with him, just to make sure he gets out."

"Very generous of you."

"He doesn't need any more shit dumped in his life," Curtis said bluntly. "I last *saw* Melinda at the same time."

Saw? "When did you last hear from her?"

"She e-mailed me from North Carolina the evening before the snowstorm and asked to see me right away. Any fool could tell OPM would shut down the government here with that much snow forecast. So I told her I'd see her the morning after the storm."

"Did she give a reason?" Jake's gut came to attenton.

"Nothing. Wouldn't expect her to, either. We couldn't discuss a classified building over our GSA e-mail system."

"Of course not. But were you expecting anything?"

"Nothing. As far as I knew, she was almost ready to make her final recommendation."

"Did she copy anybody else on the message?"

"No, but I forwarded it to the building's sponsor, just to keep him informed."

"Gotcha." Jake didn't blink. Keeping one's ass covered was, after all, the most basic of all survival tactics in this town. "Anything else?"

"No. We've only just started working through her files. Not many of my staff have her clearances."

"Very spooky stuff, huh?"

Curtis cocked an eyebrow at him and refused to answer.

"Hammond." Jake hunched his shoulder to hold his phone in place and grimaced at his voicemail's in-box. Shit, he'd only stepped out of the office for an hour or so to visit GSA. Did messages propagate like fleas?

"Murphy here."

Jake straightened up so fast his chair squeaked.

"Good to hear from you," he answered honestly. "How's everything going over at the FBI?"

"Great. Couldn't be busier, in fact." Her usually business-like voice now sounded like chocolate poured over acid.

"What can I do for you?" Were they back to the traditional arrangement, where the FBI kept all the fun and the locals handled the sweat?

"Just wanted to let you know Fisher and I have had our assignments reprioritized."

"Oh yeah?" That didn't sound good.

"Yes, we'll be working on the follow-up for that elevator incident at the courthouse."

She'd try to clean up after a magickal attack? She'd probably been trying to get close to the terrorist's bodyguards for months, given how she'd ogled them at the courthouse garage.

Jake might have laughed except he was too busy trying to figure out the consequences for his own investigation.

"What about the rest of your portfolio?" he asked cautiously.

"Your case is no longer a high priority," she said bluntly. "I recommended and my supervisors agreed—that the murder doesn't appear to link to Williams's job."

Shit. On the other hand, life might go smoother without the Feds around.

"We'll send you a summary of our findings, of course, plus everything we've found to date."

"Any loose ends?"

"For *you* to tie up?"

Her tone reduced him to dirt, and he made a rude gesture at the phone.

"No, that won't be necessary. The only thing left is our accountants' report. Fisher and my supervisor insisted we audit the paperwork for the last sites Williams worked on, from the sellers' perspective."

"A formality." Jake's hopes for a quick resolution to the case began to dissolve.

"Yeah, considering she was basically just a property developer for the government. My money's on the boyfriend. Anybody that cute"—she almost sighed—"has a right to get jealous when his girlfriend is out of the house so much."

Jake held his phone out and looked at it in disgust.

"Why do you think she worked that hard?" He kept his voice as dispassionate as when he taught unsteady rookies.

"Man, have you seen her phone logs yet? Or her e-mail records? If my man looked like that, you wouldn't get a single e-mail out of me from sundown to sunup."

Fisher coughed violently in the background but said nothing.

"What about her early return? Or the meeting she requested with her boss?"

"You heard about that? She probably wanted to go over her final report before she showed it to their high and mighty Pentagon contact."

Crap, that made far too much sense.

"Plus, she was such a dutiful daughter that she worried

about her parents making it through the snowstorm. Heck, she was probably hurrying home to check on them, even though she only lived two blocks away."

"Right."

"Now it's your job to nail the murderer. I think the fiancé hired somebody but that's just my opinion; I don't want to see anybody that fine behind bars."

"Thanks."

"Good luck." She'd gotten all the poison out of her voice now that she'd dumped the shit on him. "I'll send you my files by messenger."

"Good luck with your new assignment." If she found anything, he'd buy himself a new system to play *Argos*.

Or he'd take a week off to attend *Argos*Con with Astrid. She'd gone last year in full costume as Andromache, which was enough to make a man's head spin and libido roar. He understood now why she was fully masked in her photo but her smile blazed brighter than the marquee lights.

Another line on his phone lit up. He lifted his hand to answer it, then just let it ring until it rolled over to voice mail.

What the hell did another message matter? He'd have to answer them all before he left tonight. Plus, he needed to at least skim through his e-mail's in-box.

He stood up and arched his back. Maybe a five-minute break and a cup of coffee would make him feel more like doing his job.

Yeah, right. Melinda was less of a workaholic than he was. She'd cut back the moment she found the right person.

Now her fiancé at least had memories to help him through the long, lonely nights ahead.

If Jake didn't make a few changes in his life, he wouldn't even have a chance to see Astrid again.

CHAPTER NINETEEN

Astrid cast another long look around the stable yard before she dared raise her hand. She'd driven here since no individually powered portals were permitted within these grounds, unless guided by death throes.

The stable was built entirely from weathered gray fieldstone, set and stacked into the hillside in the manner of centuries past. A dark stone roof capped it, topped by a wrought-iron weathervane in the shape of a running horse that pointed steadily northwest.

The yard itself was paved in smoothly washed gravel, set closely in concrete, like a finer version of old-fashioned cobblestones. Chest-high walls surrounded the yard, made from the same stone as the stable. A heavy wooden gate, so closely bound in iron as to seem indestructible, provided the only entrance.

Beyond the walls, horses wandered through dappled sunshine across muddy fields. Neatly fastened rugs protected them from the mountain's crisp breezes. Two white horses stared at Astrid curiously, as if considering every article of her gear.

Only the irregular stacks of rails that Virginians called running rail fences kept them in the pasture.

Astrid knew far better than to think they'd started the day out with four legs, or would finish it that way. No, the watchers were her fellow members of the Shadow Guard, keeping watch over their order's most prized fortress.

She raised her hand to the bell and rang it once.

The silvery tones danced across the countryside and attested to her goodwill. She'd come in peace, even though she hadn't been summoned.

As soon as the echoes started to fall away, she rang it again to ask for an audience. As a member of the Shadow Guard, she had the right to come at any time and make this request.

Come on now, take me inside.

All the horses studied her now, their brown eyes uncannily thoughtful.

Only members in poor standing had to ask three times. Surely she couldn't have pushed the boundaries that far.

Before the bell's song could fade into the trees, she yanked hard. It jumped under her hand and sounded a single long note, like a hawk diving from the sky.

Space shattered around her into blackness, cut with white spears like a glacier's cold heart. She dropped for a long instant through icy winds that tore at her robe and hair until finally she landed on a solid floor in utter darkness.

She would not grovel. She should not have to grovel . . .

Light blazed into being around her, everywhere and yet nowhere at the same time, like the artificial landscapes inside *Argos*. The room itself was smaller than her living room and edged with curtains that shimmered like waterfalls. Square tiles marched across the floor in rough luminescence.

Prisms spiraled from the ceiling in one corner like the weapons they were, ready to be snatched up by guardsmen in need.

A pillar of light, too brilliant to be directly watched by farashas, stood in the center. It was both impassive and unfriendly at the same time.

Astrid's throat tightened. She'd expected to first plead her case to a lower-level officer, not be thrown straight to the top.

"Greetings, Captain." She went down on one knee, grateful for her leather trousers and high boots.

"Carlsen." His voice was both infinitely close and infinitely far. He must be physically elsewhere to run that kind of magickal link to this meeting hall.

Zing! The pillar hummed, then shrank into a man's form.

The Captain of the Shadow Guard surveyed Astrid like an eagle eyeing a peregrine falcon chick who'd dared to enter its territory. His height and raven black hair came from his Native American mother, while his skill with blades came from his English father. None of his men had ever asked who gave him the scar above his right eyebrow; they knew only that the enemy had died long before the American Revolution.

"Rise, Carlsen." The Captain gestured and she came to her feet.

He studied her in a style meant to intimidate, but she met his eyes steadily. She'd known him, worked for him, for more than a century. Surely that had to count for something now, didn't it?

"Why are you here?" An iceberg would have been warmer.

"I came to beg the Shadow Guard's help."

"Why?"

"I am investigating a murder—"

"Does it threaten the health or well-being of this country?"

"No, but—"

"Why should the Guard become involved?"

"I sense great magick at work."

"Do you have any proof?"

"No." Her stomach tightened unhappily.

"Then do not trouble us until you can offer something with meat upon it!" The light trembled and Astrid locked her knees.

"With respect, sir," she began again, "I request you consider an exception in this case."

He whirled upon her, so close he could have held a knife to

her throat. He always carried at least one under his cropped jacket.

"Carlsen, your job is to keep an eye on the FBI, not go haring off on your own adventures. You are walking a very fine line here. If you miss it by a hair, you will fry."

A hot wind blew past her. She dared a glance and saw blazing fires below her where the floor used to be, except for a single thread under her boots.

Her stomach lunged for her throat, but she beat it back down.

"Exactly," said her superior officer. "You are one of my best, so I'm allowing you a little slack."

It didn't feel like that.

She tilted her chin up stubbornly.

"Remember I spoke up for you when you broke all the rules and married that British sahir."

Too many old memories, good and bad, all of them edged in pain, slammed into her heart and she flinched.

Her captain's voice became a little gentler.

"You've chosen to play this like a lone wolf so you will finish out the game the same way. But if you singe even one letter of the Council's laws, you'll go down."

"Sir." She snapped out her assent as she'd first been taught, during the desperate days before the First World War.

Before she'd learned the true cost of failure.

Carter huddled deeper against the shopping center wall and shuddered. He'd have to dry clean—or burn—his favorite jacket when this was over.

But that didn't matter. Nothing mattered except making this phone call.

The only pay phones left in Northern Virginia all seemed to be found on either public intersections or squalid malls like this one, where the newly arrived bought their smelly staples.

He glared at a young female, who scuttled off with her three brats like startled rabbits. Much better.

He allowed himself a deep breath before he checked his watch again. Five minutes since the last call.

Next time, he could let the call go through. The first time, he'd let it ring three times before hanging up and waited one minute. Then he'd dialed again, rung five times, and waited.

Thank God this place didn't boast any cops on patrol. They might stop to ask him some questions.

Six minutes.

Who cared what a security camera thought? It wasn't illegal to use a pay phone.

Seven minutes. He pounced on the phone that he'd scrubbed so thoroughly.

"Yes?" barked Mr. Big.

"The FBI came to see me." Another cold trickle of sweat gathered inside his collar.

"So? You knew they would. I presume you said all the right things."

Soothed by Mr. Big's implacable calm, Carter's pulse began to steady, despite everything that had happened.

"Of course I did." He mopped his forehead.

"Then I'm sure they went away happy." Mr. Big's voice would have sent stampeding buffalo to sleep.

"Well, yes, except—"

"What?" The final consonant cut like a rifle shot.

"They're sending accountants to audit my records."

The phone line's silence sounded like the entrance to the abyss.

"There's nothing to worry about, really," Carter stammered. His heartbeat could have done double duty working for a hummingbird. "They'll need somebody to talk to, to understand it. But I'll be gone before they can figure it out."

"Of course you will." Mr. Big sounded soothing again.

Relief, sweet as a fresh martini, ran through Carter's veins.

"I'll call you from the Caymans," he promised recklessly. "With my connections and your money, we can do an even bigger deal next time."

"Certainly we can. But think about yourself first." The line went dead.

The phone dropped out of Carter's hand and swung back and forth like an old-fashioned hangman's noose, buzzing all the while.

He ignored it and leaned his head against the wall, his eyes shut.

Now he had time, the most precious commodity of all. He just had to use it right.

Chapter Twenty

"Carlsen?" The concierge's disembodied voice echoed through Astrid's apartment. She preferred a man's voice, so the building's services manifested themselves that way to her.

"Yes?" She warmed her hands around her stone teacup. She'd needed a long, hot bath to make her stop shaking after her visit to the Captain.

"A gentleman to see you, ma'am. Sergeant Hammond."

Jake? What was he doing here? Was she ready to deal with his questions tonight, on top of everything else? Not really—but did she have a choice?

Would he go away quietly? Almost certainly not.

"Send him up, please."

She shoved a hand through her hair and pulled a face. She didn't have the energy to get it under control before she had to face him.

Well, at least she could put her unruly locks into a ponytail. That'd give her some semblance of composure before she had to face him and whatever he wanted.

Soft chimes rang, announcing a visitor at the door. She hoped Jake wouldn't be here often enough to learn this building's elevators all traveled at the same speed—as in, immediate arrival at any floor.

"Good evening, Jake." She managed a rather stiff smile for

him. Her soft silk and wool sweater with the ruffle at the throat was feminine but not fancy, while her jeans were definitely casual.

His eyes narrowed at her lack of warmth.

"Won't you come in?"

"Glad to." He kissed her on the cheek but didn't try any other intimacies. She firmly told her heart that she was glad.

He sauntered forward, arrogant and masculine in the polished room.

"Would you like some coffee?"

"No, I'll take whatever you're drinking." He stopped by the long bank of windows. "Quite a view you've got here."

"Thank you." She wouldn't mention that the glass was warded against magick, or that her tiny balcony was a portal to anywhere on this continent.

She poured water from the still steaming teakettle. "Would you like sugar or cream?"

"Just straight up."

A flick of her fingers replenished the kettle before she served him his drink.

"Thanks." He brooded over the fragrant brew for a few minutes, his eyes hooded like those of a hawk on the hunt.

She turned her cup around and pretended to admire the stone's natural patterns. She had no pretty words left after the Captain had wrenched Gerard's loss back into being.

If Jake wanted bed play, she'd agree, but she had no energy to encourage it.

"Astrid."

"Yes?" She looked up to meet his gaze and was instantly pinned. Golden sparks glittered deep within the brown.

"Why were you really at that nudist colony?"

"I, ah . . ." She stopped, swallowed a lump the size of the Pentagon, and tried again. She couldn't lie. "I heard Melinda's scream from the Beltway."

"But that's miles away!"

"I told you before: she sounded exactly like my husband

when he was killed. She must have had a little magick in her to project it, because distance means nothing to pain and anger like that."

She shuddered, then quickly gulped the rest of her tea.

"Anything else?"

"Her last words were about duty."

"Same as your husband."

"How did you know that?" Astrid stared at him.

"You wouldn't be attracted to anybody less," he said wryly.

"What else?"

"You know the rest of it. We couldn't track the killer's car because it was warded."

"Too many protections to attack it?"

"Too many protections to see it clearly," she corrected him. "Another sahir is involved in this."

"Is there somebody important who'll help us?"

"No, because it's not a threat to our country."

"You mean the magickal cops won't take this killer on."

"Correct. We're on our own."

Totally frustrated, she snapped her fingers and steam whistled out of the teapot. Soothed by one small victory, she made herself a fresh cup of tea.

"What do you want from me?" Jake's Virginia drawl was thick enough to walk on and yet harsh enough to bring soldiers into line.

"What do you mean?" She braced her back against the kitchen wall, ready for any confrontation.

"What do you, Astrid, want from me, Jake? Why are you cowering over there when the sex is so good together that we can make the stars sing?"

Oh, shit.

"You scare the living crap out of me, Jake."

"I'd never hurt you, you know that."

"That's not the problem."

"Then tell it to me straight or I'm going to shake it out of you."

"Sahirs can die if a spell goes wrong or we try to channel too much magick," Astrid said baldly.

"Shit."

"But magick is a better drug than cocaine or anything on the street."

"Guess you want to shoot up all the time."

"Yes, which means we tend to die very young." She looked at her cup, then set it aside. Gerard had taught her to drink tea, but this wasn't a conversation for his memory.

"That didn't happen to you." Harsh lines bracketed Jake's mouth.

"We can stabilize in two ways: either bond to another sahir or a kubri. A sahir is very risky."

"Since he's as addicted to magick as you are."

"Plus, he can't provide balance by linking to Earth, the way a kubri can."

"Your husband was a sahir." Jake made the leap, of course.

"Yes, he was. The bond is equally strong between any kind of magick worker. Distance has no meaning to it."

"Did he blow himself up during a spell?" Jake took her hand.

"Oh, no. Gerard refined his magick during the First World War, and he was very canny. He never took an unnecessary risk but he knew how to drive a thrust home."

"You adored him."

"He was my life," Astrid said simply.

For long minutes, the only sound was the wood's death throes in the fireplace while Jake's expression grew sterner and sterner.

"What happened?"

"It was the beginning of the Second World War and the Nazis had started to overrun small countries. Norway, my ancestors' home, was next in line."

"We weren't at war then."

"The Shadow Guard doesn't take its orders from the White House."

Jake blinked and Astrid hurried on before he could delve into *that* disclosure.

"Norway's crown princess was very fond of America and vice versa. The British Admiralty hoped an American sahir, especially one who spoke Norwegian, might be able to convince her to evacuate."

"So you went to Oslo."

"Yes, and Gerard sailed aboard the *Heron*, a destroyer on escort duty. Everyone hoped having a sahir there would help them find one of the big German ships."

She drew her knees up to her chest and wrapped her arms around them. She'd learned to move on. But the bone-deep cold any mention of that day brought still ran deep through her.

"It worked, didn't it?"

"It helped and they stumbled upon each other in a fog bank. There was no radar back then, so nobody knew anything for certain until they saw each other."

"Too late to run, too late to hide," Jake chanted.

"The first German shells almost ripped the smaller British ship apart."

"That's when you heard Gerard die."

"A dying sahir can force his consciousness into a weapon, should it be sworn to follow the same path as he." Tears dripped down her face but her voice still held firm. Her stomach was the same tight knot it had been that appalling night. "The *Heron* wailed a banshee scream when Gerard melded with her."

"Was she invulnerable?"

"Not to the sahirs aboard the German cruiser but she became a far more deadly weapon. Her captain rammed the bigger ship so hard that it was forced out of the fight."

"The *Heron* was sunk?"

"With almost all of her crew." Astrid scrubbed her cheeks hard. "The next morning, the full German battle fleet attacked the Norwegian capital at dawn. They expected an easy fight."

"You didn't give them one."

"All we had was a few naval reservists, not even enough to fully man the guns. But they halted those arrogant ships."

Jake sat down beside her on the sofa. "What did you do?"

"I guided their torpedo to its mark and sank the biggest ship. The others retreated for a while, which gave the king and government time to flee."

"You did that without any help, right?" Jake laced his fingers with hers. "Against a warship fully guarded by sahirs?"

"Yes." Warmth flickered across her skin and brushed her veins.

"Could you have done more with a kubri?"

"Of course. But there wasn't time to call any up, even if they were willing to work with me."

"Is that what you want from me? The chance to work great spells, thanks to accessing great power through me?"

"Jake." She gripped his hands harder. "There's no safety net or guarantees for a kubri. If things go wrong and a sahir shatters, the kubri dies, too."

"Payoff could be worth it, though."

"Dying isn't fun, Jake. When the other half of your link passes over, half of you goes with him!"

"Oh damn, honey, I'm so sorry." He pulled her into his arms and hugged her close.

Astrid went stiff with surprise for a moment, then relaxed. Whatever—or however much—he meant by this, she found more shelter in his arms than she'd met anywhere else since Gerard had died.

"What do you say, we go out for beer?" Jake kissed the top of her head.

Beer?

She drew back a little and cocked her head at him quizzically.

"Or pizza? I don't know what you have here but I'm hungry. I'm paying, of course."

Men.

She opened her mouth to set his mind straight about her pantry and her talents for restocking it.

His phone rang and he snatched it off his hip.

"Hammond." His expression changed while he listened. "Oh yeah? No, I'm just surprised they arrived so fast. FBI must have really wanted to get them off their hands. Of course, I'll be right back."

He shoved the bit of electronics back into its case, his expression abstracted.

She frowned at him. Dammit, she'd almost hoped for a date.

"Sorry, but Melinda Williams's files just arrived from GSA. FBI has *reprioritized* and pulled their folks off this investigation. I need to get back to the office to read them."

"Yes, of course you do."

"FBI probably didn't find everything, fast as they went through her stuff."

"No, I bet they didn't." Her voice probably sounded as cold as she felt. "Can I help?"

"Not with this; we've got to keep it under wraps at the station."

"Pity."

"Are you mad?" he asked cautiously.

"No, I'm not angry. Just completely unsurprised." And wishing she was hungry for somebody else.

He gave her a quick peck on the cheek.

"I'll call you in the morning, if we find something new," he offered.

She cupped his jaw in her hands.

"You just keep thinking of me, okay?"

She kissed him thoroughly, long enough to drown herself in his taste. When his cock was a red-hot bar against her belly, she stepped back and gently closed the door on him.

If she was going to go through hell getting to sleep, then he could have the same damn problem.

*   *   *

Viper looked at his brand-new, prepaid phone's display and spat an extremely ugly curse word.

Next time, he wouldn't bother getting the new phone. Or maybe he'd move to a different continent where the bastard couldn't find him.

Still, he answered on the third ring.

"Yes, Mr. Big?" He kept his voice very respectful. Dammit, he still had red marks around his throat but no idea how the bastard had put them there.

If he could just find the son of a bitch, he'd make him pay—in both senses of the world. No matter what that did to the Viper's reputation with future clients.

"I have another target for you," Mr. Big said without preamble. "Same price as the last time"—*wow!*—"because the execution must occur within twelve hours."

Viper clamped a hand over his mouth an instant before he would have said impossible. He could either tell the truth and die or keep silent and get out of town fast. The third option was that Mr. Big was correct and there'd be a profit.

"Okay," Viper said. Maybe this would bring enough to get him an account in that new Luxembourg bank.

"Okay what, worm?"

"Yes, sir, Mr. Big!" Viper pumped enthusiasm into his voice. He'd greeted his sergeant's suggestions to run around hot springs in the African desert the same way, since it bought him extra water.

"There is another commission, worm."

"Yes, Mr. Big?"

What kind of accent did Mr. Big have, anyway? He kept his syllables too crisp for English to be his native language. Viper recognized that problem because it was his, too.

"After you remove this target, you will convince the buildings' residents to leave it."

"Huh?" Nobody asked hit men to evict folks.

"The methods are up to you, so long as they can't be traced

to me. But everyone must be out of there within forty-eight hours from now."

"Can I terminate with prejudice, sir?" Viper asked, using the idiotic American phrase for kill.

"Yes."

Why did he want a bunch of people knocked off? Was this too dangerous even for Viper—unlikely!—or should he up the ante?

"I will pay you triple the previous hit," Mr. Big announced.

Viper's jaw hung low enough to sweep his desk before he snapped it back into place. That kind of money would definitely get him into Luxembourg, where the prissy aristocratic bankers never spoke to American cops.

"You have a deal, sir."

CHAPTER TWENTY-ONE

Jake shot another disgusted look at Melinda Williams's files. If there was anything here worthy of murder, he sure as hell didn't see it. He'd shuffled, reshuffled, and read property titles and possible timetables until his eyes crossed. Every location seemed viable for a building large enough to hold at least two courthouses.

He lifted his head and sniffed. What was that scent? Had he worked the clock around again? Surely it couldn't be time for more—doughnuts?

A rumble of appreciation went up from the second shift, newly gathered in the squad room.

Jake shoved his chair back and opened his office door.

The delectable aroma washed over him again, twice as sweet and far more savory. Fresh doughnuts in every flavor, from sugar to cinnamon through chocolate and blueberry. Half the cops in the station were gathered around the coffee station at the far end to stuff samples down their throats, while more streamed through the doors faster than any fire alarm's summons.

Where had the goodies come from? All of the local doughnut shops cut back their baking after lunch, and nobody in the office made anything like this.

Jake took a step closer. He should eat something before he hit his e-mail. After that, he'd figure out where next to focus the Williams investigation.

Astrid backed out of the crowd, empty tray in hand.

"You're very welcome," she assured two chocolate-daubed detectives. "Try the cinnamon; it's my mother's recipe."

She turned and her eyes met Jake's. She wore a casual black jacket, black jeans, and a soft blue sweater, making her look far more like a young Belhaven detective than the rigidly correct FBI employee he'd worked with—or a heartbroken widow.

He flushed, suddenly horribly aware of how clumsily he'd left her last night.

"Hello, Astrid." He gave her a tentative smile and drifted closer. What did a guy say on occasions like this? He hadn't even had a steady girlfriend in high school. "Thanks for all the doughnuts."

"You're welcome. I was feeling a little restless"—*ouch!*— "so I thought I'd work it out in the kitchen. Glad the guys let me in; I don't know what I would have done with so many pastries, otherwise."

"Cops can always eat doughnuts," Jake assured her truthfully. "But yours smell far better than most."

"Flatterer!" She laughed, the sound far more musical than any noise pumped through the lobbies, and Jake chuckled with her.

Why the hell had he spent last night away from her? One of his team could have gone through the GSA files, while he comforted her. Then he could have woken up with her and laughed with her about some stupid new jokes on the *Argos* boards before going in to the station.

It sounded like a life, unlike the cold coffee and stale sandwich drying in his office.

Dammit, he needed to keep her around.

"How's the investigation coming?" she asked, her green eyes sparkling.

"Not much new. Why don't you grab some coffee and come see?"

Astrid hesitated and cast a glance back at the cops chatting around the trays of delicacies.

A dark-haired civilian woman came up behind her. She looked slightly older than Astrid and was also anointed with a visitor's badge. "Go on, girl. I'll make sure the crumbs hit the trash can, then visit my pal Danica. We need to talk about the Enfield House team in the Tidewater 5K."

"Thank you, Elswyth."

Jake nodded his thanks, too, but was met by a fierce glare. He stiffened before he remembered when he'd met its likeness before—the overprotective parent of a high school date.

He inclined his head to the other woman in silent acknowledgment that he'd behave like a gentleman. He hoped there were etiquette books somewhere to help him.

Elswyth's mouth twitched, but she nodded regally.

Astrid returned, balancing two cups of coffee and a small plate of doughnuts.

"What did you find out?" She offered him the sweets.

He rolled his eyes in appreciation and reminded himself not to mumble.

"Thought those would get me past your guard dogs, if you'd set any," she murmured sotto voce.

He spluttered.

"GSA lawyers gave all properties' titles a clean bill of health," he said rapidly, after he'd recovered. "Some properties had environmental problems but the three finalists had none."

"Zero?"

"Not at this early stage of assessment. Two were historic properties that have been cultivated under traditional agriculture methods and the third is an abandoned nineteenth-century warehouse. They'll undergo a full test later, of course, if selected."

"No scam there."

"Not that I can see." He shuffled his notes again. Each finalist's photo, complete with summarized description, was spread before him like a deck of cards.

"Anything on her fiancé?" Astrid tucked her legs under her.

"He's withdrawn very large sums from his bank but they've all been linked to the wedding."

"Ring, house, honeymoon." She ticked items off on her fingers. "Dress, flowers, reception. Perhaps a wedding planner?"

"How did you know he paid for so much?" Jake snatched a list out of his drawer and double-checked. "You missed something, though—her new car."

"Minivan?"

"Yes, with more horsepower than sense." He dropped the list back into its file and propped his feet up on the drawer. "So far every number on his phone bill has checked out, too."

"Which leads you back to her job."

"Yeah, and another big, fat dead end. Either that—"

"Or believe some random whacko kidnapped her on the Beltway so he could murder her in a distant stretch of river."

"Stranger things have happened."

"Yeah." Her voice said she didn't believe it either.

"We can do something else," she commented a moment later.

"Like what?"

"Any of these places make your gut twitch more than another?"

He glanced sideways at her, startled by her casual reference to his cop's intuition. Then he tapped the Northern Neck property.

"This one."

"Why?" Astrid put her feet down and scooted forward to look at it.

"It's too good to be true. Two hundred and fifty acres of undeveloped waterfront property within an hour of Washington just doesn't exist anymore, even when the only likely buyer is Uncle Sam."

"Anything wrong with the owner?"

"No, it's a bank—but that's true of several other candidates."

She steepled her fingers over the photo and hummed, her eyes half closed.

"Who owned it before the bank?" she asked dreamily.

"A trust. Astrid, why would a corporation commit murder?"

"Are either the bank or the trust here in Virginia?"

"The trustee is in Belhaven."

Her eyelids lifted and sparks danced around her head.

Holy shit. Why wasn't he scared of all that magick or her?

"Why don't we go talk to him?" she asked.

His gut surged happily into place, like a well-fed child.

"Sure thing." He wondered whether his Sig would be any use there, if affairs went south.

Astrid measured the trustee's office against the address Jake had given her. It occupied a small, nineteenth-century, brick row house amid dozens of larger, more prosperous legal establishments. Its battered masonry needed attention, just like the uneven walkway and overgrown azalea bushes.

But the brass placard bore a simple, uncompromising notation, which was undoubtedly designed to make up for any other lack: Carter & Carter, Attorneys at Law, est. 1816.

"Can you sense any evil?" Jake asked.

Astrid refocused her eyes to look beyond the current space and time. Something shimmered and was gone in an instant.

"No, just selfishness."

"Not surprising from an old law firm that specializes in estate law."

"But . . ." She headed for the door at a faster pace.

Jake caught her wrist and pulled her slightly behind him on the threshold. She cast an irritated glance at him, then scanned the door for magickal traps. Nothing.

He was inside before she could sound the all-clear.

"Hello, ma'am." He smiled charmingly at the middle-aged lady sitting behind a reproduction Victorian desk. An astoundingly uncomfortable, badly faked antique sofa and chair offered seating for guests. "Is Mr. Carter in?"

"Yes, he is." Ruth Clay, according to her cheap brass nameplate, changed from bored housewife flipping through diet recipes to eyelash-batting flirt, under his Virginia drawl's spell. "He's been in his office since lunch, working on his correspondence. I'm sure he could use a break by now."

She gave her hips an extra swing when she rose.

"Who should I say is calling?"

"Jake Hammond of the Belhaven PD." He slipped his card onto her desk, as if selling mailboxes.

"Police?" She eyed the bit of white dubiously.

"We just have a few questions about the Enfield Trust," Astrid put in and eased magick into her voice, smoother than chocolate. "Nothing serious."

"Oh." The secretary picked up Jake's card. "Well, I suppose you have every right to ask for Mr. Carter's time."

And he had every right to deny it, although the threadbare upholstery and carpet said he could use more visitors.

Ruth swayed off toward the front office, whose occupant might have heard every word they'd uttered. On the other hand, the building was very solid, even if its scent was wrong.

Jake nudged Astrid and nodded toward the wall behind the secretary's desk. Here the faded floral wallpaper was hidden by a row of steel safes, in the room's only show of modernity. Several of the drawers hung open and folders were stacked on the handy, temporary shelves, ready for filing.

Astrid made a clutching motion and he grinned ruefully. As if they'd ever have time to go through those papers.

The secretary screamed, high and wild. "Oh, Mr. Carter!"

Jake spun on his heel and raced to the office, Astrid only a pace behind him.

This office was beautifully and accurately furnished, in a baronial style suitable for a nineteenth-century president. Heavy floral velvet drapes covered the window and a rich Turkish carpet deadened any footsteps.

In the center, beside the massive mahogany desk, Ruth Clay waved her hands in the air and opened her mouth to scream again.

Before her, a white-haired gentleman gazed at the new arrivals with the blank expression of someone completely dead. His head was pillowed on his desk's leather blotter and his empty hands hung at his sides.

The foul scent of recent death explained the all-too-familiar stench creeping through the anteroom.

There was no taint of violence here, except for the thin trickle of blood from his upper ear.

Astrid cast her sight back through time.

"Miss Clay!" Jake's voice could have brought a regiment to attention.

She squeaked in a gulp of air but stared at him.

"Did you touch anything in here?"

"Oh no, never." She shook her head violently and knotted her fingers together. "I watch *CSI* all the time."

"Well, that's something to be said for TV," Jake murmured. He continued in a louder voice, "Come back here to me."

She looked at the corpse, grimaced, and waved her hands. Then she tiptoed toward the door, moving faster and faster the farther she got from the lifeless stare.

"I need a drink," she muttered.

Astrid caught her arm. "Not yet, honey."

"Just a few questions, Miss Clay," Jake added, in between jabbering code into his phone. He jerked his head toward the other office and Astrid guided the shivering woman in there.

Some basic magick produced a cup of coffee from the office supplies. The secretary drank it, without asking its source.

Jake came in a few minutes later and shut the door on the outer room, its air already sharp with police radios and technical jargon from cops flooding in.

"Can you talk to me now, Miss Clay?" Jake asked gently. "The faster we can take your statement, the sooner we can catch the killer."

"Oh, I know that." She nodded vehemently and emerged a little bit from her cocoon of layered sweaters. "I watch *NCIS*, too. I know how you guys work and I'm happy to help."

Jake managed to smile. Astrid kept a straight face.

"You said you saw him at lunch. Did he have any appointments after that?"

"No, but there was the bike messenger."

"Bike messenger?"

"He showed up about half an hour before you did. Such a fine figure of a man, too. He works out more than most of them do."

"Why do you say that?" Astrid asked, struck by Ruth's wistful tone.

"Most cyclists focus on their legs, not their shoulders. Every part of this fellow's body was impressive."

"Did you notice his face?"

She hesitated but finally shrugged. "Thirty-ish, maybe? He was only here for a minute or two. The kind of hard, dark features that can be swarthy or tanned."

"Would you be willing to work with a police artist?"

"I'll try, but I really only looked at him from the neck down."

"We're grateful for whatever you can do. I'm sure Mr. Carter's family—"

"He didn't have any unless you count the latest ex-wife. He called her the Bitch."

Jake glanced at Astrid and she shrugged. She hadn't sensed anything about this investigation that suggested a woman at the center.

"Oh, Mrs. Carter wouldn't have bothered to kill him." Ruth had caught their glance, of course. "She already took all his money after she caught him cheating."

"Really?"

"Oh yes. Every secretary on this street knows all the gossip."

A young man peeked in the door.

"Miss Clay, may I ask you to tell Detective Nagorski everything you just told me?"

"Sure. You probably want to look around the office."

"You got me there, Miss Clay."

"The bike messenger didn't touch anything in the ante-room—I like to call it my office—and he wore gloves."

"Not mittens?" Astrid asked sharply.

"I wondered about that, too. But it is the end of winter, so I thought maybe he wanted to stay warm."

She looked back and forth between them.

"Now I guess we know what he was really after, huh? No fingerprints."

Safely back in the anteroom, Jake drummed his fingers on his leg.

"I hope to God she's wrong," he muttered.

"Five will get you ten, she's right," Astrid countered promptly.

"Jake, what's going on here?" Danica looked in from the door. Elswyth, Astrid's friend, looked over her shoulder. "We came to see Mr. Carter about the mortgage."

What the fuck?

"Come over here and talk to me." He pulled them over by the hideous sofa and chair, where no sane person would ever linger. A young man of Astrid's apparent age, pretty-faced, ex-pensively dressed, and hard-eyed as a top-flight bodyguard, drifted behind them, keeping himself well away from any cop.

"Come on, give. What's up with *the* mortgage?"

"You know what's going on. I've been telling you for years and you've donated to the cause." Danica sank down onto the sofa. "We came to pay off the mortgage on Enfield House."

"The entire property will belong to the battered women and their innocent children, forever," Elswyth said firmly.

"Oh shit," said Astrid. She whirled and went for the safes, like a foxhound who'd finally caught the scent.

"Carter was the trustee, not the owner. But you paid him money." Murder usually came down to money or sex. Jake needed to understand who held the purse strings in this one.

"All of Enfield House plantation was put in trust for Civil War widows immediately after the War," Danica said patiently.

Jake nodded, generations of Virginia ancestors immediately

telling him that *the War* meant the War of Northern Aggression, or what Northerners called the Civil War.

"Carter and Carter, Attorneys at Law, became the trustees at that time," Elswyth added.

Astrid returned and started flipping through a single file. Jake decided he was better off not asking how she'd extracted it from a supposedly closed crime scene.

"When the last Civil War widow died, Enfield House was turned into a shelter for battered women and their families. The board of directors felt this was the most appropriate use, since the original will specified that it serve 'war widows and hard-pressed daughters of Virginia and their families.' "

Elswyth looked triumphant, as if she'd been personally responsible for persuading a recalcitrant group of men.

"But there's never enough money." Danica scrunched up her face in regret. "The buildings took a lot of damage from Hurricane Isabel a few years ago, and a mortgage was the only way to fix things up. We've been working hard to pay it off ever since."

"You thought you had."

"We have the receipts from Carter! He was responsible for taking the money to the bank."

"He kept it for himself." Astrid's voice cut through the room's chatter like a knife.

"He wouldn't!" Tears welled up in Danica's eyes. "He was the most marvelous man. He said the sweetest things about the babies."

"There's no receipt from the bank—and here's the foreclosure notice, dated last year."

"Foreclosure?" Multiple voices united in outrage.

Elswyth and Danica snatched the file first, as was their right. Jake read it over their shoulders.

"Wouldn't somebody local have seen the foreclosure notice?" the young man asked in a very Northern accent.

"Not if it appeared in the *Washington Post*," Jake replied. "It has enough advertising to drown the *Titanic*."

"Especially if you're talking about foreclosures in today's economy," Elswyth put in bitterly. "The sale could be held on the courthouse steps here in Belhaven, where the trustee resides, too. Not down near Enfield House, where folks would find out."

"Bastards," the young man hissed.

Jake's finger stabbed hard onto a single piece of paper.

"Judicial foreclosure—so what?" Danica said bitterly and dug deeper into her enormous purse. "The bank owns Enfield House now. They bought it for the appraised value."

"Which was probably higher than anything a local developer would pay."

"A rigged auction?" Jake reconsidered the paperwork, in light of the young man's very cynical expertise.

"Maybe, but probably not. Can't easily build houses on land bordered by a military base and a nature preserve, without any good access."

"Even so, judicial foreclosures aren't common in the Old Dominion." Jake traced the same clause over again. "You know, Judge Byrd must have been in a real pisser when he wrote this judgment."

Astrid leaned on his shoulder to read it.

"Right of redemption?" she queried. "What's that?"

"The homeowner—in this case, Enfield House Trust—can redeem the mortgage from whoever bought it." Jake tried to remember what the real estate law guy had said during his fraud class. Judicial foreclosures moved fast enough that this one had slipped past the board's annual meeting.

"In other words, if we show up with enough money, we can get the shelter back. But it's the full mortgage plus a penalty." The young man's tone was savage.

"We don't have that much cash!" Danica's eyes were enormous and damp above her tissue.

"You will—I'll give it to you," Elswyth said flatly. "How long do we have?"

"Tomorrow." Astrid looked around at them. "The right of redemption closes tomorrow."

Crap.

"The banks have already closed, so we can't get a cashiers' check now. It'll have to wait until tomorrow." Elswyth gathered her purse onto her lap. "We'll manage."

"If you're sure." Danica tried an unsteady smile.

"Once it's ours, we can put in real air conditioning, instead of those window units," Elswyth said encouragingly.

"And clean up the cemetery, where your husband's mother lies." Danica patted Elswyth's hand. Her grin gained some true wattage. "I got it."

"The new owners will need to evict their tenants, in order to take possession," the young man commented. "They'll want to do so before tomorrow."

"In case there's any question about who the actual owner is—the one with the papers or the one in possession." An all too familiar chill ran down Jake's spine.

"The bank's CEO planned to sell Enfield House to Melinda Williams, the GSA staffer who was murdered," Jake said flatly. "His name is all over her project portfolio."

"Crap, everything that made the land worthless to a regular developer makes it priceless to the government," the Bostonian breathed. "They'd never worry about nosy neighbors, not with the Army on one side and bald eagles on the other!"

"Bet he planned to make a hefty profit on it, too," Astrid snarled.

"The Williams killing was a professional hit." Danica stared around the room at the others, twisting her hands together over her purse. "Anybody who would hire a man to slice a girl's throat then toss her in the river—what wouldn't he stop at?"

What indeed?

Astrid closed the file folder with a thud, as if she wished she could finish the banker as easily.

"They're wicked men, who won't stop at violence. We've got to get the babies out of there." Danica shot up off the sofa, as if launched by NASA.

"Somebody has to stay at Enfield House until clear title is established." Elswyth tugged on her arm.

"I'll go," Astrid said calmly, her gaze distant.

"We'll go," Jake countered. Like hell would he let her take that on by herself.

"No way!"

"Nathan—Elswyth and Danica need somebody to drive them to the bank and the courthouse. The bad guys will probably try to stop them and there's nobody else to help." Astrid's voice was loaded with undercurrents Jake could only guess at.

Nathan pounded his fists together, then nodded. "Okay, I'll do it."

"Jake, will you lend him your car? Please?"

Loan his Mercedes to a strange dude? But Astrid wouldn't ask unless she thought it was vital. It still felt like giving up half of himself.

"Sure thing, honey." He tossed the keys over.

"Thanks, darling."

He gave her a twisted grin.

"Give us a call the minute you get the mortgage, okay?"

"Roger that," said Nathan.

"Good luck," said Elswyth.

Astrid's hand simply clenched tighter on Jake's arm.

Chapter Twenty-two

Jake stood on top of the grassy knoll at Enfield House and contemplated the setting sun. A century and a half ago, his ancestors had shouted insults from the same spot at invading Yankees.

"Wish we had company?" Astrid wrapped her arms around his waist from behind and hugged him.

"I've got more than enough of the right kind." He swung her around and hugged her close.

If only he'd been able to reach Logan. But the kid was off camping with an old Army buddy someplace in West Virginia where cell phone coverage was even scarcer than roads. His note said they'd be back in a few days so his pal could make it to work.

Nice to know Logan knew somebody with a nine-to-five job. Heck, maybe it was better if he sat out this action.

Since it wasn't his jurisdiction, the chief had declined to send help and said to call 911 when there was visible, imminent danger—meaning real trouble. Of course, cleaning up the courthouse incident's aftermath had stretched his resources—and temper—thinner than an elastic band around a handful of 9mm magazines.

"Bet you miss your Mercedes most of all," Astrid said quietly.

He glanced down at her, startled.

"How did you know I want a way to get you out of here safely?"

"It's pretty damn obvious, isn't it?" she countered. "Just like the view from this spot."

The plantation's big house was now a hunting lodge shrouded in thick woods downriver, where Carter had once partied with his cronies. Upriver was the military base, hidden by another dense stand of trees.

The women and their children were housed behind this grassy knoll in small cottages that had been built for the Civil War widows. Danica could spend hours discussing how she wanted to restore the little bungalows and bring back traditional farming, instead of simply mowing the grass. She thought it would be therapeutic for the children.

Jake thought it was a good idea and somebody should clean up the old cemetery, too.

"It's a gorgeous bit of country, Jake," Astrid commented, her voice deceptively soft. "Did you see the owls go past?"

"I think we're pretty damn exposed out here."

"Is your skin crawling yet?"

"No, but I don't read battlefields. That's Logan's business."

"Flatland with water running past and a few houses in a circle at the center to defend," she mused. "It hasn't changed much in the past centuries."

She tucked her hand into his elbow and allowed him to head for the largest bungalow. All of the shelter's residents had been moved to other safe houses, supposedly only for the night.

The tears shed had racked his heart.

"Who's buried here?" Astrid stopped at the cemetery gate. It was a simple place, with an arch over the gate and roses laced with thorns around the wrought-iron fence.

"Civil War dead, mostly. This was a signals post for both Blue and Gray during the War but the marsh brought a lot of fever."

She stooped and sifted her hand through the dirt, her eyes shadowed in the darkening light.

"How many men do you think will come?" he asked abruptly.

"Maybe a dozen, quite possibly more. Certainly well-armed."

"What do you call well-armed?" he asked warily.

"Fifty-cal rifles, C-5, RPGs, worse."

"No way. Any of that would tear apart those buildings like they were tissue paper. You don't use that crap against civilians because there won't be anything left of them afterward!"

"Exactly." Worlds of anguish and experience dwelt in her voice.

Full realization of his opponent hit him and his knees almost buckled.

"If the bastards are willing to kill a government bureaucrat and a well-known lawyer to put a Pentagon lab on this spot—"

"Then they won't stop at butchering unknown women and children who have already dropped out of the system. No." Astrid kissed his hand.

He held her tighter than his hope of heaven until his blood stopped running cold. It was a long time before they started walking again.

"Can you stop them with your magick?" He wanted some hopeful shit for a lullaby before he went to bed.

"Not if they're well-armed and numerous."

"I'll help you."

"Do you have the weaponry to hold them off?"

"Against that kind of firepower? I'm not SWAT. No."

" 'Fraid of that." She took the first step into the bungalow.

"But I'm a kubri." He caught her by the waist. "Lots of power there for you to work with, right?"

"Lots of chances for things to go wrong, Jake!"

"Can I give you enough magick to stop them?"

"Yes." She closed her eyes and the sun painted her skin crimson.

"Do you have a better idea?"

"No—but I don't want to lose you the way I lost Gerard!"

"You won't. I promise you, I'm going to be a pain in your ass for years."

"Really?" One emerald eye regarded him dubiously.

"I swear by the grave of every Hammond who ever defended the Old Dominion that I will stay with you."

"Okay." She blinked back tears. "Let's go practice the bond. We've got a few hours yet before they're likely to arrive."

"Where's my brother?" Logan braced his hands on his hips and glared at the intruders. Thank God he'd paid attention to his instincts and come home early.

Danica, one of Jake's coworkers, and two strangers stared back at him from *his* garage.

Worse, the dude had the keys to Jake's Mercedes in his hand.

"Easy now, big guy," the stranger crooned. "Nothing here to worry about."

"Yeah?" If he kept talking long enough, one of the neighbors should see the light and check them out. Lafferty was the biggest busybody around; he'd do. That'd be better than using guns in Jake's neighborhood. Not that he lacked those. "You want to tell me what's going on?"

"Logan, Jake said we could borrow his Mercedes." Danica edged forward.

"Jake said *what*?" Jake hadn't let anybody touch his vehicle since first Logan, then their dad had wrecked his car.

"It's an emergency and we need a very trustworthy car." She gulped.

Shit, she'd been crying.

"That's built like a tank," the other woman added flatly and came forward into the light.

"You're the lady I saw by the river, with the mother and child. Who disappeared." Damn, she was beautiful close-up.

Her mouth thinned. "Yes."

"Hammond said I could drive it," the guy contributed in the world's purest Boston accent.

"Riiight." Logan reached for his cell phone. "I'm going to see what he has to say about this."

"Not now, he's already on guard duty," the woman snapped.

Logan's hand froze millimeters above the holster at the small of his back. He couldn't even wiggle his fingers.

Danica whimpered.

"Crap." Logan counted to three and smiled at the bitch, as if nothing was wrong. He'd seen crazy shit before but not like this. Time to fall back on SF basics: improvise, adapt, overcome. "If I promise not to call my brother, will you free my hand?"

"Yes."

"Okay then." He held up his hands and waggled his fingers at them. "How about I offer you another deal?"

"What?" She sounded suspicious as an Afghani bazaar dealer. Good, that might help keep them all alive.

"I'm an excellent bodyguard and I'm very well-armed." *Especially after he got back into Jake's house.* "Why don't I come with you, wherever you're going?"

"Why would you do that?"

"Because I ain't letting Jake's car out of my sight. Call it a brotherly love kind of thing." *Like maybe it will lead to where you've hidden my brother.*

"That's crazy," the man exclaimed. "You don't know what you're getting into."

"You don't know what kind of passenger you're buying, mister. I ride shotgun real well." He eyed the woman. "What do you think?"

She gave him a long considering stare that seemed to expose all of his dirt and most of his hidden agenda.

"We'll do it. He can carry the money instead of you, Danica."

Carry the money? What the hell was going on?

"Yes? Oh yes!" Danica bounced into the air and leaped on Logan. "Thank you, thank you, thank you!"

She kissed his cheek.

He hoped he'd survive the night without meeting any MPs or cops.

Or whatever the hell else was chasing this bunch.

CHAPTER TWENTY-THREE

Mist thickened the air and lay like jewels on the tree branches. It was early morning, the start of an urban workday, but the sun was still a hazy jewel in a gray sky, not an all-powerful god.

A truck's engine rumbled in the distance, then abruptly whined to a higher pitch.

"Must have hit that patch of dirt when they came off the main road," Jake commented, keeping his voice soft enough not to carry.

"Maybe they'll get stuck," Astrid answered. Pity she didn't have enough spare magick to make the wish a reality.

They stood close to the old cemetery, far enough from most of the cottages to observe but not be seen. It also put them more than a hundred yards from where the road entered the living quarters.

But the heart and soul of Enfield House's magickal reserves slept here, shimmering deep under the dirt like a silver cauldron.

They both wore soft black wool clothing and high-topped, pure leather boots. No synthetics, not today with this much magick likely.

"They should reach the first cottage right about now," Jake said. "Polite thing to do is post a notice, knock on the door—"

Whomp! An enormous bellow roared across the meadow.

An instant later, fire jolted the low-hanging clouds and wood crackled its death throes. The water-spangled mist deepened to a darker gray and the woodlands' clean scent faded into rough-edged smoke.

Astrid closed her eyes before the tears spilled over.

"Where the hell did those bastards get a flamethrower? No other way for them to burn buildings that fast without a bomb," Jake said furiously. "Never mind; any pocket anarchist can build one. Shit, shit, shit."

"Half an hour for a cottage to burn?" Astrid wondered.

"More like five minutes, fifteen at the most. It's old wood, which hasn't been tended." Jake pounded his fists together. "Bastards can claim the property owner's right to clear unsafe buildings."

"But they didn't knock."

"We're the only ones who know that."

The rapid beating of a helicopter's blades overhead reinforced the enemy's plans for privacy.

Whomp! Another bellow and the harsh tang of smoke deepened. A man laughed and the unmistakable *chug-chug-chug* of .50 cal bullets ripping apart walls tore into Astrid's heart. Anybody left inside would be bloody sawdust.

Jake lifted his rifle and swept the field with his thermal sights.

"How many?" Astrid asked, just to confirm the bad news. Any sahir who'd murdered twice and built two excellent invisibility spells—the mask and the license plates—would probably want a solid phalanx of farasha thugs to clear his property.

"Your estimate of two dozen was pretty good, honey. None of them in full body armor."

"Wonderful."

Did she and Jake have enough magick to stop them, even with Enfield House's assistance?

"May be on the low side, though."

"Damn." Her stomach rolled over and headed for her knees.

"Do you have any magickal ways to stop them, honey? Otherwise, I'm going to use some old-fashioned cop tricks on them. You can stay here where it's safe until the local police arrive."

"Wait!" She caught his hands. There was no way one man could stand up against two dozen brutes, armed with flamethrowers or worse.

Like it nor not, she'd have to risk both their lives to summon enough power to stop the other sahir's army.

Jake's big Mercedes shook like a drunk in a California earthquake but the Bostonian still handled it like a race car driver. He made three lanes out of two, drove the wrong way down one-way streets, and turned in front of cop cars.

Logan was reluctantly impressed. He was also glad Elswyth had talked Danica into staying home. Whatever was going on here was meant for pros, not amateurs. He might not be briefed in, but he'd play out the hand.

"Holy crap!" A dozen bricks flew across their path from a construction site. "But it's foggy today, not windy."

Elswyth shot him a pitying look and said nothing.

Nathan peeled right and shot into a parking space, barely big enough for a Volkswagen Beetle, but right in front of the courthouse. He leaned over the seat. "Hurry up and redeem the damn mortgage. I have to protect the car, so I can't help you from here."

Nathan had been helping? What would it have been like if he hadn't?

Elswyth was already sliding out the door. Logan started to open his on the other side but she grabbed his hand.

Logan glanced back at Nathan, so startled at being treated like a child that any reassurance was welcome.

Nathan met his eyes in the rearview mirror. "Don't let go of her if you want to live."

Dude was dead serious. Logan almost wished he was back doing combat search and rescue where intel gave him some idea who the bad guys were.

But he latched onto the lady with one hand and his trusty Sig Sauer with the other. He could fight his way through hell one-handed.

Viper dumped a drawer onto the floor, one ear open for sirens. None yet, just the lovely sound of trash going up like firewood and some hired hands taking target practice.

He'd brought more staff than necessary but he had the cash. He needed to get in and out fast, to get the job done before any cops or firemen arrived. Not that those would stop him— but he'd always prided himself on a clean getaway and dead cops made for determined pursuers.

Dammit, didn't any of the bitches know how to steal? At least one of them should have robbed her husband before running off, then hidden the loot here. They hadn't taken any suitcases with them when they evacuated last night. So the money should still be here.

Or some jewelry. He knew a couple of fences in Europe who'd give him a good deal on diamonds. That might give him enough cash to escape from Mr. Big.

He wrenched another drawer open with redoubled zeal.

The boys would wait for him. They had to, since they wouldn't get the rest of their pay until the trip home.

"Hold onto my hands, Jake," Astrid ordered. Calm settled into her bones, the clarity of a sahir taking the first step into a spell.

"But I'd have to turn my back on them," he objected.

"We need to share our touch, our sight, our breath, our hearts. The focus is mine, as sahir, but the strength comes through you."

"Gotcha." Jake's dark eyes met hers and filled her with absolute trust.

She had to believe this would work. No matter who backed that army, she must have faith that she and Jake would win on this battlefield, not die the way Gerard had.

Jake's hands wrapped around hers in the beautiful, rough grip of a strong man. She turned her hands and caught his wrists until they were completely linked.

Power hummed at their heels and sniffed their flesh, like a torch's first tentative approach to a bonfire.

Whomp! Wood's death cry screamed through their bones as fire tore another old building away from its link to the earth.

Astrid's stomach heaved hard then settled back into place. She must *risk everything*.

"Dear God!" Jake braced his feet wider to stand fast. "Do you have your prism? We need it real soon."

"Between us." She pointed with her chin.

Summoned by its name, the crystal spun slowly between them. Rainbows of light danced through the mist in tiny sparks, only to shudder every time another gust of smoke passed by.

Astrid focused every bit of her being, every drop of blood, every dream of seeing tomorrow with Jake, until she became a creature of willpower, bright as a tall candle. She aimed herself into the prism until she found a place where time didn't exist. There she chanted a spell glimpsed in Gerard's family library, one that even the Shadow Council's Elders would have shaded their eyes against.

Boom! The universe spun like a giant kaleidoscope around her, colors shaping and reforming around her head faster than blades could carve flesh.

Afterward, the physical world gleamed in silvery-bright lines of force, shaded by brilliant shades of health and power, beyond the prism. The barren rosebushes lifted their heads when she spoke again.

"Do you feel the earth, Jake? The land your ancestors farmed and died for? Are buried in?"

"Yes." His gaze was fixed on the lights.

"Reach down and become one with it."

She opened the portal a little wider, broad enough for a

powerful trio of kubris and their sahirs. Not a rookie kubri and an unrated sahir, who might shatter and die in the attempt.

Jake's grip loosened to become a bracelet that existed in both this time and the past. His smile shifted to a seer's, which understands more than the pen can write.

Thank God. He'd entered the spell safely—but could he channel enough power?

Golden motes sparked and floated into being around him. They dove back into the earth, then spun up through his bones until he became luminous.

Kubri, the conduit, the bridge to power . . .

His eyes met hers and the golden fire leaped between them. For the first time, she tasted the earth's full power, which was only possible when a sahir freely joined to a single kubri. It whirled through her faster than light, richer than brandy, deeper than the sea.

She could have wept for its glory.

Instead she sang a single note and her prism rang like a bell.

A shockwave passed through earth and sky, not of force, but of seeing. Everything became suddenly clearer, as if a telescope had suddenly come into focus. Every color was richer and deeper, as if seen through the finest stained glass.

The fog faded slightly.

They hadn't done enough yet to cleanse the evil. Damn.

"Let all warriors within sound of this bell rise to defend Enfield House. As you fought before, may you fight again!"

She repeated the incantation twice more, each time singing the note slightly higher until she closed the chord. The shockwave ran deeper through earth and air each time until the fog faded to wisps.

Jake said nothing and his golden aura remained steady, pouring power into her, hot as a smithy's fires. She could still stand upright and focus their attack, not collapse from exhaustion or the pain lurking at the spell's edges.

She hummed very softly and waited.

A handful of men appeared at the wood's edge, half-hidden

by the rapidly evaporating fog. All of them wore the fine gray uniforms of the Civil War's early years, with the casual ease of men to whom weapons were more necessities than toys. Their outlines were clear-cut, yet their bodies lacked substance, like filmstrips held up to the light.

Jake squinted.

Astrid closed her eyes and prayed as she hadn't since she'd left Nebraska during that spring blizzard over a century ago.

"Grandpa?" he said incredulously. "Great-Grandpa Joseph?"

Chime! Another shock wave rolled the ground. Every one of the men became completely, utterly solid, as if made of flesh and blood, not celluloid or glass.

"What the hell?" Jake stared at her. "They look like people, not corpses."

"Name them," Astrid said quietly. "Name everyone you can. The more faith you pour into them, the more real they become."

She released one of his hands but the magick still wove a golden bracelet between them. Pain clawed its way closer to her skull. Yet no matter what the cost, she needed his link to the earth to bring these men into being.

Behind Jake, a brute sniggered and started to reloaded his .50 cal machine gun.

"Stonewall Jackson. It's an honor to meet you, general." Jake bowed to the general, who rode out past the ever increasing line of gray-clad men. The spell had summoned the South's two senior generals, who were buried closest to Enfield House. "And General Longstreet, I'm deeply glad you could join us."

How powerful was Jake? The spell's scarlet and gold tendrils wound deep into the earth, awakening men who were linked only by devotion to the same cause, protecting Virginia's women and children

General Stuart flourished his hat in response to his name and General Hood bowed deeply before taking his place, both of them astride beautiful horses.

Then the blue troopers strode up from the river, led by

equally bold colonels and generals. Dear heavens, Jake must have Northern blood in him, to fire up soldiers from the other side of this war.

Jake whistled softly and saluted the dark-haired, cigar-smoking general in blue. "General Grant, sir."

Now sunlight shone summer-bright across the grass, even though the air was crisp where untainted by smoke. The attackers had huddled together and were pointing at the newcomers.

One more soldier rode up, this one on a beautiful gray horse. Distance meant little to a ghostly mount, when summoned by such strong need.

Every trooper, both blue and gray, lifted his hat in salute.

"General Lee, sir, may I welcome you to Enfield House?" Astrid curtsied, as her mother had taught her so many years ago.

"Thank you, ma'am." He bowed graciously to her. But he folded his hands on his pommel, his eyes wary when General Grant joined them.

"General Lee, I would be honored to place myself and my men under your command for this engagement. We served together in Mexico and dealt the enemy many fine knocks, as I remember."

The Virginian's attitude turned gracious. "Indeed we did, Grant, and it is a pleasure to serve together side by side again."

Jake let out a soft whoop under his breath. Horses' tack jangled for the first time, matched by the clatter of rifles and swords being checked.

The generals rode forward knee to knee, and Lee drew his sword to command attention.

"Hold your fire, boys, until you see the whites of their eyes. Then I want a steady, rolling volley."

"Cold steel after that?" Jackson suggested.

"Indeed so, general."

More than one veteran's eye met another's in keen anticipation.

Fire teased the edges of Astrid's vision, more agonizing than a volcano's breath. Yet this army could not march unless she focused Jake's power.

"Quick march, now. Hold your formations!" And the voice of Robert E. Lee, the finest soldier Virginia ever produced, rang out once again to defend the homes of her women and children.

Generals and colonels, both blue and gray, kneed their horses forward to follow the erect figure on the beautiful steed. Soldiers twitched their muskets into position on their shoulders and marched to war, their uniforms brushing against each other.

Jake erupted into the Rebel yell. The ancient war cry rang out across the field, echoed by every soldier. Their booted feet suddenly shook the ground.

Astrid's heart was in her mouth. Jake tugged her forward, half-running to keep up.

The thugs stopped to look. Some hooted but most went back to burning another house.

When the small army was only a block away, it stopped and the front rank dropped to one knee.

The thugs turned a pair of assault rifles on them. The bullets whizzed through the formation and disappeared in the grass.

"Fire!" shouted General Lee.

Hundreds of minié balls, larger than most modern bullets, shot out of muskets and thudded into SUVs, jeeps, even the helicopter. They tore apart gas tanks.

Curses filled the air. The enemy sahir's army shot again, this time using both guns and the flamethrower.

"Fire!"

The second volley blew up the flamethrower, killing several men. Others turned to run, but every vehicle now had at least one flat tire. The helicopter crashed onto the meadow like a shattered buzzard and blew up an instant later.

"Woot, woot!" cheered Jake.

"Fix bayonets!"

Steel locked into place with lethal clicks and a thousand veterans smiled in anticipation. The vandals scattered faster to find cover.

"Charge!"

The Rebel yell ripped into the air once again and the army raced forward, just as one more vandal appeared on a cottage's porch.

The thugs turned to fight. But even modern weapons did little good against far superior numbers, especially when their opponents laughed off any wound. Worse, any shots from their compatriots' weapons sailed through the ghosts but decimated the thugs.

"You bastards!" The one remaining vandal raced toward Astrid and Jake, the only two people not wearing uniforms. "You're ruining everything."

He held a very ugly Steyr assault rifle steadily on Jake. One twitch of his finger and they'd both be dead.

"You killed Melinda Williams," Astrid accused, trying to catch his attention.

"Yeah, so what if I did? You won't be around long enough to do anything about it or to help me spend her big price tag." His flat gaze didn't flicker toward her.

Astrid's blood ran cold. Jake only had one hand free, since she needed the other to power her magick. Her heart said his pistol was no match for that assault rifle.

She started to tease her fingers loose but he tightened his grip.

Think logically, Astrid, remember what you know about guns. No—better yet, trust Jake.

"Viper," said Jake, a wealth of recognition in his voice. "How many hits have you made in this country? Twelve—or is it fifteen? Plus the seven in Europe and three in Argentina, of course."

The enemy's eyebrows shot up.

"You're good, cop. There's only one photo of me around."

"Two," Jake corrected him. "Every homicide cop on this continent has memorized them."

"I must be clumsier than I thought. But you'll be dead, so my mistakes don't matter."

"Yes, they do." Jake pulled the trigger.

Viper stared at them for a moment, a startled expression on his face below the small red hole in his forehead. Then he slowly crumpled to the ground, his rifle in his hands for the last time.

General Lee rode up, closely followed by Generals Jackson and Grant. "Good day to you, ma'am." He raised his hat and Astrid curtsied again.

"I perceive that all of our enemies are accounted for, Hammond?"

Astrid glanced past the officers and found corpses amid the shelter's burning wreckage. Numerous law enforcement agencies would undoubtedly be very happy.

Now, at last, she could hear sirens beyond the military base, adding their clamor to the hell wracking her brains.

The blue and gray soldiers' outlines wavered slightly.

"Precisely so, general." Jake reached up to shake General Lee's hand. "May I say what a pleasure it has been to serve with you today?"

"And mine as well, sir. If you'll forgive us for departing a bit precipitately, I do believe my men would be best released from duty under quieter conditions."

He winced slightly when another siren added to the oncoming cacophony. A silent plea lurked behind his eyes.

"Of course, general," she said quietly. "I assure you the shade will offer you every comfort you could desire."

"My thanks, Miss Carlsen. I wish you both the best of luck in all your future endeavors." He bowed deeply to her and rode off through the grass, his army behind him. It was time to end the spell and let them find peace again.

The soldiers entered the woodlands and faded into mist, to

vanish within a few paces like melting filmstrips, the way the old armies always had in the Virginia wilderness.

Astrid closed the spell and released Jake's hand. Now they could go back to being guildies again. Maybe fuck buddies, too.

It didn't feel like enough, not for her magick, especially when her legs were barely strong enough to support her and hell's bells pounded inside her skull. Why the hell did her heart want even more than that?

Jake's BlackBerry rang. He glanced at the number, and his face lit up. "What's up, little bro?"

"You won't call me that when you hear what I've been through." Logan's voice came through the tiny speaker loud and clear. "But we bought back the mortgage. Enfield House is free and clear."

Two cop cars charged out of the military base's woods and across the field, sirens roaring and lights flashing.

The cavalry was here and the enemy was defeated. Jake could go back to work. Hurrah.

Yuck.

Chapter Twenty-four

Astrid stuck out her tongue at her perfect condominium. She'd had three interior designers in, but none of their suggestions for redecorating had satisfied her. She'd gone shopping in New York but bought only one pair of shoes, instead of a full spring wardrobe.

She'd translated dozens of documents for the FBI so fast that her boss asked her to retake her competency test, in case she should be given a higher rank. Now she'd have to act stupid for a while to become invisible again, which was always a pain.

She and Elswyth had started searching for missing Nazi sahirs who might have entered the U.S. after World War II. The Shadow Council swore their immigration controls made it impossible for such a sahir to get into this country. Nobody believed them.

None of it took her mind off Jake and his absence from texting. Heck, he hadn't even made an appearance on the *Argos* boards.

He was busy. Of course, he was busy. Dude did busy the way bees did—to the single-minded exclusion of everything else, like her.

Maybe if she bought furniture that looked like his, it'd be a comfort. Yeah, right.

No, go for the real stuff—chocolate. She headed for the

kitchen. She had some triple fudge ice cream, which might just do the trick.

The doorbell rang.

Oh, crap, not another well-meaning neighbor with some bright ideas on how to perk her up.

She yanked the door open. Her jaw dropped with a thud that could be heard all the way to the Milan fashion runways.

Jake stood there, dressed in casual jeans, T-shirt, and jacket. Even more bizarre, he held a big bunch of daffodils.

"Hi." His lips twitched, like he didn't know if a smile was acceptable or not.

"Hello." She could only stare at him. He wasn't even wearing boots, just normal shoes.

He thrust the flowers at her and she accepted them.

"I'm sorry I didn't call or text you. But I've been locked up, doing the paperwork for all the criminals who died at Enfield House," he said in a rush, as if he'd memorized the words days ago.

"Okay. I figured that." She sniffed the bouquet. He'd really brought a lot.

"I took a day off today."

"You what?" The totally unexpected news brought her head up to see if he'd turned red with fever.

"The cherry blossom trees are in bloom at the Tidal Basin."

"I know." Didn't everybody in D.C.?

"I thought maybe you might want to walk around down there and have a picnic lunch with me. I brought the fixings." He pointed to the floor at his feet, where a very fancy basket rested.

Her jaw dived toward her chest again. Hope started to beat in her heart.

"That's a very frivolous thing to do, Jake," she ventured.

"I love you, Astrid. That means spending time together, starting by going on dates," he added in a rush.

She took his hand to give him courage. His smile this time was more genuine.

"I'll always be a homicide cop, but you hold my heart."

"I'm Shadow Guard," she reminded him.

"Are we going to have fights?"

"Probably. But I love you."

"Yes!" He yanked her into his arms and kissed her. She was flushed and laughing by the time he released her.

"Bed?" she asked and dragged her finger down his jaw.

"No, cherry blossoms first. Bedroom is easy but dates are hard. I need more practice."

"Plus, I can always port into your bedroom whenever I want to," she mused.

"Sounds like a great plan."

He linked hands with her, the same way they'd fought a rogue sahir's minions. They could talk about hunting down Viper's master tomorrow.

Be sure to catch A SENSE OF SIN,
the second book from Elizabeth Essex,
out this month!

The Ravishing Miss Celia Burke. A well-known, and even more well-liked, local beauty. She made her serene, graceful way down the short set of stairs into the ballroom as effortlessly as clear water flowed over rocks in a hillside stream. She nodded and smiled in a benign but uninvolved way at all who approached her, but she never stopped to converse. She processed on, following her mother through the parting sea of mere mortals, those lesser human beings who were nothing and nobody to her but playthings.

Aloof, perfect Celia Burke. *Fuck you.*

By God, he would take his revenge and Emily would have justice. Maybe then he could sleep at night.

Maybe then he could learn to live with himself.

But he couldn't exact the kind of revenge one takes on another man—straightforward, violent, and bloody. He couldn't call Miss Burke out on the middle of the dance floor and put a bullet between her eyes or a sword blade between her ribs at dawn.

His justice would have to be more subtle, but no less thorough. And no less ruthless.

"You were the one who insisted we attend this august gathering. So what's it to be, Delacorte?" Commander Hugh McAlden, friend, naval officer and resident cynic, prompted again.

McAlden was one of the few people who never addressed Del by his courtesy title, Viscount Darling, as they'd know each other long before he'd come into the bloody title and far too long for Del to give himself airs in front of such an old friend. With such familiarity came ease. With McAlden, Del could afford the luxury of being blunt.

"Dancing or thrashing? The latter, I think."

McAlden's usually grim mouth crooked up in half a smile. "A thrashing, right here in the marchioness's ballroom? I'd pay good money to see that."

"Would you? Shall we have a private bet, then?"

"Del, I always like it when you've got that look in your eye. I'd like nothing more than a good wager."

"A bet, Colonel Delacorte? What's the wager? I've money to burn these days, thanks to you two." Another naval officer, Lieutenant Ian James, known from their time together when Del had been an officer of His Majesty's Marine Forces aboard the frigate *Resolute*, broke into the conversation from behind.

"A private wager only, James." Del would need to be more circumspect. James was a bit of a puppy, happy and eager, but untried in the more manipulative ways of society. There was no telling what he might let slip. Del had no intention of getting caught in the net he was about to cast. "Save your fortune in prize money for another time."

"A gentleman's bet then, Colonel?"

A *gentleman's* bet. Del felt his mouth curve up in a scornful smile. What he was about to do violated every code of gentlemanly behavior. "No. More of a challenge."

"He's Viscount Darling now, Mr. James." McAlden gave Del a mocking smile. "We have to address him with all the deference he's due."

Unholy glee lit the young man's face. "I had no idea. Congratulations, Colonel. What a bloody fine name. I can hear the ladies now: *my dearest, darling Darling*. How will they resist you?"

Del merely smiled and took another drink. It was true. None

of them resisted: high-born ladies, low-living trollops, bar-
maids, island girls, or *señoritas*. They never had, bless their
lascivious hearts.

And neither would *she*, despite her remote facade. Celia
Burke was nothing but a hothouse flower just waiting to be
plucked.

"Go on, then. What's your challenge?" McAlden's face
housed a dubious smirk as several more navy men, Lieutenants Thomas Gardener and Robert Scott joined them.

"I propose I can openly court, seduce, and ruin an untried,
virtuous woman"—Del paused to give them a moment to re-
mark upon the condition he was about to attach—"without
ever once touching her."

McAlden gave a huff of cynical laughter. "Too easy in one
sense, too hard in another," he stated flatly.

"How can you possibly ruin someone without touching
them?" Ian James protested.

Del felt his mouth twist. He had forgotten what it was like
to be that young. While he was only six and twenty, he'd
grown older since Emily's death. Vengeance was singularly
aging.

"Find us a drink would you, gentlemen? A real drink. None
of the lukewarm swill they're passing out on trays." Del
pushed the young lieutenants off in the direction of a footman.

"Too easy to ruin a reputation with only a rumor," McAlden
repeated in his unhurried, determined way. "You'll have to do
better than that."

Trust McAlden to get right to the heart of the matter. Like
Del, McAlden had never been young, and he was older in
years, as well.

"With your reputation," McAlden continued as they turned
to follow the others, "well deserved, I might add, you'll not
get within a sea mile of a virtuous woman."

"That, old man, shows how little you know of women."

"That, my darling Viscount, shows how little you know of
their mamas."

"I'd like to keep it that way. Hence the prohibition against touching. I plan on keeping a very safe distance." While he was about the business of revenging himself on Celia Burke, he needed to keep himself safe from being forced into doing the right thing should his godforsaken plan be discovered or go awry. And he simply didn't *want* to touch her. He didn't want to be tainted by so much as the merest brush of her hand.

"Can't seduce, really *seduce*, from a distance. Not even you. Twenty guineas says it can't be done."

"Twenty? An extravagant wager for a flinty, tight-pursed Scotsman like you. Done." Del accepted the challenge with a firm handshake. It sweetened the pot, so to speak.

McAlden perused the crowd. "Shall we pick now? I warn you, Del, this isn't London. There's plenty of virtue to be had in Dartmouth."

"Why not?" Del felt his mouth curve into a lazy smile. The town may have been full of virtue, but he was full of vice. He cared about only one particular woman's virtue.

"You'll want to be careful. Singularly difficult things, women," McAlden offered philosophically. "Can turn a man inside out. Just look at Marlowe."

Del shrugged. "Captain Marlowe married. I do not have anything approaching marriage in mind."

"So you're going to seduce and ruin an innocent without being named or caught? That *is* bloody-minded."

"I didn't say innocent. I said untried. In this case, there is a particular difference." He looked across the room at Celia Burke again. At the virtuous, innocent face she presented to the world. He would strip away that mask until everyone could see the ugly truth behind her immaculately polished, social veneer.

McAlden followed the line of his gaze. "You can't mean— That's Celia Burke!" All trace of jaded amusement disappeared from McAlden's voice. "Jesus, Del, have you completely lost your mind? As well as all moral scruples?"

"Gone squeamish?" Del tossed back the last of his drink. "That's not like you."

"I *know* her. Everyone in Dartmouth knows her. She is Marlowe's wife's most particular friend. You can't go about ruining—*ruining* for God's sake—innocent young women like her. Even *I* know that."

"I said she's *not* innocent."

"Then you must've misjudged her. She's not fair game, Del. Pick someone else. Someone I don't know." McAlden's voice was growing thick.

"No." Darling kept his own voice flat.

McAlden's astonished countenance turned back to look at Miss Burke, half a room away, smiling sweetly in conversation with another young woman. He swore colorfully under his breath. "That's not just bloody-minded, that's suicidal. She's got parents, Del. Attentive parents. Take a good hard look at her mama, Lady Caroline Burke. She's nothing less than the daughter of a duke, and is to all accounts a complete gorgon in her own right. They say she eats fortune hunters, not to mention an assortment of libertines like you, for breakfast. What's more, Miss Burke is a relation of the Marquess of Widcombe, in whose ballroom you are currently *not dancing*. This isn't London. You are a guest here. My guest, and therefore Marlowe's guest. One misstep like that and they'll have your head. Or, more likely, your ballocks. And quite rightly. Pick someone else for your challenge."

"No."

"Delacorte."

"Bugger off, Hugh."

McAlden knew Del well enough to hear the implacable finality in his tone. Hugh shook his head slowly. "God's balls, Del. I didn't think I'd regret so quickly having you to stay." He ran his hand through his short, cropped hair and looked at Del with a dawning of realization. "Christ. You'd already made up your mind before you came here, hadn't you? You came for her."

If you liked this book,
try Katherine Irons' SEABORNE,
in stores now . . .

Morgan watched from the surf. Spending so long out of water this afternoon had taxed his strength, both in the energy needed to maintain the illusion that he was a human and the strain it took for him to breathe on land. He felt an overwhelming weariness of body and spirit.

Being in such close contact with the human woman should have dissolved the odd attraction he felt for her. Despite her quick wit and obvious intelligence, she was damaged, her health even more frail than the average land dweller. Although he couldn't assess her physical condition without examining her, he guessed that she was paralyzed from the waist down.

Not that it would have been a problem if she weren't human. Atlanteans had virtually no physical handicaps and possessed super healing abilities. Short of the impossibility of replacing a missing limb that had been cut off in battle or eaten by a shark, almost any injury would heal in a matter of hours. They suffered from none of the viruses, heart disease, cancers, and various illnesses that plagued humans.

Leaving the cradle of life, the sea, brought with it many challenges for the human race. The earth's force of gravity and the constant assault on the earth's surface from radiation put constant pressure on the human species. Atlanteans, who had remained in the water, were both superior intellectual and sexual beings.

The sexual part was the problem. Unfortunately, heightened sensuality was one weakness that Atlanteans suffered from, both males and females. Although some couples mated for life and remained faithful to each other, the majority, like him, took sexual pleasure where they found it. Since his kind were bound by none of the artificial human rules of morality, adults finding pleasure whenever and wherever they pleased with other adults was the norm.

Morgan reasoned that he had acquired a desire for a woman that he was forbidden to touch. It was a rare occurrence, one that he personally had never experienced, although he'd heard tales of other Atlanteans struck by this same fever in the blood. Inflamed by the unsatisfied lust for a certain object of desire—even a human one—brought weakness and both mental and physical pain.

Claire was so human that he didn't understand how he could be attracted to her. He should have felt pity for her. Instead, he wanted to take her in his arms. He wanted to touch her skin, to taste it, to nibble his way from her delicate eyelids to the tips of her toes . . . to lave every square inch of her body with his tongue. He wanted to inhale her scent until he was intoxicated by it, to run his fingers through her hair, suck her nipples until they hardened to tight buds, and cradle her in his arms. Even now, watching her at a distance, Morgan could feel his groin tightening with need. He wanted her as he hadn't wanted a female in three hundred years . . . perhaps five.

And she had been equally attracted to him. He had read the invitation in her eyes. Naturally, most sexually mature humans desired his kind. There were legends of those who walked the earth, breathed air, yet lived on the blood of their fellow humans. Vampires, they were called. It was said that vampires possessed the ability to bewitch humans with their sexuality, but the power of these bloodsuckers—if they truly existed—would be nothing compared to the sensual lure of the Atlantean race.

He sank under the waves, reveling in the powerful surge of the tide, savoring the tangy feel of the salt on his skin. This was his element; this was where he belonged. Venturing on dry land, even for a few hours, was dangerous in more ways than he could count.

But the pounding in his head and the pressure in his groin remained as strong as ever. He seemed tangled in a web of sorcery. No matter how much reason told him to leave this place, to forget her, he was incapable of doing so. He had to find a way to end this connection before it was too late.

Perhaps the only way to rid himself of his attraction was to make love to her. It would be risky. The laws against Atlanteans and humans sharing sexual favors were rigid and strictly enforced. If he were caught, he could be severely punished.

The thought that he already could have been caught watching Claire by his greatest enemy came to him. But he didn't think Caddoc had seen him spying on the woman. It was more likely that his half-brother had witnessed the near drowning of the boy. If Caddoc knew about Claire, he would have taunted him about it. Caddoc never had the self-control to hold his tongue. The offense, having romantic contact with a human, would be even greater than rescuing one from drowning.

Morgan clenched his jaw. Tonight, he would go to Claire. But this time, he would take her into his element. Once they were beneath the ocean, he could use his healing powers to temporarily give her back the use of her legs. She would be able to respond to his seduction, to feel his mouth on her body, to enjoy each shared sensation. And he knew he would satisfy her more than any human male she'd ever been intimate with. But then, sadly, he'd have to wipe away her memory of the evening.

He told himself that if she came willingly, it wasn't really abduction, and if she didn't resist, what they did together would harm no one. The argument was as full of holes as the *Titanic*, but he was in no mood to be rational. As impossible as it was to believe, Claire had become an immovable obstruction. If he was to complete his mission and return to defend himself in front of the High Court, he'd have to shatter the ancient laws and seduce her first.

There's nothing sexier than a BIG BAD BEAST.
Keep an eye out for Shelly Laurenston's latest,
coming next month!

Ulrich Van Holtz turned over and snuggled closer to the denim-clad thigh resting by his head. Then he remembered that he'd gone to bed alone last night.

Forcing one eye open, he gazed at the face grinning down at him.

"Mornin', supermodel."

He hated when she called him that. The dismissive tone of it grated on his nerves. Especially his sensitive *morning* nerves. She might as well say, "Mornin', you who serve no purpose."

"Dee-Ann." He glanced around, trying to figure out what was going on. "What time is it?"

"Dawn-ish."

"Dawn-*ish*?"

"Not quite dawn, no longer night."

"And is there a reason you're in my bed at dawn-ish . . . fully clothed? Because I'm pretty sure you'd be much more comfortable naked."

Her lips curved slightly. "Look at you, Van Holtz. Trying to sweet-talk me."

"If it'll get you naked . . ."

"You're my boss."

"I'm your supervisor."

"If you can fire me, you're my boss. Didn't they teach you that in your fancy college?"

"My fancy college was a culinary school and I spent most of my classes trying to understand my French instructors. So if they mentioned that boss-supervisor distinction, I probably missed it."

"You're still holding my thigh, hoss."

"You're still in my bed. And you're still not naked."

"Me naked is like me dressed. Still covered in scars and willing to kill."

"Now you're just trying to turn me on." Ric yawned, reluctantly unwrapping his arms from Dee's scrumptious thigh and using the move to get a good look at her.

She'd let her dark brown hair grow out a bit in recent months so that the heavy, wavy strands rested below her ears, framing a square jaw that sported a five-inch scar from her military days and a more recent bruise he was guessing had happened last night. She had a typical Smith nose—a bit long and rather wide at the tip—and the proud, high forehead. But it was those eyes that disturbed most of the populace because they were the one part of her that never shifted. They stayed the same color and shape no matter what form she was in. Many people called the color "dog yellow" but Ric thought of it as a canine gold. And Ric didn't find those eyes off-putting. No, he found them entrancing. Just like the woman.

Ric had only known the She-wolf about seven months, but since the first time he'd laid eyes on her, he'd been madly, deeply in lust. Then, over time, he'd gotten to know her, and he'd come to fall madly, deeply in love. There was just one problem with them becoming mates and living happily every after—and that problem's name was Dee-Ann Smith.

"So is there a reason you're here, in my bed, not naked, around dawn-*ish* that doesn't involve us forgetting the idiotic limits of business protocol so that you can ravish my more-than-willing body?"

"Yep."

When she said nothing else, Ric sat up and offered, "Let me

guess. The tellin' will be easier if it's around some waffles and bacon."

"Those words are true, but faking that accent ain't endearing you to my Confederate heart."

"I bet adding blueberries to those waffles will."

"Canned or fresh?"

Mouth open, Ric glared at her over his shoulder.

"It's a fair question."

"Out." He pointed at his bedroom door. "If you're going to question whether I'd use *canned* anything in my food while sitting on my bed *not* naked, then you can just get the hell out of my bedroom . . . and sit in my kitchen, quietly, until I arrive."

"Will you be in a better mood?"

"Will you be naked?"

"Like a wolf with a bone," she muttered, and told him, "Not likely."

"Then I guess you have your answer."

"Oh, come on. Can I at least sit here and watch you strut into the bathroom bare-ass naked?"

"No, you may not." He threw his legs over the side of the bed. "However, you may look over your shoulder longingly while I, in a very manly way, walk purposely into the bathroom bare-ass naked. Because I'm not here for your entertainment, Ms. Smith."

"It's Miss. Nice Southern girls use Miss."

"Then I guess that still makes you a Ms."

Dee-Ann Smith sat at Van Holtz's kitchen table, her fingers tracing the lines in the marble. His kitchen table was real marble, too, the legs made of the finest wood. Not like her parents' Formica table that still had the crack in it from when Rory Reed's big head drunkenly slammed into it after they'd had too many beers the night of their junior year homecoming game.

Then again, everything about Van Holtz's apartment spoke of money and the finest of everything. Yet his place somehow managed to be comfortable, not like some spots in the city where everything was so fancy Dee didn't know who'd want to visit or sit on a damn thing. Of course, Van Holtz didn't come off like some spoiled rich kid that she'd want to slap around when he got mouthy. She'd thought he'd be that way, but since meeting him a few months back, he'd proven that he wasn't like that at all.

Shame she couldn't say that for several of his family members. She'd met his daddy only a few times and each time was a little worse than the last. And his older brother wasn't much better. To be honest, she didn't know why Van Holtz didn't challenge them both and take the alpha position from the mean old bastard. That's how they did it among the Smiths, and it was a way of life that had worked for them for at least three centuries.

Hair dripping wet from the shower, Van Holtz walked into his kitchen. He wore black sweatpants and was pulling a black T-shirt over his head, giving Dee an oh-too-brief glimpse at an absolutely superb set of abs and narrow hips. No, he wasn't as big a wolf as Dee was used to—in fact, they were the same six-two height and nearly the same width—but good Lord, the man had an amazing body. It must be all the things he did during the day. Executive chef at the Fifth Avenue Van Holtz restaurant; a goalie for the shifter-only pro team he owned, the Carnivores; and one of the supervisors for the Group. A position that, although he didn't spend as much time in the field as Dee-Ann and her team, did force him to keep in excellent shape.

Giving another yawn, Van Holtz pushed his wet, dark blond hair off his face, brown eyes trying to focus while he scanned the kitchen.

"Coffee's in the pot," she said.

Some men, they simply couldn't function without their morning coffee, and that was Van Holtz.

"Thank you," he sighed, grabbing the mug she'd taken out for him and filling it up. If he minded that she'd become quite familiar with his kitchen and his apartment in general, after months of coming and going as she pleased, he never showed it.

Dee waited until he'd had a few sips and finally turned to her with a smile.

"Good morning."

She returned that smile, something she normally didn't bother with most, and replied, "Morning."

"I promised you waffles with *fresh* blueberries." He sniffed in disgust. "Canned. As if I'd ever."

"I know. I know. Sacrilege."

"Exactly!"

Dee-Ann sat patiently at the kitchen table while Van Holtz whipped up a full breakfast for her the way most people whipped up a couple of pieces of toast.

"So, Dee . . ." Van Holtz placed perfectly made waffles and bacon in front of her with warmed syrup in a bowl and a small dish of butter right behind it. "What brings you here?"

He sat down on the chair across from her with his own plate of food.

"Cats irritate me."

Van Holtz nodded, chewing on a bite of food. "And yet you work so well with them on a day-to-day basis.

"Not when they get in my way."

"Is there a possibility you can be more specific on what your complaint is?"

"But it's fun to watch you so confused."

"Only one cup of coffee, Dee-Ann. Only one cup."

She laughed a little, always amused when Van Holtz got a bit cranky.

"We went to raid a hybrid fight last night—not only was there no fight, but there were felines already there."

"Which felines?"

"KZS."

"Oh." He took another bite of bacon. "*Those* felines. Well, maybe they're trying to—"

"Those felines ain't gonna help mutts, Van Holtz, you know that."

"Can't you just call me Ric? You know, like everyone else." And since the man had more cousins than should legally be allowed, all with the last name Van Holtz, perhaps that would be a bit easier for all concerned.

"Fine. They're not going to help, *Ric*."

"And yet it seems as if they are—or at least trying."

"They're doing something—and I don't like it. I don't like when anyone gets in my way." Especially particular felines who had wicked right crosses that Dee's jaw was still feeling several hours later.

"All right," he said. "I'll deal with it."

"Just like that?"

"Yep. Just like that. Orange juice?" She nodded, and he poured freshly squeezed orange juice into her glass.

"You don't want to talk to the team first?"

"I talked to you. What's the team going to tell me that you haven't? Except they'll probably use more syllables and keep the antifeline sentiment out of it."

She nodded and watched him eat. Pretty. The man was just . . . pretty. Not girly—although she was sure her daddy and uncles would think so—but pretty. Handsome and gorgeous might be the more acceptable terms when talking about men, but those words did not fit him.

"Is something wrong with your food?" he asked, noticing that she hadn't started eating.

She glanced down at the expertly prepared waffle, big fresh blueberries throughout, powdered sugar sprinkled over it. In bowls he'd also put out more fresh blueberries, along with strawberries and peaches. He'd given her a linen napkin to use and heavy, expensive-looking flatware to eat with. And he'd set all this up in about thirty minutes.

The whole meal was, in a word, perfection, which was why Dee replied, "It's all right . . . I guess."

A dark eyebrow peaked. "You guess?"

"Haven't tried it yet, now have I? Can't tell you if I like it if I haven't tried it."

"Only one cup of coffee, Dee. Only one."

"Maybe it's time you had another."

"Eat and tell me my food is amazing or I'm going to get cranky again."

"If you're going to be pushy . . ." She took a bite, letting the flavors burst against her taste buds. Damn, but the man could cook. Didn't seem right, did it? Pretty and a good cook.

"Well?"

"Do I really need to tell you how good it is?"

"Yes, Although I'm enjoying your orgasm face."

She smirked. "Darlin', you don't know my orgasm face."

"Yet, I'm ever hopeful."

"Keepin' the dream alive."

"Someone has to." He winked at her and went back to his food. "I'll see what I can find out about what's going on with KZS and get back to you." He looked up at her and smiled. "Don't worry, Dee-Ann. I've got your back."

She knew that. She knew he would come through as promised. As hard as it was to believe, she was learning to trust the one breed of wolf her daddy told her never to trust.

Then again . . . her daddy had never tasted the man's blueberry waffles.

"But do me a favor, Dee," he said. "Until I get this straightened out, don't get into it with the cats."

Dee stared at him and asked with all honesty, "What makes you think I would?"